A GLOW OF CANDLES

AND OTHER STORIES

CHARLES L. GRANT

Author's Dedication

For Kirby, in memory of the breakfasts at the Sabre Luncheonette when we had to pool our change to buy a muffin and orange juice; thank God those days are over; those muffins were lousy.

Contents

Preface..1

A Crowd of Shadows 5

Hear Me Now, My Sweet Abbey Rose 19

Temperature Days on Hawthorne Street 35

Come Dance with Me on My Pony's Grave.......................................47

The Three of Tens 63

The Dark of Legends, The Light of Lies..77

Caesar, Now Be Still 105

White Wolf Calling 125

The Rest Is Silence..141

When All the Children Call My Name...167

Secrets of the Heart 189

A Glow of Candles, A Unicorn's Eye 199

Preface

In 1974, Damon Knight held his annual Milford Conference (by invitation only, a sweatshop for professional writers who think they know it all and find out they don't) in Florida. I drove down with Gardner Dozois, and spent a week listening to some very fine prose of mine brutally, expertly, and sometimes marvelously mangled by the likes of Damon, Kate Wilhelm, George Alec Effinger, Ed Bryant, Gene Wolfe, and Joanna Russ (among others). During one of the less hectic, more personal, evening sessions, Damon asked me if I could characterize my protagonists, not only those in the stories I'd brought to the Conference, but also those in works published or about to be. I hesitated only a moment before saying, "They're lonely."

That isn't quite right. Most of them, the strongest, are alone, not always lonely. They're also deliberate attempts to use ordinary people, rather than the so-called Heinlein man, who isn't ordinary at all, no matter what job he holds when the story opens. Ordinary people—that's most of us, in spite of our dreams—speak more eloquently, I think, than do superheroes about what frightens us daily: bills, employers, employees, the Bomb, the anti-Bomb, the younger generation, relationships that somehow work for Rock Hudson and Doris Day but don't work for us, the reflections in our mirrors.

When I step off that deliberate path, I fail. I can look back on fifteen years of work and see it as clearly as I can see the Jill Bauman fantasy paintings on the wall above my typewriter. Not that I'm a raving success when I stay on the path, either, but I feel better about those pieces. I feel as if I'm dealing with people who are more than dark inkspots on white paper that just happen to form words that just happen to form stories that just happen to be books. And because they're more, they seem at their best to create a reaction with the reader. In my case, that reaction is a shudder, or a glance over a shoulder to check the lock on the door.

That's fine with me.

That's what I'm here for. I didn't always know that, of course. I was going to be an Episcopal priest like my father. Then I was going to be a teacher. Now I'm…whatever this is that publicists call it.

It makes for strange, sometimes unsettling, reactions from my banker, those who don't know me all that well, and from editors who think I can live very well, thank you very much, on $5000.00 a year.

It also gives me a great deal of satisfaction. More so when my stories, not me, are recognized beyond the occasional fan letter or call. For example (if you don't mind me blowing the horn a little here): of the stories in this volume, five have been nominated for the Nebula Award from the Science Fiction Writers of America, one for the Hugo Award, and two for the World Fantasy Award. That all breaks down thusly—"A Crowd of Shadows," and "A Glow of Candles, A Unicorn's Eye" were nominated for the Nebula in their respective categories, and won; "Secrets of the Heart", "White Wolf Calling", and "The Rest Is Silence" were also nominated for Nebulas, and lost to Fritz Leiber and a Greg Bedford/Gordon Eklund collaboration; "A Crowd of Shadows" was nominated for the Hugo (my one and only nomination there) and lost to Joe Haldeman; and "When All The Children Call My Name" and "Hear Me Now, My Sweet Abbey Rose" were nominated for the World Fantasy Award, and lost to Fritz Leiber and Ramsey Campbell.

I mention the other winners, not out of respect for their superior works (which they are), but because I want them to know I don't want it to happen again.

But beyond all that, if the truth be known, there's an even greater satisfaction. Part of it comes when an eventually successful piece is rejected the first time by an editor saying, "Who wants to read nine thousand words about a nebbish?" (Damon Knight, re "The Rest Is Silence"), which I admit up front is a totally selfish part at best; and the greater proportion comes from the fact that some people out there really and truly enjoy reading what I do. And what I do for a living is exactly what I want to do. That makes it extraordinarily special; there aren't a lot of folks out there who can make the same claim.

I wouldn't begin an attempt to characterize those readers, but I can say one thing about them—they're seldom Heinlein men, men or women who Save The World with a twist of a screwdriver, the jiggle of a toggle, the brainstorm of a latent genius. Instead, they enjoy slipping out the real world now and again, enjoy remembering what it was like to go to a Saturday matinee and be delightfully, deliciously, heartstoppingly scared.

They know, and I know, that none of this dark stuff is real.

They know, and I know, that the above statement isn't necessarily true, but it damned well better be or we're all in deep trouble.

They know, and I know, that being alone doesn't mean lonely.

Barry Malzberg once said about a story of mine that it wasn't a horror story, it was about the dissolution of a marriage and the breakup of a family. After the (writing) fact, perhaps that's true. But what comes first is the story, the slipping away for a while; when *that* works, the rest is gravy.

When *that* works, I've done my job.

Charles L. Grant
Budd Lake, N.J. 1981

The evolution of this story has already been chronicled in the Afterword to its novelization, A Quiet Night of Fear *(Berkley, June 1981). And it was to be the first in a series of stories taking place in Starburst, a community I'd developed deliberately placed out of Time and the range of the laws of physics. Thus. I could safely combine science fiction and dark fantasy in identical settings—or so I thought. Unfortunately, the other stories materialized at less than proficient levels, and someone out there gave a candy bar the same name. I've not tasted it, but I have a feeling I'd prefer my own product...especially since a candy bar couldn't possibly win the Nebula Award (unless they change the rules again).*

If arm-twisted to unearth a theme, however, that would be simple: bigotry is a bitch.

A Crowd of Shadows

Of all the means of relaxation that I have devised for myself over the years, most required nothing more strenuous than driving an automobile, and not one of them had anything remotely to do with murder. Yet there it was, and now here I am—alone, though not always alone, and wondering, though not always puzzled. I'm neither in jail nor exile, asylum nor hospital. Starburst is where I am and, unless I can straighten a few things out, Starburst is where I'm probably going to stay.

I had long ago come to the conclusion that every so often the world simply had to thumb its nose at me and wink obscenely as if it knew what the hell was making things tick and for spite wasn't about to let me in on the secret. When that happens, I succumb to the lure of Huck Finn's advice and light out for the territory: in my case, that turns out to be Starburst. Where the luncheonette is called The Luncheonette, the hotel is The Hotel, and so on in understated simplicity. Where the buildings, all of them, rise genteelly from well-kept lawns on full-acre lots, painted sunrise-new and no two the same shape or shade—a half-moon-fashioned community that prides itself on its seclusion and its ability to sponge out the world from transients like me. It's a place that not many can stand for too long, but it's a breather from every law that anyone ever thought of.

At least that's what I thought when I came down last May.

It was a bit warm for the season, but not at all uncomfortable. Wednesday, and I was sitting on the grey sand beach that ribboned the virtually waveless bay they had christened Nova. The sun was pleasantly hot, the water cool, and the barest sign of a breeze drifted down from the misted mountains that enclosed the town. I had just dried myself off and was about to roll over onto my stomach to burn a little when a thin and angular boy about fifteen or so dashed in front of me, kicking up crests of sand and inadvertently coating me and my blanket as he pursued some invisible swift quarry. I was going to protest when there was a sudden shout and he stumbled to a halt, turning around immediately, his arms dejectedly limp at his sides. Curious, I followed his gaze past me to a middle-aged couple huddled and bundled under a drab beach umbrella. The woman, hidden by bonnet, dark glasses, and a black, long-sleeved sweater beckoned sharply. The boy waved in return and retraced his steps at a decidedly slower pace. As he passed me, looking neither left nor right, I only just happened to notice the tiny and blurred sequence of digits tattooed on the inside of his left forearm.

I'm sure my mouth must have opened in the classic gesture of surprise, but though I've seen them often enough in the city, for some reason I didn't expect to see an android in Starburst.

I continued to stare rather rudely until the boy reached the couple and flopped face-down on the sand beside them, his lightly tanned skin pale against the grey. The beach was quietly deserted, and the woman's voice carried quite easily. Though her words were indistinct, her tone was not: boy or android, the lad was in trouble. I supposed he was being told to stay close, paying for his minor act of rebellion.

I smiled to myself and lay back with my cupped hands serving as a pillow. Poor kid, I thought, all he wanted was a little fun. And then I had to smile at myself for thinking the boy human. It was a common mistake, though one I usually don't make, and I forgot about it soon enough as I dozed. And probably would never have thought of it again if I hadn't decided to indulge myself in a little fancy dining that evening.

Though my stays are irregular, they have been frequent enough to educate the hotel staff to my unexciting habits, and I had little difficulty in reserving my favorite table: a single affair by the dining room window overlooking the park, overlooking, in point of fact, most of the town since the hotel was the only structure in Starburst taller than two stories, and it was only six. The unadorned walls of the circular room were midnight-green starred with white, a most relaxing, even seductive combination, and its patrons were always suitably subdued. I was just getting into my dessert when I noticed the boy from the beach enter with the couple I had assumed were his parents. They huddled with the maître d' and were escorted to a table adjacent to my own. The boy was exceptionally polite, holding the chair for mother, shaking hands with father before sitting down himself. When he happened to glance my way, I smiled and nodded, but the gesture quickly turned to a frown when I heard someone mutter, "Goddamned humie."

The threesome were apparently ignoring the remark, but I was annoyed enough to scan the neighboring tables. Nothing. I was going to shrug it off to bad manners when suddenly an elderly man and his wife brusquely pushed back their chairs and left without any pretense of politeness. As they threaded between me and the boy, the old man hissed "robie" just loud enough. Perhaps I should have said something in return, or made overtures, gestures, something of an apology to the boy. But I didn't. Not a thing.

Instead, I ordered a large brandy and turned to watch the darkness outside the uncurtained window. And in the reflection of the room, I saw the boy glaring at his empty plate.

In spite of the ground that fact and fiction have covered in exploring the myriad possibilities of societies integrated with the sometimes too-human android, the reality seemed to have come as a surprise to most people. For some it was a pleasant one: androids were androids; pleasant company, tireless workers, expensive but economical. Their uses were legion, and their confusion with actual humans minimal. For others, however, and predictably, androids were androids: abominations, blasphemies, monsters and all the horrid rest of it.

They had become, in fact, the newest minority that nearly everyone could look down upon if they were closed-minded enough. Ergo, the tattoos and serial numbers. For people not sensitive enough to detect the subtle differences, the markings served as some sort of self-gratifying justification, though for what I've never been able to figure out exactly. I have a friend in London who has replaced all his servants with androids and has come to love them almost as brothers and sisters. Then, too, there's another friend who speaks of them as he would of his pets.

It's true they haven't brought about the Utopia dreamed of in centuries past; they are strictly regulated in the business community—always clannish, job preference still goes to the human, no matter how much more efficient the simulacrum might be. Still and all, I thought as I emptied my glass and rose to leave, there's something to be said for them: at least they have unfailing manners.

So I smiled as graciously as I could as I passed their table. The boy smiled back, the parents beamed. The lad was obviously their surrogate son, and I was slightly saddened and sorry for them.

I spent the rest of the evening closeted in my room, alternately reading and speculating on the reasons for their choice. Death, perhaps, or a runaway: as I said, the androids' uses are legion. It puzzled me, however, why the parents hadn't kept the boy covered on the beach. It would have at least avoided the scene in the dining room. Then I told myself to mind my own stupid business, and for the last time I slept the sleep of the just.

The following morning my door was discreetly knocked upon, and I found myself being introduced to the local detective-in-chief by Ernie Wills, the manager. I invited them in and sat myself on the edge of the still-unmade bed. "So. What can I do for you, Mr. Harrington?"

The policeman was a portly, pale-faced man with a hawk nose and unpleasantly dark eyes. Somehow he managed to chew tobacco throughout the entire interview without once looking for a place to spit. I liked the man immediately.

"Did you know the Carruthers family very well?" His voice matched his size, and I was hard put not to wince.

I looked blank. "Carruthers? I don't know them at all. Who are they?"

Harrington just managed a frown. "The couple sitting next to you last night at dinner. The boy. I was under the impression that you knew them."

"Not hardly," I said. "I saw them once on the beach yesterday afternoon, and again at dinner." I spread my hands. "That's all."

"Some of the other guests said you were rather friendly to them."

By that time I was completely puzzled and looked to Ernie for some assistance, but he only shrugged and tipped his head in Harrington's direction. It's his show, the gesture said. And for the first time, I noticed how harassed he seemed.

"In a detective novel," I said as lightly as I could, "the hero usually says, 'You have me at a disadvantage.' I'm sorry, Mr. Harrington, but I haven't the faintest idea what in God's name you're talking about."

Harrington grinned. His teeth were stained. "Touché. And I apologize, okay? I didn't mean to be so damned mysterious, but sometimes I like to play the role. I read those books, too." He settled himself more deeply into the only armchair in the room and reached into a coat pocket for a handkerchief which he used to wipe his hands. "You see, there's been a murder in the hotel."

I looked at him patiently, but he didn't say anything else, apparently waiting for my reaction. I almost said, so what? but I didn't. "Am I supposed to guess who was murdered, or who did it? My God, it wasn't one of the Carruthers, was it?"

Harrington shook his head.

Ernie swallowed hard.

"Well, surely you don't suspect one of them?"

"Wish I knew," Harrington said. "An old man was found outside his door on the third floor about three o'clock this morning. His throat was, well, not exactly torn...more like yanked out. Like somebody just grabbed hold and pulled."

That I understood, and the unbidden image that flashed into my mind was enough to swear me off breakfast, and probably lunch. I shuddered.

"Some people," the detective continued, "said they heard this old guy call the boy 'robie.' Did you hear it?"

"Yes," I answered without thinking. "And I heard someone else, I don't know who, call him a 'humie.' There were other remarks, I guess, but I didn't hear them all. That kind of talk isn't usual, you know. The Carruthers may have been offended, but I hardly think they'd have murdered for it. I smiled as nicely as I could because I felt sorry for them, and the boy."

Harrington kept wiping his hands; then, with a flourish, deposited the cloth back into his pocket and stood. "Okay," he said brusquely. "Thanks for the information."

As he turned to leave, I couldn't help asking if he really believed the boy or his parents had done it. "After all," I said, "the boy is an android. He can't kill anyone."

Harrington stopped with his hand on the door knob. He actually looked sorry for me. "Sir, either you read too much, or you watch too much TV. Andy or not, if ordered, that kid could kill as easily as I could blink."

And then he left, with silent Ernie trailing apologetically behind. Slowly I walked to the window and gazed out toward the bay. The sun was nearing noon, and the glare off the water partially blinded me to the arms of the coast that came within a hundred meters of turning Nova into a lake. Below was the single block of businesses that squatted between me and the beach. Leaning forward, I spotted a milling group of people and a squad car. I watched, trying to identify some of them, until Harrington strolled from the building and drove away. The crowd, small as it was, disturbed me. Starburst wasn't supposed to deal in murder.

"Christ," I said. "And I wanted to punch that old guy in the face."

I shook myself and dressed quickly. At least Harrington didn't tell me not to leave town. Not that I would have. I still had four days of vacation left, and though I was sorry for the old nameless man, and sorrier for the shroud the crime must have placed on the Carruthers, I still intended to soak up as much sun as possible.

And so I did until a shadow blocked the heat, and I looked up from my blanket into the face of the boy, the face turned black by the sun behind him. Specter. Swaying. I imagine I appeared startled because he said, "Hey, I'm sorry, mister. Uh, can I talk with you a minute?"

"Why, sure, why not?" I shifted to one side and sat up. Today the boy was fully dressed in a sweatshirt, jeans, and sockless sneakers. His dark hair was uncombed. He squatted next to me and began to draw nothings in the sand. Since I'm single, I guess I haven't developed whatever special rapport a man can have with a younger version of himself; and when that youthful image isn't even human, well, I just sat there, waiting for someone to say something.

"You were nice to me and my people last night," he said finally, his voice just this side of quavering. "I think I should thank you."

My mind was still not functioning properly. Part of me kept up a warning that this kid was suspected of murder, and my throat tightened. The other parts kept bumping into each other searching for something to say that sounded reasonably intelligent.

"They, uh, treated you rather unkindly, son."

He shrugged and wiped the sand from his doodling finger. "We get used to it. It happens all the time, though I guess that's not really true. Not all the time, anyway. Maybe it just seems bad here because it's so small. I'm…we're not used to small places."

He began digging into the sand, tossing the fill up to be caught and scattered by a sharp, suddenly cool breeze.

"People can be cruel at times," I said unoriginally. "You shouldn't let it bother you and your folks. Small people, you know, and small minds."

The boy stared at me from the corner of his eyes, his face still in shadow. "Aren't you afraid of me?"

"Why? Should I be?"

He shrugged again and worried the hole with the heel of his hand. "I think that detective thinks I killed that old man. He talked with us nearly two hours this morning. He said he was satisfied. I don't think so."

I shifted around to face him, but he continued to avert his face. I couldn't remember seeing such a shy boy before, though I supposed that the shock of the crime wasn't the easiest thing in the world to accept with nonchalance, especially when he was on the receiving end of the suspicion. I made a show of searching the beach, stretching my neck and gawking like a first-time tourist. "I don't see your, uh, parents. Are they as unconcerned as you?"

"My people are inside. They don't want anyone staring at them."

My people. That was the second time he'd used that wording, and I wondered. In the silence I found myself trying to place his accent, thinking it was perhaps a custom of wherever he came from, but there was nothing to it. Curiously so. He could have lived anywhere. On impulse I asked if he and his mother and father would care to join me for dinner. He shook his head.

"Thank you, but no. We'll eat in our room until something happens to change their minds. The doorman almost slammed the door in my face."

That figures, I thought as the boy struggled to his feet. He looked down at me and said, "Thank you again," and was gone as abruptly as he had come. It was then that I noticed the few sunbathers staring at me, their hostility radiating clearly. I grinned back at them and lay face down, hoping they hadn't seen the grin twist to grimace.

As I lay there, I considered: unlike members of most minorities, androids had no recourse to courts, education or native human talent to drag them out of their social ghetto. They were as marked as if their skin had been black or brown, only worse because whatever rights they had stopped at the factory entrance. And I wasn't at all pleased to have to admit to myself that even I couldn't see handing them the same rights and privileges as I had. I was beginning to wonder just how far above the crowd I really was for all my ideas. I thought of the people who'd glared at me: you'd better stop casting stones, I told myself. Don't feel sorry for the boy, feel sorry for the parents.

And then I dozed off, which, for my skin, is tantamount to stretching out on a frying pan. When I awoke again, my back felt as if it had been dragged over hot coals. And in feeling the burning pain, I surprised myself at the foul language I could conjure. I tried to put on my shirt, gave it up as the second worst idea I'd had that day, next to sunbathing, and gathered my things together. I walked across the sand and between the buildings that had their backs to the bay. When I reached the street, I stopped dead at the curb. There was the squad car again and an ambulance. A crowd getting noisy. And the flashing red lights. I spotted Detective Harrington staring at me, and I waved and crossed. He met me by the police car.

"Heart attack?" I asked, indicating the ambulance.

"You could say that," he said dryly. "A man has had his head bashed in."

I found it difficult to believe. It was as if someone had drilled a pipeline directly from the outside world into Starburst and was pumping in that which we were all here to get away from. Some wonder the people milling around us were in such a foul mood. I tried a sympathetic smile on Harrington, received no reaction and turned to go. I hadn't taken a single step when he placed a gently detaining hand on my arm.

"Somebody said you were talking to the boy."

"Somebody?" Suddenly I was very mad. "Just who the hell are these somebodies that seem to know everything, every goddamned thing that I do or say?"

"Concerned citizens," he said with a slight trace of bitterness, as if he'd had his fill of concerned citizens. "Were you?"

"Yes, as a matter of fact, I was." I looked at my watch. "About an hour ago. On the beach."

"For how long?"

I tried to ignore the people trying very hard not to appear as if they were eavesdropping. "Hell, I don't know. Fifteen minutes, maybe twenty, twenty-five."

I looked at Harrington closely, trying to snare a clue as to what he was thinking. I did know that, for some reason, he still felt the boy had to be involved with these two appalling crimes. Yet, if the boy had committed them, he would have had to have been ordered to do so. And that meant the Carruthers. Somehow I couldn't see those two becoming entangled in something quite so lurid. I was about to say as much when a flower-shirted man shoved through the crowd and confronted us. The stereotypes come crawling out of the woodwork, I thought and immediately wished there was something I could do for the big detective.

"If you're the police," the man demanded in a voice as shrill as a woman's, "why aren't you doing something about this?"

"Sir, I am doing what I can."

"I don't like it."

Harrington shrugged. The man was evidently a tourist, and the detective obviously felt as if he had more important people, like the natives, to be answerable to. "I'm sorry you feel that way, sir, but unless we can—"

"I want some protection!" the man said loudly and was instantly echoed by several of the crowd who had paused to listen.

Harrington smiled wryly. "Now how do you expect me to manage that with the force I have here? Did you know the man?"

"Of course not. I only arrived yesterday."

"Then what exactly are you worried about?"

"Well, that killer's obviously a maniac. He could kill anyone next."

The detective stared at him, then glanced at me. "No," he said quietly. "I don't think so."

"Well, what about that andy." someone else demanded. "Why the hell don't you lock it up? It's dangerous."

With that bit of melodramatic tripe, Harrington's patience finally reached its end. "Lady," he said with exaggerated calm, "if you can give me the proof, I'll snap that kid's tape faster than you can blink. But he belongs to someone, and there isn't anything I can do without proof. So why don't you, and all the rest of you, why don't you just go about your business and leave us alone. You want me to catch this man, boy, woman, whatever, I can't stand around here answering your hysterical, stupid questions."

For a moment I was tempted to applaud. In fact, one or two people did. But I just stood aside while the crowd dispersed, far more rapidly than I thought it would. Most of the people disappeared into the hotel, muttering loudly. The rest scattered and were gone within a minute's time. When it was quiet, Harrington signaled the ambulance driver, then slid into his own car. He rolled down the window, chewing his tobacco slowly. He spat. "Middle-class backbone of the race," he said to me and drove off. The ambulance followed and I was alone on the sidewalk. I don't remember how long I stood there, but staring passersby reminded me that I was dressed only in my bathing trunks and still carrying my beach paraphernalia. Embarrassed, I darted inside and rushed up to my room. In the bathroom was a first-aid kit, and after many painful contortions, I managed to empty the can of aerosol sunburn medication onto my back.

I felt flushed.

Feverish, nearly groggy as if in a nightmare.

Despite the air conditioning, the room felt warm, but I didn't want to go out again. Not for a while. A long while. In spite of some of the other hotel guests' fears, I realized I hadn't once felt as though I were in the slightest danger, and when that fact sunk in, I was horrified. I didn't believe I was in danger because I knew I had never been anything more than polite to the Carruthers and their son. *Guilty*. Jesus Christ, I thought they were guilty.

You son of a bitch, I told myself. You're as bad as the rest of them. Would a grown man murder for an insult as common as the ones Carruthers must have been getting for as long as he'd had the android? To strike back so drastically was too immature for the owner of a simulacrum—he would be too vulnerable.

Hell! It was not a pleasant day. It had not been a pleasant vacation. I hesitated and finally tossed my things into my bag. I decided to wait until after dinner to leave. Until then, I lay on my bed, and it wasn't long before I fell asleep.

I dreamt, but I'd just as soon not remember what it was I saw in those dreams.

In Starburst, the dark is not quite the same as in the rest of the world. Because of the mist on the hills, the slate and stone roofs, the moonlight and starlight glinted off more than just water, and the result was a peculiar shimmer that slightly distorted one's vision. When I awoke to that unnatural light, I had a splitting headache. Groping around on the nightstand, I found my watch and saw it was close to ten o'clock. Hurriedly I swung off the bed, thinking that if I were as good a patron as the hotel led me to believe, I might be able to squeeze in a meal before the kitchen closed for the night. The clothes I was going to wear home were laid out on a chair, and without turning on the lamp, I dressed, standing in front of the window. The moon was hazed, and what stars there were challenged my schoolboy knowledge of constellations. I was staring out over the building at the bay when I caught movement on the beach. All I could see was a group of shadows. Struggling.

I leaned forward, straining to make out details, curious as to who would be playing games this time of night, since Starburst was definitely not noted for its evening festivities. As I clipped on my tie, the shadows merged into a single black patch, then separated and merged again. But not fast enough to prevent me from spotting one of them lying on the ground. The figure didn't move, and for no reason other than an unpleasant hunch, I dashed from the room and, not wanting to wait for the elevators, ran down the fire stairs and outside.

Once on the sidewalk, I hesitated for the first time, realizing I could very likely be making a complete ass of myself. There were no sounds but the evening wind in the park trees. As I crossed the street, my heels sounded like nails driven into wood and I self-consciously lightened my step. I became more cautious, though feeling no less silly, when I entered an alley and could see the beach and bay beyond. By the time I reached the far end, I was almost on hands and knees, and now I could hear: grunting, and the dull slap of body blows, struggling feet scraping against the sand. It didn't take a mastermind to figure out what was happening, and, for all my professed cowardice, I burst from the alley shouting, just a split second before I heard someone gasp, "Oh my God, look at that!"

The group of people were close to fifty meters from me, and when they heard my racket, they scattered, leaving me behind, motionless on the beach.

I vacillated, then ran to the fallen body. Closer, and in the dim moonlight I could see it was the boy.

Standing next to him, I could see he was bleeding.

And kneeling, I knew he was dead.

A boy.

I panted, my breath shuddering.

A boy.

I'm not sure exactly what I felt at the moment. Shock, anger, sorrow. Anger, I suppose, the greatest of these. Not so much for the shadows who had killed him, but for the ruse he had perpetrated on us all. Callously I stared at his bloodied face and thought: you tricked me. Damnit, you tricked me.

Slowly I rose. I brushed the sand from my knees and walked swiftly back to the hotel. Just before I stepped into the lobby, I saw the whirling red light on a squad car, and I was glad I wasn't the one who had made the call.

The fourth floor, like the lobby and elevator, was deserted. I walked to the end of the hall and knocked on the Cartuthers' door. When there was no answer, I knocked again and turned the knob. The door opened to a darkened room, and I stepped in.

The man and woman were sitting motionless in identical chairs facing the room's only window.

"Mr. Carruthers?" I didn't expect an answer, and I received none.

I moved closer and gathered what nerve I had left to reach down and touch the woman's cheek, poised to snap my hand back should she flinch. The skin was cold. She didn't move, didn't react. She and the man stared directly into the moonlight without blinking. Carefully I rolled up her sleeve, and though the light was dim, I found the markings easily. There was no need to do the same to the man.

I was still standing there when the lights flicked on and Harrington lumbered in, followed by a covey of police photographers and fingerprint men. The detective waited until my eyes adjusted to the bright light, then pulled me to one side, away from the strangely silent activities. It was as if they were investigating a morgue. Harrington watched for a while, pulling out his handkerchief and again wiping his hands. I never did learn how he'd picked up that habit, but at that particular time it seemed more than apropos.

"You, uh, saw the boy, I take it?" he said.

I nodded dumbly.

"Didn't happen to see who did it, I suppose."

"Only some shadows, Harrington. They were gone before I got close enough to identify them. Any of them."

One of the men coughed and immediately apologized.

"Would it be too much to ask who called you?" I said.

"What call? I was coming over here to question the kid." He pulled a slip of wrinkled paper from his jacket pocket and squinted at some writing. "I checked on the, uh, parents, just for the hell of it, just to keep those people off my back. Seems he was fairly well off—the kid, I mean.

He is, was eighteen and from the time he was six was shunted back and forth between aunts and uncles like a busted ping-pong ball." He shook his head and pointed a stubby finger at some line on the paper. "When he reached majority and claimed his money, he bought himself some guardians. Parents, I guess they were supposed to be. According to some relative of his, this was the first place he brought them. Trial run." He shoved the paper back into his pocket as though it were filth. "I'm surprised nobody noticed."

I had nothing to say. And Harrington didn't stop me when I left.

My people.

He had deliberately exposed the false identification on his arm and had never once looked me straight in the eye. It was all there, but who would have thought to look for it? He had been challenging me and everyone else, using the simulacra to strike back at the world. Maybe he wanted to be exposed; maybe he was looking for someone as real as I to stop the charade and give him a flesh-and-blood hand to shake. Maybe — but when I think of going back to a city filled with androids and angry people, I get afraid.

And worse…my own so-called liberal, humanitarian, live-and-let-live armor had been stripped away, and I don't like what I see. As much as I feel sorry for the boy, I hate him for what he's done to me.

That crowd of shadows could have easily held one more.

I'm always being asked why I seem to lean toward the long, poetic-type titles. I honestly don't know. In this particular case, the title came first, out of nowhere, and I linked it with a notation in one of my journals that quoted what was to be the story's last line in its more popular form, with a suggestion to myself that perhaps the sentiment isn't as accurate as justice may demand. I do that quite a bit, actually. One of my greatest pleasures in writing dark fantasy is to take what one believes is "normal" and prove that it isn't. And in my world, the world of Oxrun Station, it never is. That's the fun of it. Otherwise, life would be as dull there as it is on the outside.

Hear Me Now, My Sweet Abbey Rose

Dusk; a haze of drifting light that keeps the eye from resting too long on a single tree, a faint star, a leaf that bumps over disused furrows poking out weeds. It drops a lace curtain over the farmhouse and blinds the windows, stills the dog, stirs the cat, makes the kitchen seem far warmer than it is. It takes the freshness from the daylight and returns the evening to the memory of winter. And summons the rolling black that follows a breeze from the surrounding hills. And by the time nightfall is full, and heavy, the only sound is a flock of geese invisible, calling, guiding, sweeping over the land and the house and the hills and the breeze.

Nels leaned against the kitchen door frame and shivered when he heard the birds. Beautiful in the bask of the sun, they were unpleasantly lonely in the hours past nine. Too lonely by far, and he slapped a hand to his thigh, closed the door and moved to sit at the table in front of the iron-black stove. Kelly turned from the refrigerator and held out a bottle of ginger ale. He nodded and pushed back in the hard wooden chair, swallowing at air, idly scratching at the traces of wattle at his throat. He said nothing. He liked to watch his wife move from place to place, within or without the confines of the house, knowing that other men envied him without reservation, knowing that he envied himself in his fear of losing her. She filled a glass, waited for the bubbles to settle, topped it and set it in front of him. Then, and only then, did she sit opposite him with a cup of tea protected by her palms.

"They're late," she said, blowing upward to fend off a strand of black hair drifting down toward her right eye. "I told them before dark."

"The place is still new," he answered, wrinkling his nose at the carbonation splashing into his face while he drank. "If they get lost, they'll call."

"Grace will," she said with a smile, "but not Abbey or Bess. They've got dollar signs in their eyes already, or didn't you notice."

He laughed and swept a plate of shortbread toward him, picked up one of the flour-and-butter cakes and bit into it. "They take after me. Grace is all yours." Then, with a frown: "Are you worried?"

She shrugged. "Not really, I guess. I just don't want them to have all their fun before the vacation is over, that's all. To get it all out on the first big night in town will make everything else seem…well, quiet."

"Dull," he said. "What you mean is, dull."

It was her turn to laugh, lightly, mocking the sigh of the breeze now turned to wind.

Ten o'clock, and the muttering of a car coughing into silence. Nels hustled Kelly into the front room, grabbed at a magazine and switched on the television. Then he thumped at the cushions on the dark quilted sofa, waved his wife to an armchair, and snapped open the first page before the front door swung in and his daughters arrived.

Physically, they were Kelly; from the black hair and eyes to the dark lips and slender figures to the nearly sickly pale complexions made disturbingly erotic by the nips of pink at their cheeks. Twenty, nineteen, eighteen, all in college, all with glasses, all standing with hands on hips staring in at their parents. Grace tsked, Abbey sighed, and Bess walked deliberately over to her father and turned the magazine right side up. "You're impossible," she said, kissing him on the cheek. Nels shrugged and asked how it went.

Grace and Abbey slumped to the braided rug by the raised brick hearth and pulled their heavy sweaters over their heads, shook their hair back into place, and folded the sweaters neatly in their laps.

"They may be rich," Grace finally said, "but you cannot believe how incredibly dull they are."

"God, Pop," Abbey said, pulling at her lower lip, "we went to some place called the Chancellor Inn. There's a restaurant upstairs—it's an old farmhouse, see, I think—and there's a poor excuse for a disco on the first floor. Lots of noise. No action."

"They thought we were rubes or something," Bess said, knocking his legs away so she could sit on the couch with him. "Hicks. I think they think we're going to move in here forever. Raise chickens or ducks, or whatever they do on a place like this."

Kelly looked up from her knitting—a sweater for Nels in muted blues and greys—and smiled sympathetically. Then she looked to her husband, frowned when he lit a cigarette, but said nothing when he studiously avoided her glare.

"Did you guys have a good time?" Abbey said, looking to her father.

"We watched the sun set over that tree in the field."

"Great," Bess said. "That's really…great."

"We heard some geese, too."

"Oh my God," Grace said, "I don't think I can stand any more. I'm tired, folks. I think I'll go to bed."

"Me, too," Bess said quickly. "It's the country air, or something."

Abbey alone stayed behind when the footsteps on the stairs faded into running bath water and the shouts of who gets in first and who uses what towel. She picked up a long splinter of kindling and drew roads between the bricks, connected them, drew them again.

"What's the matter, Abbey?" Nels said softly. "Aren't you tired?"

"Nope," she answered without taking her eyes from the hearth. "Just… I don't know. I guess I was expecting something different."

Nels stretched out on the couch again and pillowed his hands behind his head, stared at the dark-beamed ceiling and the shadows that lurked there from the lamp next to Kelly. The vacation in May had been his idea, what with all his daughters' schools ending early and he and Kelly climbing the walls from a particularly harsh winter. The farm had been a quick-growing inspiration, sparked by a friend at the office who had lived in this same house once and remembered—so he claimed—the great times he and his own family had had. Rediscovering the land, roots, the whole mystique of a Nature without city. Not to mention, it had been added slyly, the preponderance of wealth in Oxrun Station and the young men who were attached to it. Kelly thought that part of the argument crass and almost unforgivable; Nels didn't think of it at all. His daughters were, in temperament, much like himself—what came, came, and if it didn't—whatever it was—well, there was no use crying. Time never cried for a flower that died. But Abbey was his special flower, hence her middle name, and it disturbed him that she should be disappointed, that the unusual vacation had turned sour for her already. Normally, she was prepared for anything, to try anything, to at least give everything half a chance to prove itself worthy of her attention. But this, he thought, had somehow killed her enthusiasm before she had given it that one half chance.

"What?" he said finally, as she knelt on the hearth and arranged the logs to start a fire. "Come on, girl, what's up?"

"They told us there was a lynching here, back before the Civil War. Some abolitionists were hanged from the tree in the field out back. Four of them, I think. I didn't know they did stuff like that in Connecticut."

"You think the farm is haunted, then?" Kelly said, her disbelief evident and marked with the nail of her practicality.

"No, Mother, of course not."

Kelly looked to Nels, set her knitting in the carpetbag by her side and folded her hands in her lap. "Then what, dear?"

"I don't know, I told you! Let's just say the place doesn't feel right, okay?"

She rose then and hurried from the room, up the stairs and into the giggling storm that erupted when she opened a bedroom door. Nels listened to the laughter for a while and allowed himself a drop of sweet reminiscence, when they had lived in another house in another state, when the girls were younger and going to bed meant only another opportunity to invent new games and friends and create chaos from careful order. And now they were drifting away. It made no difference that he understood the inevitability of it, that young ladies and fledglings soon enough stretched their legs and their wings and discovered that the horizon moved when you approached it. That didn't make any difference at all when the sun had set and his girls were asleep and he could remember pajamas with feet and dolls with calico dresses, carriages and plastic tea sets and braces and boys.

Maudlin, Nels, he told himself; watch it, or you'll next be thinking how close to fifty you are, and that would crimp this week faster than you can sneeze.

———————

Nels, it doesn't feel right, Kelly said with her hands roaming gently over her swollen stomach.

Nonsense.

A mother knows these things, Nels.

All right, then, we'll call Dr. Falbo and see what's what.

It's not that kind of feel.

Then it's the Irish in you and the Norse in me. A combination of fey not seen since the world's creation. Don't worry about it, love, he'll be fine.

And what makes you so sure it'll be a he?

Fey, I told you. I have the sight, in case you didn't know.

And what if it's another girl?

Two girls? Are you kidding? How the hell can I possibly afford two weddings? But...if it's a girl, we'll name her Kelly Rose, after you and your mother.

Abbey Rose, she said with a grin. After my mother and the theater in Dublin.

If it is a girl, I'll want another shot at it.

You'll keep your distance, Nels Anderson, or you'll be singing soprano in some damned fey choir.

———————

Early the following morning, Grace and Bess took the car into Oxrun to, as they explained, see what was so special about all the fancy jewelry stores clustered there. Kelly ensconced herself in the kitchen to test the reputation of homemade bread. Alone, then, Nels wandered across the fallow field, jumping at startled grey mice, watching a pair of hawks riding the wind beneath a softly blue sky. He stopped every few yards to overturn a rock, dig around a burrow, marvel at the life no city ever maintained, marveling more that such continual amazements could become so mundane that the previous owners of the farm had given it up and moved to Los Angeles. At last, at noon and in no hurry, he reached the tree he had claimed for his own. It was a chestnut squat with age and broad with a crown that was flecked with new green. Weeds and grass grew up to its bole, surrounded knees of roots that nudged through the rocky soil. He had never seen anything quite like it, and as he grabbed at a twig dangling in front of him, wondered if even the yard of their suburban home would ever seem the same.

"Gruesome," a voice said behind him, and he jumped, a hand to his chest, his mouth open.

Abbey laughed delightedly, clutching at her stomach, stepped backward and fell, her legs splayed and her hands behind her to prop her up. Nels shook his head in rapidly diminishing anger, somewhat embarrassed, and pleased that she had come. He sat where he stood, crossed his legs and rested his palms on his knees. "Now that you've assured me ten years less of a magnificent life, kid," he said, "you can tell me what was really bothering you last night."

She had been having dreams of dying the past few months, each one sending her screaming into her parents' bed; in the last one, she had risen from her coffin at the church to sit beside her father.

Nels prayed they hadn't started again.

"Come on," he said gently, leaning forward slightly. "Come on, Abbey. You can tell me and the tree. We're old friends, the three of us."

Abbey puffed her cheeks. She was ready to deny him, then sagged and began pulling at green blades by her thighs. "They thought we were hicks," she said. "Kind of a reverse snobbery, I guess. Dumb country folk from the city, if you know what I mean. First they tried to get us drunk. Then they tried a few old-fashioned wrestling holds. We'd left the car at one of their houses...Frank's...he's the one who came out and introduced himself so nicely, remember? We left the car at his house. By the time we got back there, we were a mess. But..." and she grinned broadly, suddenly, "our virtue was, for the moment, ladies and gentlemen, still intact. Speaking for myself, that is." And her grin became a laugh.

Nels felt the warmth rising from below his collar, saw that she'd recognized his protective anger and coughed to keep himself calm. He reached blindly over his head, caught at a thin branch and pulled until his fingers had stripped a handful of leaves into his palm. He rolled them into a cylinder, pressed, rolled, and felt the moisture released and rubbed into his skin. It was a good feeling and an uncommon one. When he looked up, he saw his daughter staring at him.

"You're all right, though," he said, awkwardly.

"If you're asking if you have to buy a shotgun, the answer is no." She twisted until she was kneeling, took the crushed leaves from his hand and laid them to her cheek, her neck, across her forehead with her eyes closed. Then she stared at the tree and back to him. "Dad," she said, "if you only knew how natural you looked, sitting there."

"Ah," he said. "The primeval in me, that's what it is. One with the land and all that."

"No," she said, frowning as she puzzled it out. "Not quite. But it feels right for you to be here."

"Like it doesn't feel right to be in the house?"

She nodded, quickly shook her head and rose. "It's more like my room back home. I belong there more than anyplace else. You, though…I think you belong here."

"So I'll quit my job and we can play farmer for the rest of our lives."

She grinned, brushed at her jeans and smoothed her plaid shirt over her breasts. "Dad, what would you do if I got married?"

"I'd cry a lot and wish the boy luck. Lots of it."

"You'd let me? You'd let me go?"

He swallowed quickly the wisecrack that rose, sniffed and spread his hands helplessly. "I'd have to," he said quietly. "But I sure wouldn't want to."

"Neither would I," she whispered, knelt and kissed him on the cheek. "I love you, Dad. I don't say it enough, I know, but I love you."

Nels watched her leave. And the sadness that suddenly cloaked him grew when his hand absently touched at his close-cropped hair, blond turning white. That, he thought, is what New England does for you, pal; autumn in the spring. He knew there was a tear in his left eye, but he refused to acknowledge it by wiping it away. Soon enough, too soon, far too soon, it was gone, and he turned on his buttocks to stare at the bole, to follow its winding configurations and ease his mind into a state of near-trance. And it wasn't until a shout floated across the field that he came out of it, pushed himself to his feet stiffly and trotted back toward the farmhouse. He saw Grace standing on the back porch, waving her arms, and the trot became a run, the run a dash when his eldest leapt from the steps and raced toward him. She was crying as she dropped into his arms, sobbing out a garbled story of the three men they had met the night before; they had cornered her and Bess in a luncheonette, pressing until the girls had become frightened, following them to the turnoff from the main road and sitting there in their convertible, waiting.

"I'll have a look," he said as he led her back into the house. Kelly was not in the kitchen, but he heard soft sounds from upstairs and knew she was busily contorting the youngest. Grace sniffed loudly and borrowed his handkerchief. Ordinarily, had it been Abbey and Bess, he would have fallen instantly into the comforting father role he played for skinned knees and elbows, nightmares and thunderstorms. But Grace was twenty, a woman, and not easily shaken. Those men must have been more than simply crude, more than only playfully threatening. He set his daughter in the living room's armchair and slipped into his windbreaker.

"Stay there," he said. "Get yourself a brandy and light a fire. It'll be cold tonight. A Connecticut May is more like March."

He waited until she had reached for the decanter on the sideboard, then unhurriedly stepped outside and slid in behind the wheel of the car. The keys were still in the ignition, and he fired the engine, turned round the oval drive marked with a birch in its center, and drove the half-mile to the stone pillars that flanked the farm road's entrance. He braked, got out and walked to the main road that led in a direct line back to the village. There were no cars, no trucks, nothing at all that he could see save another field across the way and the faint rise of the low hill that marked the village park. Not a hill, really, he thought incongruously; more like a bump that the trees came to like.

He waited for nearly half an hour, leaning against one of the low brown pillars and smoking. When the twilight chill finally numbed his hands, he gave it up and drove back to the house, went inside and found all his women in front of Grace's fire. They were playing a word game found in the bookcase built into the back wall, and when they noticed him, they laughed, waved, and ordered him into the kitchen to make a sandwich supper.

"Done," he said, shucking his coat and tossing it to the couch. "Just don't complain if I'm not as good as Bess."

———

So she isn't the smartest in the world, Kelly, so what? She's got brains enough to make it through any decent college, and that's all that counts.

Suppose Abbey doesn't want to go to college?

All right, so she doesn't go. It's her choice, isn't it. It's her life, not. mine, for crying out loud.

Nels, sometimes I think you love her too much.

Kelly! Are you…are you saying that I spoil the girl?

God forbid, no, dope. I just mean…well, sometimes I think she's closer to you than any of us are, that's all.

Good Lord. Kelly, do the other girls…do they resent it? I mean, have I—

Failed them? Nels, you're beautiful when you're worried. No, you haven't failed any of us at all. You worry too much. That's your problem, you know, you worry too much. Especially about Abbey. It's fine to say it's her life, not yours, but whenever she's out, more so than with Grace or Bess, you lose more sleep than anyone I know.

I hate to admit it, but you're right. God, that's frightening, you know it? But sooner or later, she'll leave us. She'll grow up and the ties will be gone before we know it. It'll happen so slowly we won't even notice.

Maybe, I hope so. I hope it is slow.

It always is, isn't it?

I suppose so. Anyway, she'll probably be the first to get married, and then it'll be her husband's problem.

Maybe, but I'd hate to be the man to try her out.

Now why did you say that?

I don't know. I really don't know.

They were carrying no weapons that he could see, but the fact didn't make him any less nervous. He had heard the tires on the dirt road long before anyone else, had excused himself from the game to walk out onto the porch for an ostensible breath of fresh air. He refrained from lighting a cigarette, leaned against a post and waited until the car, a low black convertible, had glided without headlights around the birch and parked in front of his own. Three men climbed out, one of them giggling into a fist, and he knew instantly they were drunk and therefore too dangerous to reason with, unless he were lucky.

They arranged themselves at the foot of the porch steps. Steady, not weaving, but the stench of beer was as strong as their obvious sense of masculine outrage.

"Gentlemen," he said, more to hear his own voice than to make them aware he was there, "I don't recall any invitations being sent out for a party tonight."

"Want to see Gracie," said a stocky sweatered man. It was too dark to make out their features; they stood just beyond the diffused glow of the living room lights, were irregular black holes against the black of the evening. "I want to tell her something."

"Grace," he said evenly, "is busy right at the moment. I'll give her the message. Who shall I say is calling?"

"Oh my, 'who shall I say is calling,'" mimicked the one in the middle. "You're very polite, aren't you? Well, I can be polite, too, you know. That's Brett over there, and I'm Frank. See? I can be polite if I want to."

"Thank you," Nels said.

The one on the right, the unnamed one, stepped toward him, a man Grace's age but without the lines that would give him age and personality. He raised a fist. "Abbey has a date with me, old man, and I want her out here."

"My goodness," Nels said, pushing away from the post. "I don't think she remembers. And since she doesn't remember, perhaps you ought to find another place to play, all right, boys?"

Brett laughed, then, lunged and tripped over the bottom step as Nels whipped a shoe up into his chest, spilling him back into the unnamed one. They sprawled, cursing, and took a long time getting up. Frank just stood there, glaring, until Nels took a step down, and another. Then he swung a wild fist that Nels easily trapped with his hand, flung it aside contemptuously and pushed the man's face back sharply with his palm. He kicked out again to catch Brett between his legs, grinning at the anguished howl while he spun toward Frank, who was trying to dash past him. He caught the man's jacket, spun him back and into the side of their car, grabbed his legs and dumped him into the back seat. Brett, on his knees and retching, was hauled up by his collar and spilled into the passenger side. The third man turned to run when Nels faced him, shrugged and slid in behind the wheel. When Frank rose from the car floor and glared, Nels smiled at him politely.

"Don't say it," he said. "If you're going to come back and teach me a lesson, just come back. But don't say it, all right? It's much too corny."

He was back in the house before the car thundered away, surrounded by his wife and children whose amazement at his reaction was only slightly less than his own. He quickly dropped onto the couch, gladly took hold of an offered brandy and sipped at it until his hands stopped their trembling. When the tale was told, then, the girls preened proudly and Kelly clucked in admiration. Only Abbey, however, stood to one side, staring at him as though he were a stranger, yet not a stranger but rather someone she had known and had not recognized before. Her expression bothered him, but he thought nothing of it until he was in bed and Kelly was tracing promises across his chest.

"Scared?" he said into the darkness, feeling the cold of her hands.

"A little."

"Maybe we should leave in the morning. I asked for trouble and they'll probably give it to me. And I don't want you girls hurt, Kel."

"You did all right out there, Viking."

"They were drunk. A boy could have done it. Bess could have, for that matter."

"That's sexist."

He laughed dutifully, fell silent, a moment later sat straight up and leaned against the headboard.

"What?" Kelly said, her fear too soon open to hide. "What is it?"

"We will go on a picnic tomorrow," he said. "A regular old-fashioned picnic in the field beneath the tree. Complete with mice and ants and flies and all that good jazz."

"For God's sake, Nels, go to sleep."

"But damnit, I'm a hero! Don't I deserve some kind of a reward?"

Her quiet laughter infuriated him until she yanked him down by the hair to kiss him.

He said nothing at all about the look on Abbey's face, the look that was part fear, part question, a large part astonishment: you really *won't* let me go, will you, Daddy?

He said nothing.

He only shuddered.

For crying out loud, Kelly, I don't see any real problem.

But, Nels, she won't go. She's been accepted and she won't go!

All right, so she won't go, so what? If she wants to stay at home and go to the community college, that's fine with me. In fact, I'd rather have it that way. I don't think she's ready to leave just yet.

But what if she—

Kelly, will you please leave her alone?

No, Nels, you leave her alone!

The brown-and-blue blanket still smelled of the attic, but no one seemed to mind, and he sat with his back against the tree and watched them struggling with the lumps in the ground as they set out the food, the bottles of wine, the paper plates Kelly had bought in the village that morning. The air was slightly hazed with uncaring clouds that occasionally blinded the sun, but the day stayed warm and the breeze kept the light from baking too hot. They had discovered a battered soft tennis ball in a closet and had played run-the-bases, man-in-the-middle, and anything else they could remember or devise for the best part of three hours before their hunger rebelled and forced them to eat. The wine spilled freely, then, and Nels felt expansively patriarchal as he fed and was fed, joked and was laughed at, listened for the hundredth time to stories, the gossip, a vivid reenactment by his three daughters of his protection of the fortress the evening, the century, the lifetime before. Then they made solemn plans for Grace's birthday at the end of the coming week, for Bess's sophomore year, for Kelly's new furniture in their bedroom at home.

Then Abbey announced it was wild flower time, and the girls rushed off in a scattering while Nels brought his wife to his lap and nuzzled her hair, stroked her arm and watched as a black-bottomed cloud threatened the sky.

"Let's go for a walk," he said suddenly; and they did, wandering away from the three and the house until the latter was gone and the former a shadow.

"Abbey had another nightmare last night," Kelly said.

"It was those men," he said quickly. "They'd be enough—"

"No," she said, stopping, turning in the circle of his arms and looking into his eyes. "She dreamt she was dead, again."

He shook his head. "She would have come to see me, like always."

"I heard her crying, Nels. She didn't want to, and she did. There's something wrong, Nels. She's...she's afraid of you."

"She's had the dreams before," he said, ignoring her.

"Nels, this is serious, and you know it."

"It's the Irish in her."

"Dammit, Nels!" And she slapped his arms down and away, stalked back toward the picnic. He watched her go, his fists clenched, then hurried to catch up, saying nothing but remaining at her side. He would have tried an epigram or two, something appropriate or entirely non sequitur, but a sudden *crack* made him glance up at the sky. The wind had risen, cold and sifting through the trees at their back like some stalking beast at midnight. He hunched his shoulders and rubbed the back of the neck. Another *crack*, and Kelly stopped, her eyes wide and staring toward the tree. He followed and saw his daughters huddled around the bole, clutching at each other, heard then their screams in atonal harmony and...was running.

Kelly shouted behind him.

He ran, nevertheless.

A burrow snagged at his ankle and he fell, barely getting his hands into position in time, feeling his cheeks scrape across the rough ground to let out the blood.

Kelly was past him by the time he had regained his feet, and the shooting continued, the screaming continued, and as the tree grew closer than a hundred yards, he realized that no strike was meant, no killing…only a scare; and he began looking for the three men who had been beaten and were now sniping back. It was possible, he thought, that they were still behind the treeline at the edge of the field, hidden and laughing, but he only ran faster, toward the tree and his children. Kelly's arms were waving them down when they rose to greet her, and then…she was stopped.

She fell as though tripped, but Nels saw the spurt of blood at her left shoulder and fell beside her, shouting to Grace to keep the others down.

"Don't die, Kel, for God's sake don't die," he whispered repeatedly as he tore at her sweater, his jacket, his shirt, to ball up cloth and jam it against the wound. It came from a fair distance away, some part of him noted, or the shell would have gone through. As it was, she was too stunned to do more than whimper, too astonished to yet feel the pain. When he was done, he lifted her in his arms and carried her awkwardly, suddenly shouting in angered panic when Abbey stood to help him.

And was stopped.

With a scream.

She stood motionless for a second that lasted much longer, toppled with one hand grasping at a branch for support. Her fingers closed on a leaf. It held. Tore. She was face down on the blanket.

Bess broke and ran for the house, but there was no more firing.

There were images, then, of no certain continuity: of red flashing lights and white-coated men and men in blue uniforms and men in dark suits and a man intoning and a man moaning and a sling for an arm and a bandage for a face, and a printed sympathy card from the real estate agent in town.

Abbey was buried in the cemetery in Oxrun.

Grace took Bess back to their home, to clean and to wait for their parents and school.

Kelly wandered the house.

Nels wandered the field. The three men had had alibis, and none were arrested. Revenge gave way to sorrow to rage to a feeling that something…something was not right, not right.

"Nels, we have to go home. Your job—"

"I can't, Kelly. Don't ask me why. But I… can't."

Nels wandered, sat beneath his tree and wondered.

"Nels, they're giving your job away. I…we have to go back now. Grace and Bess need us. Dammit, Nels, it's been almost a month!"

He wanted to tell her to pack, that it was over at last; he wanted to say that life must go on, though, with Millay, he wondered just why. He wanted to. He could not. Kelly left the next day on the first morning train.

And he sat in the kitchen until the sun went down, drinking coffee, drinking tea, shaking his head and waiting for the tears, until just before ten he stiffened.

Oh, Jesus, no, he thought.

He pushed away from the table and stumbled to the door, opened it, crossed the porch and walked to the field. He was frightened. More frightened than when he had heard the first shot and knew what it was, more frightened than when he had stood on the porch and faced three drunken men. He looked back over his shoulder and saw the single light in the kitchen, warm, slightly blurred, and fading.

He told himself to stop. He did not, and could not, until he had reached the tree.

There was no wind.

The branches stirred.

"Abbey?" he whispered.

Stirred, and scratched.

"Abbey, I have a family still. They need me. You've got to let me go."

Leaves trembled.

"Abbey, please, I'm your father!"

Trembled, and curled.

He expected a voice on the wind that did not blow, a young girl's voice that would touch his mind with melancholy and a final good-bye.

What he did not expect was the muttering of anger, and finally the voice that hissed *turnabout, Father, is not always fair.*

This was my tenth published story, and the first to deal with the people who live and/or work on Hawthorne Street. Curious place, that. It seems to me now to be awfully damned long for all the stories written about it. But it has served more than one purpose. When I finally hit upon an idea whose supernatural horror didn't seem to fit into the neighborhood (for reasons which even now are thankfully nebulous), I had to take it somewhere else. In addition, the idea blossomed into a novel-length plot, and before I knew it I had created another setting—Oxrun Station. And to answer the question before it's asked—no, Hawthorne Street is not in the Station. I don't know where it is, to be honest. What I do know, however, is that "wishing will make it so" is something I wouldn't wish on my worst enemy.

Temperature Days on Hawthorne Street

The half-moon porch was partially masked by untrimmed arms of fully green forsythia and juniper dying at the tips. What breeze there was in pressing heat only caused to quaver the languid drone of hunting bees. A spider, working steadily in the shaded corner of a peeling post and sloping roof, ambushed a fly while a mantis lurking on the lattice flanking the steps watched, praying. There were ants, marching, but the man on the bottom step ignored their parade, waiting instead for the sounds of anger to drain from the house. He rubbed his face, tugged at his chin, blaming the summer-long heat for the pots he heard slamming onto the stove, the crack of cabinet doors, the thud and hollow roll of an empty can on the linoleum floor. He hunched at the sharp noises and glanced up the block, wondering why none of the houses to the top of the gentle hill had emptied at the aftermath of the fight.

Sounds carried on a street like this, he thought, like the night the week before when Casper Waters had ordered his wife to pack and leave just before the late evening news. By the time she had limped with a suitcase to her car and had driven around the corner, not a porch was deserted, not a lawn flickering flashlights carried by men ostensibly searching for lost tools. So now where are they, he wondered at the blank facades of Hawthorne Street. They're no better than I am. Why the hell don't they come out?

The milkman, he answered himself. They've figured the bogeyman milkman has done it again, and some of them believe it, and they're as afraid as I am.

A robin landed silently beneath one of the front yard's two ancient willows and cocked a brown eye toward the lawn.

"Gerry?"

It pecked twice and fluttered, hopping rapidly across the slate walk to the other side where it pecked twice again and flew off.

"Gerry?"

He leaned backwards, feeling the ragged edge of the step pressing against his spine, and tilted his head until his neck stretched close to choking. Ruth, her night-soft hair twisted back to a ponytail and wisping around her temples, looked down at him, trying to manipulate muscles that once made her smile. One softly tanned hand lay flat against her stomach, and he suddenly wished the baby would hurry up and show itself; his first daughter had kept Ruth slim, and had died before birth. He closed his eyes briefly, then stretched up a palm, holding it open until she covered it and came down beside him.

"They must be tired of men beating their wives," he said quietly, waving his free hand toward the street. "Not even old lady Greene's left her precious garden."

Nearly four years ago he would have been a father for the second time.

"Gerry, I'm sorry."

"Don't be silly, lover," he said. "You've nothing to be sorry for. I'm the one who started it. I guess I'm not used to such heat in September."

Smiling, then, she rested her cheek against his damp shoulder, and they watched for an hour the shadows of the willows glide away from the house. A lawn mower sputtered, a gaggle of small girls shrieked by in pursuit of a dream; there were birds and clustering gnats, and a Siamese cat that disdained Gerry's enticements for the stalking of a jay.

Then, explosive, a trio of boys sped past on bicycles, shouting and gesturing to one another before separating at the block's center, one to swerve widely and thump over the curb, mischievous bravado in the skid that came to a halt inches from the juncture of step and walk.

"Hi," he said, with Ruth's thin lips and Gerry's heavy jaw. "I'm too young for a heart attack," Gerry said, noticing absently the clotted mud on the boy's jeans. "Put the bike away and wash up. We're going out to eat; your mother's tired."

"She asleep?" his son whispered loudly.

"No," Ruth said, keeping her eyes shut. "I'm recovering from shock. One of these days you're going to hit these steps and wind up in pieces all over the porch." It should have been a joke, but the boy knew it wasn't. "Your father," she added, aware of the strained silence. "Your father just painted it last summer."

"It'll never happen," he said, laughing as he walked the bicycle around to the side of the house. "How much time?"

"Not enough time for you to call that girl," Gerry said. "Just wash up and get on out here. And change those pants."

"Maybe the milkman will bring me a new pair. I've sure messed this one up."

Ruth immediately sat up, preparing to stand, when Gerry grabbed her firmly by the wrist. "Relax," he said. "Sandy didn't mean anything by it. He doesn't know for sure. None of the kids do."

A joke, Gerry had thought in a long-ago May when the grass was new and the smell of it cut filled the neighborhood like meadowed incense. In addition to the family's usual order for milk, eggs and butter, he had added at the bottom of the note a mocking request for a clean shirt when Ruth had forgotten to do one up for him the evening before. They had laughed and gone to bed, and the following morning a package lay beside the milkbox. Inside was a shirt the proper size and perfect color for the suit he had been planning to wear.

"Now this is the kind of milkman I like," he said, but Ruth, though laughing, was uneasy. "Oh, come on, woman," he said. "This guy obviously appreciates a joke. I'll just leave the box if it'll make you feel better, and I'll bet it will be gone the next time he comes. Okay?"

He did, and when the plain-wrapped package remained, he only shrugged and shoved the shirt to the bottom of his dresser drawer. Ruth asked him to get up early enough to give it back personally; she was wary of gifts from a man they'd never seen.

"Now you're being silly," he said, more stubbornly than he had intended. "I'll be damned if I'm going to get up before dawn just to give a stupid milkman back his shirt. Besides, it's a pretty nice one, you said so yourself. I'll just wait for the bill and see how much he nails me for it."

There was a week before the payment notice arrived, itemizing nothing more than the dairy products they'd consumed. Gerry shrugged again and decided the shirt was a present. He assumed it was a clever bit of maneuvering for a whopping Christmas gift, but did not mind since he had planned after the first delivery to do it anyway. The Sweet Milk Dairy Farm was a firm he'd never heard of and decided was an independent farmer. Since he was willing to patronize the little guy over the big guy, especially one whose service provided unexpected benefits and the best tasting buttermilk he'd had since he was a kid, he ignored Ruth's misgivings.

Shortly afterward, he needled Ruth into asking for something, and when she proved as intransigent in her refusals as he was in his insistence, he petulantly added a request for a tie to match the shirt. And when it came, in a plain-wrapped box, he laughed all day, shaking his head and telling his friends at the office what a tailor he had. Bolder, then, he decided to ask for a suit to go with the shirt and tie; and this time, when the hand-tailored-to-fit-no-one-else sharkskin garment hung on a nail over the milkbox, he stopped laughing and began wondering what kind of racket he was getting himself into. Ruth, he noticed with some relief, had not said a word but placed the suit at the back of the closet, still wrapped in its clear plastic bag.

"You got to admit," he said at dinner one evening when Fritz Foster and the Yorks had joined them, "the man's a go-getter. I just wish he'd send me a bill or something. Ruth here thinks he might be peddling stolen goods. I've been thinking about asking around the police myself, to tell the truth."

Syd York, puff-cheeked and portly, glanced at his wife who nodded, and Gerry's eyebrows raised in question. "Yeah, yeah," Syd admitted. "We've been picking up a few things here and there ourselves. Like you, we figured it was some kind of joke but…what the hell, right? I don't ask questions and I get what I want. There was a set of golf clubs, a pair of shoes and…what else, dear?"

Aggie, her husband's twin, pointed at her mouth with her fork apologetically. Syd snapped his fingers. "Of course, how could I forget. Silverware! Aggie was complaining about the stuff we use in the kitchen and when I got my clubs, she snuck in a note for the knives and forks. Damn, but didn't we get real silver."

Aggie grinned, and Ruth only stared at her coffee.

Fritz placed his utensils on his empty plate and leaned back, his fingers tucking inside of his belt. "I asked for money." The women looked at him. Syd laughed, and Gerry only shook his head, not surprised that the block's resident investment broker would be the one to get practical with their dawn genie.

"How much?" he asked. "That is, if you don't mind me getting personal."

"Let's just say substantial, and I received every dime."

"Well, didn't you ask him where he got it?"

Fritz grinned at Ruth and shook his head. "I don't ask, my dear, I just take. The money was in large bills, and when I took it to the bank, it was good. As long as I don't see his face in the post office, what do I care how he operates as long as he keeps up the good work."

"Besides," Syd added, "how would you know him? None of us have ever seen him."

It had been like moving into another country, Gerry recalled thinking when he and Ruth deserted the city and the routine of the neighborhood settled over them like a worn and welcome sweater. The mailman knocked at every door and knew all the streets by name; a policeman walked the beat three times daily and was covered by a patrol car whose brace of blue was as familiar as the century-old maple on the corner. Through traffic was negligible, and the street was covered with markings for baseball and hopscotch and spur-of-the-moment games comprehensible only to the young. And the milkman, who might have used a fly-bitten horse for all the inhabitants knew, passed each dawn, and only the early-risers and insomniacs heard the clatter of empty bottles as he left each back door more silent than shadow.

No one tried to wake early enough to see him; an unspoken warning about breaking their charm.

As June released summer, children, and, sporadically, husbands, Gerry thought he noticed increasing reluctance to try their luck again. Indeed, they all seemed rather guilty about suspecting their good fortune and began ordering more dairy products than most of them could use. Then Syd, after drinking himself into melancholy on Gerry's porch, asked for a raise, and two days later he was promoted.

"Now that was definitely a coincidence," Gerry said. "I can understand a guy trying to pick up an extra buck peddling goods from God knows where, but there's no way a stupid milkman can get a guy a raise like that."

Ruth immediately agreed, but her face was drawn and he didn't learn until it was too late that she had finally contributed her own request. It was a Saturday morning when he backfired into the driveway and saw the sleek and gleaming automobile parked in front of the house. In the kitchen, Ruth was crying at the table. Confused, since there didn't seem to be any company in the house, he cradled her softly while she explained that she could no longer stand the daily wait for the call from the police saying he and their twelve-year-old car had died in the traffic.

"I thought about Syd, Gerry, and I was scared, but I put a note in and this morning this man comes up with a receipt saying we won this car and we have to pay the taxes but we have a week from this Monday, and I wish it was gone because I'm frightened."

Ridiculous, Gerry thought, coincidence. But nevertheless, he went to bed early and set the alarm for an hour before dawn thinking, the hell with the charm if it was going to do this to his wife.

In not entirely unpleasant contrast to the daylight's enervating heat, the morning was cold, and a residue wind from an evening thunderstorm hunted through the neighborhood for wood to creak and leaves to sail. Silently dressing in the clothes he'd left in the kitchen, Gerry sipped on hot coffee and rubbed his arms briskly. A groan from Sandy's sleep made him motionless, then he slipped a blanket over his shoulders and carefully opened the front door, picking out a chair on the far end of the porch where he could watch the walk that wound round the house to the back. He lighted a cigarette when he was settled, and he was startled by the flare of the match and shook it out quickly. He listened and heard nothing, watched and saw only the dark. The air was still damp and he hugged himself tightly but would not walk, knowing the floor boards made near as much noise as the children playing in the afternoon. Finally, he tried to count gorillas to pass the time and when he awakened, the sun was full in his eyes, and blinding.

Ruth was standing over him, smiling sadly. "Big brave watchdog," she said, offering him a steaming cup. "What were you going to do, sprinkle garlic over his horns or tackle him like the football star you thought you were?"

"Knock it off," Gerry said, feeling bad enough that his soap opera plan had failed without his wife telling him how foolish he looked wrapped in a blanket in the middle of August. "Did he leave anything?"

"Nothing."

"Well, damnit, he must have magicked me to sleep, or something. And I asked for a hundred dollars."

"Maybe he figures you were testing him," she said, leaning against the railing and huddling her arms under her breasts. "Maybe he doesn't like testing."

Gerry, suddenly angry because he was more than afraid, stood abruptly and started pacing. "You know, I should have listened to you because you were right from the beginning. This guy is up to no good. I think I'll cancel the contract, and we can get our milk from the store from now on." Then he glared because his wife was laughing. "Well, what's so funny, damnit? I spent a miserable time out here, I could have maybe even caught double pneumonia, and you think that's funny?"

Shaking her head, Ruth pressed into his arms and quieted. "No, dear, I don't think it's funny. In fact, I think it's kind of sad. Things are just so different out here, I can't really explain it. The city was bad, but at least we knew where we stood. Here, we get a little boost from an invisible milkman and we go into melodramatic hysterics. Maybe country rules are different, I don't know, but there's something wrong with us."

"What?" Gerry said.

"I'm not sure," she said. "But this isn't right."

A short exclamation from Ruth and a dry flurry dragged him reluctantly back to the present where the world appeared to be turning black at the edges of his vision. Feeling a shudder from Ruth, he looked down and saw a praying mantis disappearing over the side of the steps with what looked like the remains of a spider in its jaws.

"Do you want to change before we go out?" he asked quietly, wondering what was taking his son so long. Ruth shook her head slowly and he was dismayed at the ridges of darkened skin beneath her eyes, cursing himself for not noticing her condition sooner. To adjust from the city's frantic years had been difficult enough when she saw the proliferation of little girls Hawthorne Street had spawned, but the addition of the pregnancy in the century's worst summer was draining her of laughter; she had been claiming since the beginning that the baby hadn't felt right, and no amount of persuasion from husband or doctor could change her mind. And if I told her about the milkman, Gerry thought, she might literally kill me. Finally he eased a solicitous arm about her shoulders and drew from her a melancholy smile.

"I spoke with Syd on the golf course this morning," he said after calling for Sandy to get a move on. "We've decided to confront the dairy company—"

"Please, Gerry, I don't want to hear it."

"Oh, come on, Ruth, let's not start again, please? This milkman business is getting all out of hand. I don't see why you're letting it get to you like this. I mean, no one else is all that bothered."

"Well, maybe nobody else cares whether or not they're doing the morally right thing by letting this farce continue the way it has," she said angrily, shrugging away his arm. "I told you before I don't want that man, beast, whatever the hell he is, coming to my house anymore. Suppose Sandy starts sneaking notes to him? Suppose the other kids find out this isn't a game? Suppose..." She turned to him and he flinched at the hardened lines destroying her mouth. "Suppose one of you big brave men gets tired of his wife and asks for a new one? What happens then?"

Her hands went protectively across her stomach, accusing him with their barrier and he realized that she suspected what he had done.

Suddenly angry to camouflage his fear, he paced to the sidewalk and back, his hands fisted in his pockets. "What the hell are you talking about," he demanded as slowly and flatly as he could. "A few ties, a few shirts, one lousy set of golf clubs and everyone—no, you go flying off the goddamned handle. Tell me, do you see anyone else on this block worried? Do you see the place crumbling in moral decay just because a milkman runs a shoddy little business on the side?"

"What about Syd's promotion, and the new car?"

Gerry spun around, frustration at his wife's persistence threatening to erupt in shouting. "Syd has been with that firm for fifteen years, and a promotion was just plain due. I won that bloody car in a raffle at the office and what the hell more explanation do you want anyway, Ruth?"

"The hundred dollars."

"For crying out loud, I didn't get it."

"Yes," she said. "Yes, you did."

Gerry stopped just as Sandy ran out the front door and flopped next to his mother, grinning. "Well?" he said. "We going or not?"

"In a minute," Gerry said to him before turning back to Ruth. "What are you talking about, Ruth? What hundred dollars?"

Ruth obviously did not want to continue the argument in front of their son, but Gerry's face, in an uncontrollable sneer, forced her to ignore him. "In the mail while you were out with your precious friends on that precious golf course. A check from the insurance company. Overpayment."

Gerry froze, the sun suddenly chilling as he loosened and began waving his hands impotently in the air. "Nonsense," he said. "Pure nonsense."

"Then what about this baby?" she said, throwing the question like scalding water into his face. She stood, then, swaying, crying silently, her head shaking away what answers he might have had. Sandy gaped before reaching up to her, but she only cried out and ran into the house.

"Dad?"

Gerry fumbled in his hip pocket, pulling out his wallet from which he yanked the first bill his fingers could grip. "Here," he said hoarsely, extending the money blindly, "take the bike and grab some hamburgers or something. I..." He looked helplessly at his son who nodded and left without a word. When he returned with his bike, Gerry looked at him. "Your sister," he started but could not finish.

"I know, Dad," he said. "Today should have been her birthday, right?"

Gerry nodded mutely and stared as his son wheeled into the street and vanished around the corner; the boy seemed so old. He watched the empty sidewalks until his legs began to tremble, then he shuffled to the porch and sought out his chair in the far corner, remembering the night he had waited and slept, and the morning when Ruth had smiled and laughed at him. Though he didn't see how it was possible, he was positive Ruth knew he had asked the milkman for a daughter to replace a daughter. He had done it, he told himself every evening in freeflowing nightmares, because she needed it, because the two of them had been too afraid to try again only to renew the pain.

"Insane," he muttered to a hovering bee.

And did she know, he wondered, that Casper Waters had asked for his freedom and had found his wife naked in bed with Fritz Foster?

"Insane."

"I'll tell you," Syd had whispered confidentially at the course that morning, "If I had the nerve, I'd dump Aggie in a minute for a twenty-year-old girl without ten tons of fat."

Perversely, the temperature climbed as the sun fell, and perspiration on his neck trickled warmly to his chest and back. Cicadas passed him a childhood warning of the next day's heat and he dozed, fitfully, swiping flies in his sleep, flicking a spider from his shoulder. Up the street there was music, and Sandy drifted back for permission to accept a last-minute invitation to a block party over the hill. Inside, the house was dark though he had heard Ruth stumble once in the living room.

Embryos floating through ink and white blood, their faces not his, not hers, blank and unfilled and waiting for a wish from unarmed despair.

There was a rattling far back in his dreams that twisted his head until he snapped awake and heard the footsteps on the walk.

"Hey," he said sleepily, and the footsteps halted. "I, uh, was just kidding about the daughter bit, you know." He shook his head but remained groggy and nodding, his speech slurred though he heard himself clearly. "I mean, let's face it, shirts are one thing, a kid's another, you know what I mean? Hey, you know what I mean?"

There was a silence before the clinking resumed and Gerry slept on, dreaming pink and white lace, until he awakened, the sun barely rising, to Sandy's shouts for help and Ruth's hysterical screaming.

In 1968, six months before my twenty-sixth birthday. I was drafted into the Army. In that same month I had also sold my first story, a pastiche of Burroughs in a horror setting (for the record, it's "The House of Evil," published in Fantasy and Science Fiction, *December 1968). I wasn't sure whether to laugh or cry, and I suppose I did both. Especially when, the following December, I found myself in Vietnam. Quy Nhon, to be exact, serving as an MP. We had many duties in that port "city," among them were guarding prisoners, doubling as infantry, and working the convoys. A year later, thanks to a sniper working out of the graveyard that fronted our camp, I was in the hospital. While there I saw a tiny, smoke-skinned girl whose chest urn being held together by large, gold pins. I was told she was a victim of the Viet Cong, who'd invaded her Montagnard village and slaughtered all but her. She never smiled. She never spoke. She sat in her bed all day and held a tiny rag doll one of the nurses had given her.*

This is the first and only time I've written about that war.

Come Dance with Me on My Pony's Grave

November, and an aged slate sky; a wind snapping across the fields like a bullwhip and cracking around a golden brown house that squatted warmly on the grey landscape.

Aaron, huddled in a winter-worn and crimson jacket, was slumped, seemingly relaxed, against the jamb of the open front door, his hands flat in his pockets. His eyes were narrowed against the wind, and they shifted quickly along the partially wooded horizon, blurring the Dakota spruce and pine to a green-and-grey smear of almost preternatural fear.

Behind him the house was empty, and silent. There was only the wind and an occasional wooden creak.

He shivered.

Suddenly an explosive gust caught him unprepared, and shoved him off balance; a magazine was blown to the floor in the living room, and a shade snapped against glass. Reluctantly he closed the door and cut off the warmth from his back. His lips twisted into a half-smile. A good thing Miriam's not here, he thought as his mind mimicked her laughing scold: Aaron Jackson, what do you think we are—Eskimos? Just look at my curtains blown all over, and the cold, Aaron, the cold… He grinned, shook his head and closed his eyes briefly to allow her face to flash before him reassuringly. The wind gusted again, and his smile faded. Come home, Miriam, he thought (nearly prayed), come home soon—the boy frightens me yet.

Then he resettled himself to wait, arms folded and pressed tightly against his chest. He squinted into the cold, his eyes moving, moving as they had once been trained to do, watching and waiting…

… under a multigreen canopy of broad leaves, twisted vines and knee-high, waist-high brush beside the paths he and his men rarely used as they climbed for hours through the bugs sweat heat dirt world. A ragged clearing ahead where the village so often visited was hidden, and the smoke-skinned, half-naked Montagnards who gave them the news that the enemy had long since fled—all save one who, this time, belonged to them, not the soldiers. Water, then, with iodine tablets to kill the bacteria, and orange flavoring to kill the taste. While he watched the jungle and his men relaxed, finally. And the boy—eight, perhaps nine—stood by a black patch of earth where several men were racing the sun, digging what looked to be a grave. A shout…

… and Aaron blinked and watched a slight figure break from the trees and zigzag swiftly across the field, arms waving wildly in greeting. He grinned and, pushing himself away from the house, limped heavily toward the fence as grass crackled sharply beneath his feet. He shivered and wondered how the boy had managed to adapt so rapidly to the four seasons so radically different from the hot and not-so-hot of the mountain jungles.

At last the boy reached the yard and with a melodramatic gasp draped himself over the faded white rail, his face darker, but not red, from exertion.

"Hey, Dad."

"Hey, yourself."

"Boy, am I…bushed?"

Aaron nodded. "Bushed, pooped, beat, tired…in fact, you look like all of them rolled into one." He was tempted to ask where his adopted son had been, and thought better of it. "Come on inside, David, and get yourself warm. Your mother'll kill me if she finds I let you catch cold the minute she decides to go visiting."

The boy was thirteen and still quite short (would never be much taller), and as he dashed back to the house ahead of his father, his long straight black hair whipped his shoulders and the air, while Aaron watched carefully for hints of the past until he realized what he was doing and scolded himself silently for behaving like a damned fool. The boy, he insisted to his shadow, was an American now. But he could not help the growing feeling that, without Miriam, David thought of him only as the lieutenant who took him away. He glanced back at the trees and shut the door.

"Sit down, Dad," David called from the kitchen. "I'll make you some hot tea. Did Mother call today?"

"Yes, I'm afraid she already has," he answered. "About ten, ten thirty. You were out with Pinto, I think."

"Nuts."

Aaron laughed and, after shucking his coat, stretched out on the sofa, letting the room draw the cold from his skin to die in the dark glow of the beams and paneled walls. And everywhere, the scent of Miriam.

Then he heard a cup shatter, and he sighed when David, none too quietly, began muttering to himself. "Hey, in there," he shouted. "We speak English in this house, remember?"

The boy poked his head out of the kitchen and grinned broadly. "Sorry, Dad, but that's all I remember any more."

"The swearing?"

"But, Dad, they're the best kind, don't you know? I heard the GIs use them all the time."

There was a sharp silence before David finally giggled and thrust out an open hand. "Look, Dad, I was only counting. I don't remember any more than that, honest." He waited a moment, staring, then frowned and disappeared.

Now that's got to be a crime, Aaron thought, recalling all the tedious, impatient hours he had spent scraping together enough of the tribe's language to make himself, and his mission, understood; there were still a few isolated words and phrases that returned to him when he pressed, yet the boy had forgotten a lifetime. So he said. Once, when Aaron had been feeling particularly moody over his crippled leg, he had asked David if he minded being away from his old home, toppled through a sargasso of red tape and interviews into a country and life style as alien to the boy as the jungle was to Aaron. David had smiled, a little softly, and shook his head. But the black eyes were expressionless; they always had been since the death of his father.

"Hey, Dad! Quit daydreaming, please? This stuff is hot."

Aaron smiled and took the steaming cup from the offered tray. David sat cross-legged on the rug, watching intently as Aaron tasted the tea and nodded his approval. "Your mother," he said, "will be jealous."

David finally returned the smile, then turned his head toward the bay window as if he were plotting the darkening sky, listening for the invisible wind. He squirmed. Coughed. Aaron amused himself with the boy's impatience as long as he could; then, softly, "Pinto must be starving. Is he on a diet or something?"

And the boy was gone. To a pony named Pinto, horse enough for a youngster who would never be tall, not even average. They had both arrived on the same day, and five years later they were inseparable. Wind, Aaron thought. Both of them.

The telephone shrilled. Aaron grunted away a cramp that knifed his mine-shattered leg as he headed into the hallway and picked up the receiver.

"Jackoson, that you?"

Aaron winced. "Yes, Mr. Sorrentino, it's me."

"Damned good thing. Want to tell you those wolves are back again. Went after two of my rams this morning. Saw them. Big as horses they were. Chased them into the woods, I did." Right to my place, Aaron thought bitterly, thanks a lot. "I got a shot at them."

"You what?"

"Said I got a shot at them."

"Damn it, Sorrentino, my boy was playing there today. You know he always—"

"Did I hit him?" The voice was singularly unconcerned.

"Christ, no! If you had, do you think I'd be—"

"Then don't worry about it, Jackoson. I'm a perfect shot. I hit what I aim at. That kid—"

"My son."

"—won't get hurt, don't you worry about that. But one thing, Jackoson…I, uh, don't want to make any trouble, you understand, but I wish you would straighten out your kid about where your property ends. Him and that damn pony scare hell out of my sheep."

"If I didn't know you better, Mr. Sorrentino, I'd be tempted to think that you were somehow trying to threaten me."

A raucous laugh and a harsh gasping for breath. Aaron wanted to spit at the phone. "Just wanted you to know, Jackoson, don't get so worked up. You soldier boys get excited too easy."

"I just don't like the tone of your voice, Sorrentino."

"So sue me," Sorrentino said, and hung up.

Aaron breathed deeply and grabbed the edge of the hall table. "I could kill you so easily, Mr. Franklin Sorrentino," he said to the wall. "So goddamned easily."

"Dad?"

Aaron spun around to face the boy standing in the hall…

… standing by the gash of a grave while the jungle severed the sun's scattered light and a pit fire substituted shadows for trees. Lt. Jackoson shifted uneasily on the ground and lighted a cigarette as the boy stared at him. There was no recognition in the black bullet eyes though the man and the boy had often played together whenever the squad came to stay and use the friendly village as

a base. Now Jackoson saw only a new, weary emptiness, and deeper: a purpose. The grave was for the boy's father, the shaman of the tribe...

... the boy's voice was quiet. "I don't like him, Dad." The words spun high, and Aaron shivered a remembrance while he stood in the tunnel-dark hall. David moved as silently as he spoke. Even on the Shetland he was noiseless—in the early days, when the boy was still learning, Miriam had said: he's like a ghost, Aaron, and he frightens me. In the early days. There were still remnants of the mountain in him, but Miriam no longer saw them. "He's greedy, Dad, and doesn't...feel for things."

Aaron nodded, just barely stopping himself from patting the boy on the head. He had learned early that "sin" was too weak a word for such a gesture. Instead, he grabbed his shoulders. "Go watch some TV, son. Forget it. It's not worth worrying yourself."

They walked, the son just behind, into the living room and dimmed the lights. Before Aaron switched on the set, David curled into a corner chair where the age in his voice belied his thin body. "Why doesn't he like me, Dad?"

Aaron knew this was not a time to smile away a question. Five years before, his greatest fear had been what the other youngsters would think of his adopted son, but the smoke-grey skin and the hint of Polynesia in his features had given him instant acceptance, especially with the girls; David, however, was only always superficially friendly. "I don't know, son. Perhaps he's lonely with no children of his own, and that wife of his is enough for any man."

"He thinks I'm different." The tone said: he knows I'm different, and you're afraid that maybe he's right.

"Perhaps."

"I don't like him."

"David, he's not going to be the only one in your life to think you're...well, not the same as others. You're quite a unique young man."

"He hates Pinto. He say, last week when he run me away, it was a silly name for a horse. Pinto doesn't like him either. He try to kick his stomach once."

"Oh." Aaron, forgetting to correct the boy's English, thought he was beginning to understand Sorrentino's surliness.

"He missed."

In spite of himself, Aaron said, "Too bad."

The boy laughed quietly.

"Listen, David, Mr. Sorrentino doesn't really understand how you can…can *be* with animals. Most boys…do you know what rapport means?"

"No, Dad, but I think I can make guesses."

"Well, good. Rapport, you see, isn't always explainable. Sometimes it's something that just happens or belongs to a way of life that people just can't grasp. Like…" and he stopped, thought and decided not to mention the shaman. "And, if you don't mind me asking," he said instead, falsely lighter, "why did you name him Pinto?"

David laughed again. "It suits him."

"How? He's all brown?"

"It feels right, Dad. It suits him. He runs and leaps and …he's like me in many ways. His name is right."

"Well, Sorrentino can't understand that, son."

"I know. He doesn't…feel. I don't like him."

Aaron frowned in concentration, seeking the speeches that would stifle the hatred he knew the boy was feeling. It was wrong to allow this to fester, wrong not to show the boy that some men must be tolerated, that, as the saying goes, it takes all kinds. He tried, but he took too long.

"I'm going to bed, Dad. Good night." David uncurled from the chair, stayed out of the light until his bedroom door closed behind him. Always closed. Sanctum.

Aaron hesitated in following, then sat again. For the first time since they had been together, David had lied to him. So blatantly, in fact, that its very obviousness pained more than the deceit itself. The language. He knew David had not forgotten all but the numbers. Once in a while from behind the door, a muttering filtered through the house and filled him with dreams. Songs chanted on horseback across the fields and through the half-light in the pines; the whisperings to the animals. Black hair and black eyes and a strength in slender arms that contradicted their frailty. Montagnard. Mountain dweller. Outcast.

Christ! he thought and chided himself for allowing his mind to become so morbid. The weather, his leg and Miriam's absence were getting to be too much. He decided to call her first thing in the morning and ask her to cut her visit short. Her mother wasn't that lonely, and he needed her laughter.

He dozed fitfully until the telephone twisted him stiffly from the couch. His watch had stopped. He stood, scratching his head vigorously, then stretched his arms over his head. "All right," he mumbled. "All right, all right, for God's sake." *Daylight*, he thought in amazement. That little dope didn't even wake me so I could sleep in a bed; how the hell did I oversleep? Glancing at the front window, he noticed streaks on the glass and the shimmer of ice on the walk. Rain, freezing rain was the last thing he needed with David pouting and his wife gone. For a moment he was ready to let the phone ring and crawl into bed to hide. The house and that damned phone were making him nervous.

Still rubbing the sleep from his face, he leaned awkwardly against the wall and snatched up the receiver. "Yeah, yeah, Jackoson here."

"Aaron, this here is Will."

He stiffened. "Yes, Sheriff, what can I do for you?" There were excited noises in the background; a man was bellowing angrily.

"I'm over at the Sorrentino place. You'd better get over here."

"David?"

"No, nothing's happened to the boy. But Sorrentino accidently shot the pony. He's dead."

"I'll be right there." No thought, then, only an endless stream of cursing accusations: half in relief for his son's safety, half in anger at the rancher's murder of the boy's pet. His coat, first jamming on its hanger, refused to slide on easily. The pickup stalled twice. He shook uncontrollably, and his leg throbbed.

The truck skidded on the icy road, but Aaron, barely aware that he was driving at all, ignored the warning. Twice in two days he had wanted to kill, and twice he was unashamed for it.

There were two town patrol cars parked on the shoulder of the road when he arrived, and he nearly ran up the back of one as he slid to a halt and scrambled out. There was a small crowd hunched coldly in the vast, well-tended yard: police, several neighbors looking ill-at-ease, Sorrentino himself pounding his arms against the air by the sheriff, and David standing quietly to one side...

...while the oldest men carefully lowered the body of the shaman into the oversized grave. They scuttled away, then, and the boy stepped up to drop in the trappings of his father's profession, a lock of his own hair, a brown seed, a young branch freshly cut. They buried the war-murdered man beneath black earth and passed the remainder of the night mourning. Lt. Jackoson continued to watch the boy—a one-time, now distant friend. He watched the boy sitting calmly on the grave, staring at the prisoner, a scarred man in a tattered blue uniform. Jackoson had warned his men to mind their own business this time, and they did, gratefully; but few slept and all were uneasy. And still the little boy stared...

...at the ground until Aaron placed an arm lightly around his shoulders and he looked up. No greeting. A look was all. Sheriff Jenkins, a scowl and sympathy fighting in his face, walked hurriedly over with Sorrentino directly behind him. Aaron glared at them, barely able to contain the rage he felt for his son. "How?" he demanded without preliminaries. Sorrentino tried to bull forward, but Jenkins held up a hand to stop him.

"Frank here called me about forty-five minutes ago, Aaron. Said he was afraid he'd shot your son."

"I was just inside the wood, Jackoson," Sorrentino said, his voice oddly harsh. "I was chasing them wolves. I heard this noise right where I spotted them last, so I let go—"

"Without being sure?" Momentarily, Aaron was too appalled at the big man's stupidity to be angry. "You know kids are playing in there all the time. My God, Frank, you're a good enough shot to have waited a..." He stopped, seeing the retreat in the other man's eyes. "You..." He shook his head to clear it. "You... no, you couldn't have. Not even you."

"Now wait a damn minute, Jackoson."

"Shut up a minute, Frank."

"But, Sheriff, that man just accused me of deliberately killing that kid's animal!"

"He didn't say that, did he?"

Sorrentino sputtered, then wheeled and stalked away, muttering. Jenkins didn't watch him leave; Aaron did. "Listen, Aaron, I couldn't find any evidence that it happened any other way than he said. I know how you two feel about each other, but as far as I'm concerned, his story holds up. I'm sorry, Aaron, but it was an accident."

Aaron nodded, though he was just as sure the sheriff was wrong.

"Look, if you want, the boys and I will take the—"

"No," David said.

Aaron saw the look on Jenkins's face and knew it was the first thing David had said that morning. Against his better judgment he agreed. "We'll take him, Will. But thanks anyway. I'd appreciate it if some of your men would help me put him in the truck."

The sheriff started to say something, but the boy walked between them, past the neighbors to the truck where he let down the gate and stood by, waiting.

"The boy wasn't on the pony," Will said. "It must have wandered off while Davie was playing."

Aaron nodded. And what, he thought, was David playing?

Pinto's head had been hastily wrapped in a blanket now matted with blood. David sat stroking the animal's rigid flank. Through the rear-view mirror, Aaron could see the hand moving smoothly over the cooling flesh. In his own eyes were the stirrings of tears. For once he thought he knew how the boy felt, to lose a friend much more than a pet. He drove slowly, turning off the road just before his own land began. There was a rutted path leading into the wood to a clearing where the boys of the surrounding farms had erected forts and castles, trenches and space ships. At its western end was a slight rise, and it was there that they sweated in the cold noon of the grey slate day and buried Pinto. The wind was listless, the rain stopped. When the grave was filled, Aaron walked painfully back to the truck to wait for David, and an hour passed before they were headed for home, and all the way Aaron tried vainly to joke the boy back into a fair humor, even promising him a new pet as soon as they could get into town. David, however, only stared at the road, one hand unconsciously working at his throat.

Immediately they arrived at the house, the telephone rang and Aaron grabbed for it, hoping it was Miriam. It was Sorrentino, apologizing and sounding unsettlingly desperate; and Aaron, eager to talk, eager to turn from his son's depression, profusely acknowledged the other's story, and damned himself as he spoke. Sorrentino kept on. And on. He was babbling, Aaron realized, very often incoherent, and in his puzzlement at the rancher's behavior, he responded in kind, knowing he sounded like an idiot, trying not to admit that he was somehow, inexplicably afraid of his own son.

When Sorrentino at last rang off, Aaron felt rather than saw the boy's bedroom door open. He would not turn. He was not going to watch grief harden the young face. "It'll be all right, son," he said weakly. "In time. In time. You…you have to give it time."

The boy was a shadow. "He could see, Dad."

"We can't prove that, son."

"He could see everything. The brush isn't that high."

"David, we cannot prove it. Things are different here, you know that. We have to prove things first."

And still he did not turn.

"He did it on purpose. You know that, and you won't do anything. You know it and…"

Turn around you old fool. He's only a boy. He's only a boy, for God's sake…

…for God's sake, the lieutenant thought as he watched the hoy sitting on the grave, how long is he going to stay there? His eyes, burning from the darkness and the fire's acrid smoke, shifted to the prisoner. The man was staring at the shaman's son, entranced, it seemed, and unmoving. He was unbound, but none of the tribesmen seemed to care. They were confident with knowledge that Jackoson didn't have, and Jackoson didn't like it. He tried instead to think of home and a place where people behaved the way they were supposed to…

… behave yourself, stupid, he thought, and send the boy to bed. He'll feel better in the morning.

"You'd better lie down, now, Dad," the shadow said. "Your leg must be hurting after all that digging."

Aaron closed his eyes and nodded, feeling for the first time since leaving the house eons ago the painful strain that nearly buckled him. A moment later he felt the boy's arm around his waist, guiding him firmly to the bedroom. In the dim curtained light, he watched David prepare the bed, then stand aside while he eased himself between the cold sheets. David smiled at him.

"We'll...we'll see the sheriff again in a few days, son. We'll talk to him."

"Sure, Dad."

"And David, don't...I mean, you know, don't try to do anything on your own, you know what I mean? I mean, don't go off chasing his sheep into the next county or smashing windows. Okay?"

The boy paused in the doorway. "Sure, Dad. You want your medicine?"

"No, thanks. I'll be all right in a little while. Just call me for dinner."

"Okay. I'm going to read or something. You need anything, please call."

Aaron smiled. "Go on, son." And after the door closed, he wondered, not for the first time, if he had been right in taking the boy away. Neither, in half a decade, seemed closer to understanding the other than when they had started out on the plane from Saigon. They spoke the same language, shared the same house, but the rapport David had with the animals, with Pinto, was missing between father and son. The war was no longer a threat, its use as a bond had dissolved.

I don't know my own son, he thought.

A part of his mind told him to stop feeling sorry for himself: the problem wasn't a new one.

I'm not feeling sorry for myself.

You sound like one of Miriam's soap operas.

I don't.

He's an ordinary boy who needs time. He's seen war.

He's had five years, and so, by the way, have I.

And when he slept, he dreamt of a slight mound in a path supposedly cleared and the sound he felt and heard before waking screaming in a hospital in Japan with a leg raw and twisted. He had refused amputation. He needed the leg.

When he opened his eyes, it was dark. He tried to fall asleep again, but a rising wind nudged him back to wakefulness. Finally he swung out of bed and dressed quietly. He was hungry and thirsty. Cautiously, he crept into the kitchen to fix a snack and unaccountably remembered a rancher he knew in passing who had a string of Shetlands he rented to pony rides during the summer fairs. Maybe, he thought, he could persuade this man to part with one of his animals on credit. It would be easy enough to explain what had happened to Pinto. The man would have to help him. Slowly the idea grew, hurrying his actions, making him grin at himself. Without stopping to drink the coffee he had poured, he hastened down the hall to David's room.

It was empty. His boots were gone, and his jacket. There was a hint of panic before Aaron realized that David, still mourning, had probably gone out to the barn to Pinto's stall. Snatching his coat from the closet, he rushed outside, gasping once at the cold air and the strong wind that slid across the now-frozen ground. A digging pain in his thigh caused him to slow up, but long before he'd fling open the barn door, he knew the building would be empty. He stood in the barnyard, aimlessly turning, seeking a direction to travel until he saw the faint orange glow over the trees. He stared, hands limp at his sides, squinting, thinking, denying all the fears that founded his nightmares. He knew his century and still refused to believe what he had seen on the jungled mountain, dreaded what he might see if he followed the light.

It was just before dawn…

…and Lt. Jackoson was the only squad member still awake, the others sleeping in luxurious safety for the first time in days. Night noises. Night wind. He was drowsy and rubbed the blur from his eyes. Curiosity prodded him; he rubbed his eyes again. The fire burned sullenly at the side of the grave. The boy was naked, now, and standing…

…running over the ice-crusted ground, Aaron was pushed from behind by the wind. He ignored his leg as long as he could, concentrating on the wavering line of trees ahead. Then, just inside the tiny wood, his foot pushed through a hidden burrow and he slammed to the ground. Palms, knees, forehead stung. When he tried to stand, his leg wrenched out from under him, and he cried out. Before him, trunks and branches, brush and grass twisted slowly in the light of the fire, weaving darkness within darkness. Aaron pushed himself to one leg, his teeth clamped to his lips and, using the trees for support, hobbled toward the clearing. His left leg went numb, the pain felt only from the hip, and finally he collapsed.

Not now, he begged, not now!

He crawled, forearms and one foot, seeing his breath puff in front of his face, seeing his hands turn a dry red from the cold. Then there was a break in the pine, and he saw the boy...

...on his father's grave, shuffling slowly from side to side, humming to himself as he stared at the mound beneath his feet. The tribe had reassembled, squatting in the shadows, silent. The pit fire cracked...

...on the rise, and the smell of burning pine pierced the brittle air. And beneath himself and his son, Aaron saw...

...the prisoner seemingly rooted in place, turned so his face was hidden. The boy, not looking up, not acknowledging the world's existence, muttered something and the man shuddered...

... beneath his heavy, fur-trimmed hunting jacket. There was a rifle, useless now, dangling from one hand. Aaron tried to push himself up, to stand, but the agony was too great, and at the moment all he wanted was the heat from the fire that silhouetted the boy...

...shuffling faster, mumbling in rapid bursts while the prisoner swayed, slipped back, then lurched forward. Slowly, toward the grave, in the light of the fire. Jackoson thought he was dreaming...

...but the cold was too real, and he wondered how the boy, so lately his son, could stand the wind that whipped the flames from side to side and drew...

...the prisoner toward them, stiff-jointed like a grotesque marionette. The jungle...

...the clearing was quiet, and Aaron could hear the boy, chanting now, urging, taunting the big man forward. Aaron tried shouting, but his throat was too dry, his mind unable to break loose his tongue. All he could see was the rifle glinting. Sorrentino moved. Lumbered. Silent.

Prisoner/rancher reached the grave.

The boy, still chanting, reached out, palms up, waiting until the other grasped them (the rifle dropping soundlessly). A pair now, circling in slow motion. Dirt shifted beneath their feet. Aaron watched...

...more drowsy still from the fire's heat and the boy's monotonic voice, still undecided whether or not he was dreaming ...

...numb from the cold and drawing blood from his lips as he fought the pain enshrouding his thoughts. He lay flat on the ground, his head barely raised, his eyes glazed.

The boy abruptly dropped his hands and stepped down from the grave.

The prisoner waited, standing, and made no attempt to resist when the shaman's hand/pony's teeth reached through the earth and took hold.

Jackoson slept, thought he was dreaming.

Aaron fainted, thought he was screaming.

David, smiling, picked up a shovel.

For two summers in a row, while I was still teaching, I chaperoned a group of students while they were ostensibly studying college-level courses at various universities in Europe. One of them was in England— Royal Holloway College, in a small town called Egham. It's a gingerbread confection that has to be seen to be believed, originally built as an asylum and dedicated to Queen Victoria. Just outside Egham was Runnymede, and during the first summer the kids (who were eighteen and nineteen, mostly) and I took in a tiny carnival that had set up shop on the green, next to the Thames River. Most of it was pretty dreadful, but there was an elderly man sitting next to a caravan that sold goldfish in tiny glass bowls. Nothing else about this story is true, I sincerely hope.

The Three of Tens

It was no more than a week past midsummer when I came home from playing and my mother said to me, Jaimie, how'd you like to go to the fair tonight? Well, I looked at her, wondering if something had gone wrong, but she seemed no worse or no better than she always did since Dad died. Her hair, not yet gone grey, was pushing into a knob at the back of her head, and there was always little bits like feathers flying about in the breeze she made rushing from one place to another. She seemed no more tired than usual, though her hand was shaking a little when she lifted the kettle from the burner. So I looked around the kitchen thinking maybe she'd been down to the King's Arms and had carried home a pint or two. But there was nothing there, either.

"Jaimie," she said again, "don't you hear me, son? I said, do you want to go to the fair tonight?"

"Why, Mum," I said, "do you have a caller coming?"

I grinned, taking away the bite of what I was saying, and she waved me a quick no while she poured the tea and laid out the scones.

"I just want you to get out of the house for a while. You've been staying in every night past supper, and it's not like you."

I shrugged and sat at the table. "I don't want to go," I said.

"And why not, if you don't mind me asking?"

I shrugged again and fiddled with my spoon. "I don't know. I just don't want to go, that's all."

"Michael down the road is going," she said. "You could stay by him if you're afraid, you know."

"I'm not afraid," I said, a bit angrier than I wanted. "And I am so big enough to cross the road, you know." Then I saw the tease in her eyes. "Ain't I been taking care of you this past year, then?"

She sat down opposite me and took my hand, patted it once when she saw I didn't go for that, and leaned back. She tucked at her hair, brown like mine only longer, and fluffed the dress around her front as if it was too tight. "You have indeed been doing that, Jaimie," she said, "and to look at you now, nobody'd think you haven't even seen a dozen winters."

"Well, what do you mean by that?"

"I mean, Jaimie, that your friends aren't your friends anymore. I never see your old chums coming round, and you're getting a hard look a child shouldn't have your age. You go to school, you come right back and change and go to Mr. Harrow's for the errands he has for you, then back to eat and straight on to bed." She shook her head and let it drop forward slowly like it was too heavy for her to hold up anymore. "It isn't like we need the money, what with your dad's pension, and it isn't what I want for you, Jaimie. And I know he wouldn't want it, either." She jerked her head in the direction of the picture on the wall next to the Queen's, and then she pushed a pound note to me. And when I didn't take it up straight away, she laid it in my palm and closed my fingers around it.

"Go," she said. "Stay until after dark and see the lights. Then come on back and tell me what they look like. Michael'll be by about half-past eight."

It was ended then, and whether I wanted to go or not, she had already made the decision and there was nothing I could do about it.

She's funny that way, she is. And when I come to think about it, I decided I wouldn't mind spending a few pennies at that.

So, when Michael came around practically dragging that girl of his, I was dressed and scrubbed and ready. The girl—Charley, they called her because her stupid name was Charlene—takes my hand right off, and before I knew, they were hustling me between them to the fair.

In case you don't know the place, there's a roundabout directly past the town's center, and two roads coming off it have between them this big field of grass that stretches toward Windsor and climbs up a hill into a lot of trees. Off the road on the left is Egham, where I live, and off the road on the right that goes to Windsor is the Thames. Well, dead in the middle of this field was a large circle of caravans with their inside walls open for games of chance and things like that. There was a Big Wheel, some rides for kids littler even than me, and on the side of the circle with its back to the river was a wagon that was supposed to have a scary Fun House. Only it wasn't scary. I went through twice, and I know. There was a lot of people, it being Saturday night and all, and as soon as Michael and Charley walk me into the place where all the colored lights were, they patted me on the head, said ta and made me promise to look for them once an hour to see that I was all right.

This didn't bother me, though, because they know I can pretty much take care of myself, and I didn't always care for the way Charley liked to mother me.

So I changed my quid for pennies in the gambling arcade and played a few of the machines and lost a bit, then did a ride on the bumper cars, which wasn't much fun because there was no one there I knew good enough to really bump into. I tried throwing some hoops around these blocks of wood to win a goldfish for my mother, threw a couple of darts at some balloons, and just was mucking about when, during my wandering, I saw this small wagon tucked in sort of by the side of the Wheel. There was this sort of old man sitting on a chair under a sign that said he could make me a ten if I wanted to pay.

"Hey, mister," I said to him. He looked up and smiled. He hadn't shaved in a while, and his eyes kind of looked like my dad's when he'd had one pint too many, but I didn't smell nothing in the air. So I took a step closer and asked him what a ten was and how much did it cost.

"Well, lad," he said, reaching into his hip pocket and pulling out a pipe what looked like it'd been dropped a hundred times from the top of Windsor Castle. "I'll tell you something you don't know," he said, "a ten is whatever you want it to be. You want it to be a special wee gift for your mum, then that's what it'll be. You want it to be something not so fine for the chappie what steals your lunch, then that's what it'd be, too." He laughed, then, and I backed away a bit. I wasn't scared or nothing, you see, but when you get to be the man of the house at my age, you got to learn pretty quick who wants to do you out of a fiver and whose hand you'd better shake quick before he slips it into your pocket.

"That don't make sense what you said," I told him. "That's silly."

"No, it don't make sense," the old man admitted, sucking on that pipe and staring at the blue smoke coming out of the bowl. "And that's the gem of it, you see. It don't make sense, and that makes it better than some flippin' doll or a bag with a goldfish in it, don't it?"

I didn't really know what he was saying, but there was something about him that wouldn't let me get away. It was then he waved me closer, and I realized we'd been near shouting all the time to be heard over the people laughing and shouting, and the music and the noise. So I moved right beside him, and he reaches into a sack by his feet and pulls out a big handful of little boxes no bigger than my thumb.

"Tens," he said. "They cost tenpence each," and he laughed, and I could see his yellow teeth and smell the dead leaf smell of his tobacco. I kind of gave a shudder, and he stares at me before holding up the boxes. "They're numbered, you see," he said, "one through twenty. The odd ones are for your enemies, the others for your friends."

I tried to look close, but he pulled them back just enough so I couldn't touch. For tenpence maybe I could get something nice for mum, I thought, and I was going to pick out number twelve when I looked into his face. He was still smiling, the old man was, but there was nothing behind it, and when I saw those eyes the color of the river at night, everything kind of went away and I just stood there. Then I got awfully hot, and I started to feel dizzy and sickly like I'd had too many sweets. I felt myself holding out a hand and saw him picking out the pennies before he grabbed my other hand and dropped a box into it.

"What do I do with it," I said, sounding like I was far away at the top of the hill.

"You'll think of something," he said, "and mind you be careful with it, brat." Suddenly the smile went away and he pushed at me with the end of his pipe. "Now go away, boy, and let someone else have a go."

"But—"

"Go on," he said, "before I have to call the manager."

I got mad and wanted to ask for my pennies back, but he kept staring at me all the time, and so I quickly turned away and went to look for Michael and Charley. I didn't feel so big anymore, and I wanted Charley to take my hand for a bit. The lights, the noise of the rides, the people's faces all twisted and funny—the fair wasn't much fun anymore. When I finally found them at the shooting gallery, I asked Charley to take me across the road to the river, and she did it without asking why because that's the way she is. We walked along the bank past where they mow the grass for people to sit and watch the pleasure boats go by, and then I stepped into the weeds a little ways and threw the box into the water.

It wasn't heavy at all, but it sank right away.

"Now why'd you go and do that?" she said as we walked back to the fair.

I shrugged. "It weren't worth nothing," I said.

"Where'd you get it, Jaimie?"

"Over there," I said, pointing when we reached the Wheel. But when she asked again and I looked, the old man was gone and the sign was away, too. Even his small wagon.

"I think you've been taken, Jaimie m'boy," she laughed, and I felt bad at that for a minute, but then she grabbed me under the arms and lifted me over her head. "You'll not get down until you give me a kiss," she said, and when I stuck out my tongue at her, she laughed again.

"Hey," Michael said, coming up behind us while I was pretending to hit Charley after she let me down, "do you mind if I hit her a few myself, or is this a private party?"

"Jaimie got taken," said Charley, dodging around him to get away from me.

"Who?" Michael said, suddenly very mad and kneeling down to look at me straight on.

"I don't want no trouble," I said. "I shouldn't have done it, but he looked at me funny, and it was only tenpence—"

"I don't care if it was a hundred pounds, Jaimie," he said. "You got taken and that wasn't right."

I looked at him, saw his black eyes frowning, and grinned; I think that if I had any friends left in the world, Charley and Michael would be all of them.

"He was over by the Wheel," I said, "sitting by a wagon. There was a sign, too, but they're all gone now."

He put a hand on my shoulder, and we moved over and could find nothing but the smoking leftovers of the pipe tobacco in the grass. "He was right here," I said, looking around. "He was—"

Suddenly there was a scream, louder than the ones from the dumb girls on the Wheel, one that made the ones close to it turn around and look.

It was getting dark outside the caravan's circle, and the lights in the middle made it so bright that nobody could give a good account later of what they saw. But there was this man, this…something standing just in the shadow of the Fun House wagon, getting up from a bundle lying on the ground. Charley told me not to look and pushed me behind her, but I had already seen that the bundle was a lady and her face was all red and shining, and you couldn't see her eyes or her mouth for all the red.

Then the man-thing ran away across the field toward the hill, and it was a long time before anyone got enough nerve to follow him or call the police.

Of course, Charley took me home straight away and dragged my mother into the kitchen, but she was so excited and crying and looking at the back door that mum calls me in, knowing I was hiding in the hall listening.

"Tell me, Jaimie," she said.

So I told her.

She gave us a kind of funny look and said, "What did he look like?"

"Big," I said, "tall as a house he was. He had a black thing on, like a greatcoat, but it was all wet. And, and his face was all…bones…and…"

And before I could help it, I was crying worse than Charley with shivers that wouldn't quit even when mum held onto me.

I didn't sleep well that night.

I kept seeing that face.

It had no eyes.

Well, the next day my aunt and uncle took us to Windsor Great Park to see the polo matches, and everyone there was talking about the excitement at the fair, and when we got home we saw in the papers all the stories about the murder. The police finally came after we'd left, and they chased after the guy, but they never caught him. They lost him, it said, in the forest park at the top of the hill. The funny thing was, a lot of people must have seen him, like me, but in all them papers there weren't no pictures at all. Not the camera kind, but the kind like they have them artists draw. All they said was: a man of unusual description.

Two days later, over in Englefield Green, a pharmacy was broken into and the two people living upstairs were killed. The papers said their faces were smashed.

The fair was still on, but hardly anyone went. Even my mother decided she didn't want to go, even when I told her I had a good time.

Since we was into the summer holiday, I didn't have to go to school. So when I wasn't running errands for Mr. Harrow's shop, I spent a lot of time in the small front yard helping my mother with our roses, which were the largest ones on the whole street. The neighbors were always coming over and asking me how I do them so well. Then, all they talked about was the killer. My nights hadn't been all that good since that day. So when they started into talking like that, I always left. But one day Michael came around and told us that the killer had murdered a whole family, parents and two kids, on the other side of town. Egham being the size it is, that wasn't too far away. He said they weren't going to put it in the papers anymore because of the terrible things done to the people and the police didn't want to scare anyone. But he knew a chum in the station who told him everything that was happening.

I started to ask Michael some questions about it, but my mother all of a sudden got mad and sent me inside to put on the kettle. She always did that when she didn't want me to hear anything bad.

It rained that night, and I could hear the police sirens just a couple of blocks away, down by the train station.

I kept having those dreams about the box.

That face.

One night I told Mum I had to go out for a quick errand for Mr. Harrow, but instead I ran over to the fair. There was maybe ten people there, not counting the hawkers, but when I asked a couple of the workers where the man with the wagon was, they only shoved me away and told me I was too little to be out so late. I could see they was getting ready to pack it in, but then one man said I was too young to drink, that there wasn't any old man like I said, and there never had been.

"Then what about the box I bought," I said, grabbing at his coat before he could walk away like all the rest.

"What box?"

"The one I bought from him," I said. "For tenpence."

"Oh? Well," he said with his face telling me he thought it was all a joke, "well, where is it?"

"I threw it in the river," I said.

"Oh, well, then," he said, patting me on the head like I was a little boy. "It'll come back to you, then. Anything you drop in there always comes back. Didn't you know that?"

I ran all the way home.

When I finally got to my block, I started to walk, trying to keep my face from getting all red, otherwise mum would think I'd been up to doing wrong. All the houses were close together, you know, with two families in a house side by side, and unless you knew the numbers or the colors of the shutters or something, you really couldn't tell one place from another.

But when I turned into our gate, I saw the box.

It was sitting in the middle of the walk. There was a puddle of water around it. I looked at the roses, but they were dry. So was the little bit of grass we had.

I looked up at the house, then across the hedge to Mrs. Daniels' yard. Then I kind of snuck up on it, feeling my heart getting ready to break through my shirt and my fingertips getting all tingly. It wasn't hot that night—there were clouds and all—but a drop of sweat stung my eye, and I jerked my head to clear it away. I moved another inch and stuck out my foot to tip the box over. The number three was still on one side, but the bottom had been ripped off. I kneeled down so I could look inside, but it was just at sunset and I couldn't see anything very well.

And when something tapped my shoulder, I let out a horrid yell and fell over the box, felt it under me and rolled away, trying to crawl to the front door before that man-thing could get me. But these hands grabbed me and pulled me to my feet, and I started punching and screaming until I opened my eyes and saw Michael ducking away from my fists.

"Hey, come on, come on." he said. "Settle yourself, Jaimie, it's only me, it's only me."

I got mad at him then, just as Mum came running outside to see what all the noise was about.

"Why'd you go and scare me like that," I said, puffing like I'd just run in from London. "I could have done you harm, Michael."

He looked at me dead serious and nodded before turning to my mother, who was demanding that someone please say something she could understand. "Sorry," he said, "I guess I spooked him a little."

"Well," she said, wiping her hands on her apron, "you come in for a cuppa. The state he's in, I'm not going to spend the rest of the night alone with this vicious devil. And bring Charley with you."

I poked my head around Michael's waist, and there she was, leaning against the front hedge trying not to laugh at me. I frowned and poked a fist at her. She poked one back and came through the gate.

"You're out to kill my man," she said, cuffing the side of my head.

"No such thing," I said, pushing her away.

"Inside, all of you," Mum said, and we were pushed into the kitchen before she really got mad. And we attacked some scones until I remembered the box and Michael said something about the fair closing down because no one was going. So I told Mum what had happened outside, and Michael got up right away and went to the front, and I could hear him on the stoop before he suddenly slammed the door and came back in. His face was more white even than mine, and he told mum real quietly to bolt the latch and check all the windows. Charley he sent upstairs to do the same, and he waved for me to follow him into the parlor where he picked up the telephone and dialed 999.

"Michael, what's happening?" I must have sounded scared because he put an arm around me and pulled me close while he told the policeman who answered the emergency number that there was a prowler around our house and would he hurry and send a man round to check it. There was a mumbling I couldn't hear, and Michael nodded and rang off.

"Jaimie," he said, "I want you to go into the kitchen and turn off all the lights. You don't stop for anything. You come right on back."

"Michael?"

"It's all right, son," he said, and for the first time I didn't mind him calling me that even though he'd just started going to university himself. I did what he said as fast as I could, grabbed a tin of biscuits from the cupboard and ran back. Charley and my mother were sitting on the sofa when I came in. And even though it was still summer, someone had lit a small fire. I didn't say anything; I was cold, too. The curtains were drawn tight over the windows, and the only light other than the fire was the small lamp in the corner.

"We'll just have to wait now, for the police," Michael said, "and I'll show them that box." He was standing in the middle of the room, his hands behind his back, kind of rocking on his heels like he was a mate on a ship. On the mantel over the fireplace I could see the box. It still looked wet.

Suddenly there was a smashing of glass, and mum says, "That's Mrs. Daniels."

Michael ran to the window and pulled back the curtain a little, but he said he couldn't see anything. But we could hear enough. There was a thumping, and one long scream that made me drop to the floor. We could hear plates breaking against the wall, and then something heavy, and it sounded like that whole half of the building was going to come down on Mrs. Daniels's head. There was another scream that Charley made, quietly, and then there was nothing.

Michael licked his lips and pointed me to stand by the fireplace. Charley and Mum were holding onto each other tight, and Charley looked like a little girl and Mum like she was a hundred years gone. I could see there were tears on her face, too. I watched while Michael picked up the poker and held it like a bat, but I could see he was almighty scared, and that made me scared, too, because if Michael couldn't do anything to help us, who could?

"Who is that man?" Charley said, stuttering so bad I couldn't understand all her words.

Michael shrugged, but I said that I knew and told them what the man at the fair had told me about the box, and the river. He gave it and me a look, and mum said that it was nonsense and only the Gaels believed in things like that, but I could see she was just talking because she couldn't take her eyes off the mantel.

Now, I know there's a real lot of things that can happen whether you believe them or not, and if that box had something in it that could make the river give up one of its dead, then I didn't see how we were going to get away from it. But I didn't say all that out loud because I was scared enough, and I didn't want to make Mum feel worse.

Then we heard the window in the back door smash onto the floor.

"It's your box, Jaimie, your box!" Charley shouted and jumped to her feet and pressed herself against the wall.

"No!"

Another smash, and the door slammed back against the stove, and there was the rattle of the soup pot falling onto the floor.

And wet noises. Like someone walking in out of the rain.

Michael turned out the lamp and whispered to the women to get behind the sofa. All there was when I got used to it was the light from the fireplace; I was on one side, and Michael was on the other.

Wet noises, dragging. And it came around the corner.

Charley and Mum whimpering behind the sofa.

The light was moving from the fire, shining off the thing's coat that was dripping water. I could hear it. Nothing else.

All I could see was its hands and its face. The hands had no skin, the fingers sharpened from years of scraping along the riverbed; they were huge and clung to with lots of little things like pointed scales. It held them up and took a step into the room.

Its face. Bones. Hanging green-black things. Grey, like the belly of a dead fish in the market. And nothing, nothing at all where the eyes should have been.

Michael made a noise and the thing moved to him. quicker now. It reached out and Michael swung with the poker, hitting it near the elbow and making it lean back. Then it came at him again, like I wasn't even there, and Michael aimed for its head, but he missed and it grabbed him like they were going to wrestle. Its hand came up and Michael started screaming, and the women started screaming, and there was a pounding on the front door, and all I could hear was Charley shouting how it was my box, my box. I started shaking all over, and Michael and the man-thing bumped into a table, knocking it over with a lamp and a candy dish. I started looking around for something to throw, anything at all, when I remembered the mantel; and I stretched up and grabbed around until I found the box.

The thing was making noises and Michael was still screaming. I didn't like the sound of a man screaming, and I crushed the box under my foot and threw it into the fire. Then I don't know what happened to me, but I started shouting terrible things and ran to try to jump on its back, and suddenly there was this awful smell and the fire went bright for a second, so bright I could see the blood splashed on the wall, all over the thing's coat.

Then everything stopped.

The river-thing let go of Michael, who dropped back a step and fell onto his back, and his face was cut so much I couldn't look. And then it turned around to me, and I ran into the hall just as the door broke in and policemen started pouring into the house. They stopped, though, when they saw the thing standing there, but before one of them could use his gun, the coat folded like it was over nothing but air. The next thing I knew there was a pile of coat at my feet running out water and everyone talking all at once. I tried to get to Michael, but then all the lights went out, and the next thing I saw was myself in a hospital bed and a nurse bringing in Mum and Charley, and they were carrying all kinds of sweets.

Charley leaned over me and kissed me hard and said, "My second hero."

"I didn't do anything," I said. "How's Michael?"

Her smile went away, but she said he was going to be all right except they would have to do a lot of work on his face before it could look good again. Not, she said, that it ever did. But it was a sad kind of laugh she gave me, then, and I could see the crying in back of her eyes.

"Hey, Mum," I said when she bent over to take my hands and kiss me. "What am I doing here? I'm all right, honest."

"You are that," she said. "The doctors say it's for observation."

"What's that mean?"

"It means they want to be sure you're all right. You've had yourself quite a shock for a little boy, Jaimie."

"Well, what about—"

"The police took what was left away."

"Will I get my picture in the papers?"

"No, Jaimie. They're saying they shot the man while he was escaping capture. No pictures. No one would believe it."

"It was the box, Mum," I said.

"I know, dear."

"Something in the box, Mum. It got into the water and—"

"I know, dear. Don't tax yourself."

"The ashes! Charley, you got to be sure she throws out the ashes. Bury them. Get metal, a tin or something, and bury it in the yard. You got to do it, Mum. Charley, you got to see she does it."

I guess I was getting kind of loud because Mum put her hand on my lips gently and nodded.

"I'm way ahead of you, Jaimie. It's done, don't worry. Not exactly like you said, but done just the same."

"Mum, what did you do?"

"I shoveled it all in a sack and flushed it. Nothing to fear, Jaimie. All the ashes are down in the sewers, stretched from here to London, most likely."

She winked. Charley smiled. Then the nurse came and said they had to leave, and I was left alone in the ward. Thinking about what my mother had done.

So, if you come to visit, if you come to find my house, knock loud and call out your name. But don't be surprised if nobody's home.

Anywhere.

By the time this story appeared in 1977 I was well into the writing of an extensive future history series, which had by then been more elaborately described in two novels (The Shadow of Alpha, and Ascension). I was intrigued by this world of mine, and it seemed as if every time I turned around there was something else to uncover, to explore, like a cave that has too many branches to count, each one as fascinating as the last. I was also attempting to extrapolate the fate(s) of one of my abiding passions — the Arts, from writing to acting to sculpting to whatever.

But my career, by this time (and such as it was), had taken a direction I should have foreseen — deeper and deeper into the delightful midnights of dark fantasy. "The Dark of Legends…" is one of the last pieces I did about the Arts, and that future world, and it's a conscious attempt to write a supernatural horror story that has its setting in the future. Whether it works or not depends on how many jolts your suspension of belief is willing to take.

The Dark of Legends, The Light of Lies

The hills of October are laden with ghosts, and that lone stand of birch is a white cage for a whisper.

To mark that now as a beginning is simple enough when hindsight lends its not-so-calming torch to the confusion of fear; but to mark it as an ending is something to which I will not let myself repair, not yet. Not even now, not even beneath the fading to brown golds and reds where the wind has stopped and shadows still drift, where the wind has died and sighs still hover. Perhaps it's because I refuse to admit it, or perhaps it's because I admit it, finally and will not fight it. To fight implies a possibility, a chance, an unexpected twist of Fate in my favor that will bring me the win, the victory, or at the very least…the pause. Yet, not to fight likewise implies that I have been beaten, I have lost, I have no hope at all that there is a waiting Fate. Confusing it is, and I am confused to be sure, but the one thing I still know, the one thing my senses will

not rob me of in this twilight of too many things, is the assurance that what has been done has been done because the future came to pass and I was not ready.
    Assurance.
    Or judgment.
    No matter.
    It ends.

1

There are very few things convincing and real that will force a man to a mirror and show him the absolute truth of his talent. I had resisted, both stubbornly and childishly, not only the blandishments of my employer, but also the sweet sympathy of my friends; resisted the damnation of my dreams until, as always, the incongruous and the unlikely came to their aid. And again, as always, I didn't know it until it was over.

I was still in my office well after hours, working on a manuscript flashing slowly across the desk screen of my comp. With litepen in hand, I was trying to make a masterpiece of something that should not have even been dreamt of, much less written. That part wasn't unusual. I did it for a living, such as it was, along with two other editors in a Philayork firm, one of less than a similar dozen still in existence, still plodding, still dreaming of the days when people held books instead of each other. The words flowed across the screen and I corrected almost automatically, paying no attention to the plot because I'd read it eight times already, and it wasn't much different from the dozens of others I'd read that year. Admittedly, it was realistic—as it had to be to get anywhere—and it even had a romance that boded well to last beyond the final page. That was all right, too. That would help it sell. The trouble with this novel (not to mention those dozens of others) was, it was both too short and too bare, and I was attempting to correct that, too, when Neil Benson slammed into the small room and did not stop running until he came up hard against the front of my desk.

I looked up and smiled. Neil was beefy and jowled, and when he laughed his ghost-pale eyes vanished into purple-shadow folds. This time, however, he was glaring, and my greeting smile drifted to one side hesitantly before it disappeared.

"You're still working," he said.

I shrugged, but restrained from pointing out the obvious.

"Damnit, why haven't you finished, Simon? Don't you know we have a deadline on this one for tomorrow? This thing has got to be at comprint before noon. My God, man, don't you have any sympathy for me at all?"

Sympathy for him I would never have. He was the editor-in-chief of BenEl Publications and the publisher of five novels a month, five novels that vanished into the cityplex and were never heard of again. It wasn't his fault, though, I'll give him that much. All the firms were the same, struggling manfully if not gainfully against the floodtide of extinction. But sympathy? For the others, perhaps, but not a whit for Benson.

"Simon," he said when I didn't answer immediately, "I'm beginning to think you've delayed me for the last time. I've already looked over what you've done on this one to date, and instead of doing what you're paid for—and you surely remember what you're paid for, don't you, Simon?—instead of doing what Joanna and Alex do without giving me any trouble, you've made this thing at least twice as long! Twice, Simon! Twice!"

"Well, it should be, Neil," I said, miraculously sounding more calm than I felt. "It can't be told in fewer words than that."

Neil shook his head, almost in sorrow, and might have said something more to carry out his threat of dismissal had we not been interrupted by a forced cough at the door. Two heads—one framed in soft black hair that curled at the ends and was Joanna; the other desperately struggling against baldness, and losing, and was Alex. Neil straightened and glared at them, turned back to me and jabbed a stunted thumb at my compterm's segmented hood.

"You will finish this before you leave, Simon. Finish it and be ready for the next one in the morning."

"I thought I was fired."

He rolled his eyes, closed them, and I thought I had finally pushed him a shade too far. "How," he said, "can I fire you? If I did, you would only go somewhere else and do the same to the next man." His eyes closed again, his features softened, and for a moment I thought he would slump to the floor. "Simon," and now his voice was quiet, "when you're

79

not lugging that banner for your crusade, you're one of the best men around here, and you know it. Your trouble is, among other things, you worry too much about the novels and not enough about the firm. You care too much for the authors."

"Maybe that's because I'm one myself."

"No, you're not, Simon. I wish you were, believe me, but you're not."

I traced my forefinger over the screen while I thought about what he'd said. But before I could compose a reasonably strong retort he had sniffed, grunted, jabbed the hood again for emphasis and turned on his heels. At the door he muttered something to Joanna and Alex and pushed between them to vanish into the dim light beyond.

Alex, as lank as I but looking ten years older, rubbed a palm over his mouth and chin. Then he tapped a finger lightly against the jamb. "You going to be long?" he asked.

"Long enough it looks like," I said.

"Simon," Joanna said, "why don't you quit now and come in early tomorrow? We've been waiting to have dinner with you, if you want to come."

"I want," I said, swearing at Neil through my regret, "but I can't. You heard the man. I have to cut out everything I put in and have it all ready for comprint by morning."

Alex clucked, Joanna blew me a kiss, and they pulled back into the corridor, leaving me alone.

It has been said by those who emulate birds and foolish butterflies that the nightlights of Philayork are enough to rival any other cityplex in the known world, the universe, even that bold infinity beyond. I accept the hyperbole for what it is: a prideful celebration of one of the largest Noram population centers on the continent. But as for the universe and the immeasurable infinity beyond…that judgment I'll leave up to those who live in the Colony Domes scattered throughout the solar system. Myself, I was just as glad that BenEl had interior offices so I didn't have to look out and see those famed lights. Neil's anger had produced a reaction of my own, and I was in no mood for poetics, rather needed only a slight shove more to send me home for good.

Damnit, I thought as I turned back to my desk, now I'll probably have those damned dreams again!

But I did the work required, and did it well. Though the taste in my mouth was something else again.

Then, instead of rushing directly back to my Key, I decided to walk.

Alone.

Not nearly as bad as one would think. There's a hell of a difference (the old cliché goes, and rightly) between alone and lonely; the former is mine by choice and preference, in lifestyle and thoughts; the latter seldom touched me save when I tried to be more than I was (if Neil is any judge, and the others an objective jury). But I couldn't help it. At thirty-seven, habits resist dying. Besides, I had been raised in the Fringe, the outer limits of the cityplex that ended in blank walls facing blindly the hills and the trees of the country's Outland. The Fringe isn't a gutter by any means, but neither is it the elegance of City Prime. The Fringe is…the Fringe; and when my mother died giving birth to a stillborn sister, my father took the easy way out (though not so easy for him, I admit), and I was left to beg and scrounge and thus skipped entirely the compulsory University most Noram children were shuttled through.

Without a trade, then, and without a legal means of accumulating creds and coin, I wandered for years from doorway to doorway, from Keyloft to Keyloft whenever a woman took pity and coveted my lovemaking. I learned, though, damn but I learned. From the women, from the newses in the streets and the newshawks on the comunit, from the ed channels when I could watch them, and from dozens of battered bound books I found in alleys, in homes, wherever I could. Some were texts long outdated and not even University used, many of them were novels, and many of those were old enough to intrigue and puzzle. They were long, they were wordy, evocative and moody, and in numbers of cases the print was incredibly small. A puzzlement, as I said, but an incredible fascination.

Eventually, however, I grew tired of living vampiric and I tried writing, liked it, but sold not a word.

There is one book, however, that I…

Later.

Later.

Not having sold, then, I decided to work from the inside out, and hoped to bide my time with BenEl until my time finally came.

And each time I thought that it had, there was always Neil and Alex and the dark-eyed Joanna to smile and pat and wash me behind my ears.

———

The sidewalk was crowded with gaily dressed peds heading for the joyhalls and cinema bowls; the air was barely tinged with a warning approach of October; and I felt for a delightful moment as if Philayork were indeed the greatest plex on earth. I ambled, and passed children crouched over a sparkling spinning toy, a couple listening to a joyhall advoc enticing them into the game and the gambling and the holofilm adventures. The Blues were out, too, walking their patrols and pointing directions, always polite, always imposing. A lousy job being a cop, I thought as I passed one, and gave him a bright smile that nearly rocked him off his feet.

When I strolled away I was laughing, and when a hand touched my arm, I turned and the laugh faded in nearly a choke.

A stranger, a man, in a black lapelled suit edged in muted gold, a dark face with dark hair fashionably tipped blond and curling over a deep-lined forehead. He was tall, taller than any man I'd ever seen, and before I could question his intent he handed me a card. Relaxing and thinking him a shill for a Lover, I made to slip the card into my pocket and be on my way. He stopped me with a look. I read the card.

"All right, Jonathan Dare," I said, and he nodded. "I'm sorry, but as they say, you seem to have the advantage. Do I know you from somewhere?"

"In a manner of speaking," he said, his voice not quite matching the heft of his bulk. "You're Simon Wallace."

"True. That's true. And now that we know each other...so what?"

I didn't like being curt, but then I didn't much care for his expression. I'd seen it once before, just before Neil had fired the last fourth member of our so-called editorial team. A look of complete satisfaction at a deed well done; no matter how bloody or awful, it was a deed well done.

"If you're Simon Wallace—"

"Come on, I just told you I was."

"—then you're the man who works on my books."

Had I the chance then I would have turned and run, or flown, or searched for a hole I could crawl quickly into. But under the circumstances, I could do nothing but gape at him stupidly. Jonathan Dare. He was the giant who wrote small books, small books that sold and kept BenEl afloat. Not that he was any different from any of the other authors in Noram; he simply followed the lucrative formula of simplicity and large print better than most.

"All right," I said, "that's me. But I'm off duty now, if you'll excuse the expression, and unless it's really important I'd like to go on home. Where I was heading, by the way, before you stopped me. Home. I have my own Key, you see—"

The man had frightened me into babbling, and I feel no shame for it. His height was imposing, his heft unbelievable, but his face and the glaring white teeth in his feral smile gave him an aspect of the Reaper I didn't need knowing. I edged away, hopefully unnoticed, and he took a pace to close the gap, took my arm and pulled me closer.

"I just want you to know, Wallace," he said, "that we've been told what you're trying to do to us."

"We?" I must have announced my fear, because his smile broadened and he leaned closer, his breath warm, his grip now tight enough to make me gasp.

"Let me put it to you this way, Mr. Wallace. In simple terms. You are long out of date, way too long out of date, and we do not appreciate you trying to drag us down with you. It's difficult enough trying to make a living without your meddling and your so-called editorial discretion. Benson told me you've delayed my new novel for the second time. I can't afford that, Wallace, none of us can. If the books stop coming out, no one will pick them up again. So why don't you just do us all a big favor and get the hell out, go find a grave and write yourself an epitaph."

"I'll call a Blue," I said.

"Do that, Mr. Wallace, and he'll never know what you wanted."

He released me abruptly and strode into the crowds that jostled me as I tried to follow his departure. My hands were wet, my neck stiff with tension, and I could feel blades of perspiration stabbing down my chest and back. A Blue marched by and I almost grabbed his arm, stopped myself when I realized I had no legal cause. The threat was between Dare and myself, and no one else had heard it; and if someone had, they couldn't have understood it. Instead, I hurried down the boulevard toward my loft building and saw nothing on the way but shadows that trailed me and that foul dark face grinning at me from every shop window.

And when I had finally, centuries later, reached my own neighborhood, the fear had drained and anger had taken its place. An anger I had grown used to over the past several months, an anger that surged whenever I read those books I'd saved and compared them to the books whose accomplice I was in letting them out. I kept telling myself, of course, that a country's population moves with the times, and the times had been moving too rapidly for the leisure that novels needed. Why sit and read when you could catch the comunit and learn, play the joyhalls and win, be safely immersed in bloody spectaculars by paying the price at a cinema bowl? That was nothing new, nor was it original with my generation; it was as ancient as the idea that Columbus had been the first to cross the ocean and sight Noram's ancestor.

No, that's not what angered me, not entirely. That part was the inevitable result of advancement and regression. What angered me was that I still did not know why men like Jonathan Dare, understanding all that they did, continued to write.

I took the liftube to my floor, went inside the three-room Key and leaned against the door. Tans and browns worked to calm me. A sprinkling of red at chair and couch, the black grey face of the comunit's wall screen a meter square, the lamp that glowed golden as soon as I entered. But I wasn't calmed. I would have to, once again, do my own purging.

I made a fist of both hands and clasped it to my forehead, pressed hard, pressed harder, gathered the acid anger into my throat and tightened my lips. Grunted. Once. Loudly. And it was gone, all of it gone, and I sagged onto the couch, thankful that one more time I had stopped myself from screaming.

I dreamed that night.

I dreamed of shadows and things, of dark corners and things, of shadows and dark corners…and something that waited to spring.

It was a familiar dream, too familiar and too frequent.

And when I awoke, I thought I saw a shadow in the corner.

2

Several days later, Joanna and I left a poorly renovated theatre well beyond the regular entertainment strips. We'd just seen a revival of a fifty-year-old play, and we were more than slightly depressed. She had feathered her hair over both shoulders, was wearing a soft cotton tunic suit of light grey and greens, and in the silence that cloaked us I realized for the first time (after dreaming of it often enough, wistfully enough) that I loved her. Her left hand grasped my elbow, and I hugged her fingers to my side, breathing deeply to stall time and perhaps the moment and us with it.

"It's sad," she said finally, her dark lips in a pout, a glance over her shoulder.

"No kidding? I thought it was supposed to be a comedy."

She slapped playfully at my arm without laughing, and for the briefest of moments rested her cheek on my shoulder. The briefest of moments.

"No, Simon, I mean the whole thing about all these plays. They try to bring them back, and they don't work. Did you see that audience back there? They didn't know what to do, Simon. They were waiting for volcanoes and hurricanes, things like they get on the regular stage. They didn't even know when to laugh!"

"So? A play fifty years old is fifty years old. They weren't putting floods on stage back then, remember."

"I know, and that's what makes it so sad somehow. Those poor people, and us included I guess, weren't used to just actors saying lines. I heard some guy keep asking when the earthquake would start."

"All right," I said, frowning, "so they're used to having things done for them, and to them. So that's the way things are, Jo. What can I say?"

"Nothing," she said after a disturbing pause. "It's just like your books."

I nodded without thinking, knowing she was referring not only to those BenEl novels we worked on every day, but also my own abortive attempts to copy the old ones I'd read when I was fighting to get out of the Fringe. I had written three...but they were far too old.

"Like my books," I repeated. "Well...I'm not all that sure, actually. Partly, that's true, I guess. But there's something else, Jo, and I don't have a name for what it is, something more than just big letters and simplistic plots. I'm going to figure out why things have turned out this way, I've been trying on my own, but..."

She stopped suddenly and put a hand to my chest. "And so what if you're right, Simon?" she said, nearly angry. "What if you do come up with whatever that 'something else' is? What good's it going to do? It won't change things. Books won't change, plays won't change... What damned good is it, Simon, that you're ruining yourself trying to find something no one cares about?"

"The good is that we *might* be able to change things, make things like...well—"

"No." There was no equivocation, no leeway for argument. Just a statement of fact. "No, Simon, and that's why you're sad, too. There's no room for that kind of change anymore."

My hands reached for her shoulders, but she turned and walked away from me. A few moments later, swallowing to keep the anger down, I hurried to catch up, this time not touching. "Look, Jo," I said earnestly, "if you helped me read those old books, and read my new novel, maybe the two of us could find out why this has all happened and what we can do to fix it."

"Alex was right," she said, more to herself than to me. "He told me yesterday you were driving yourself toward a firing and a breakdown. He was right. Blessed priest, Simon, he was right. Your trouble is, you won't accept things the way they turned out to be, things that can't change no matter what you do."

"Jo, that's unfair. There're all kinds of ways we—" But I never finished. I looked across the street and saw a shadow standing in a doorway on the other side. At first I thought it was Dare or one of his friends after me again, but it wasn't. It was only a shadow, standing, waiting, but I'll be damned if I knew for what.

But I said nothing to Jo. She was still angry with me, and I knew she wouldn't believe me if I tried to point the shadow out to her. And to show her there were no lights over there, nothing from which a shadow could be born.

Later I tried to talk to her about finding out what happened to the books, and why my attempts at writing were not working, but she refused to listen. "Simon, just take me home, all right? I'm tired, and I don't want to have to fight with you."

I did, reluctantly, and when I got home and grunted away my anger, I fell into bed without disrobing, kicked my clothes off sometime after midnight and almost, but not quite, slept.

———

I dreamt again. And could not fight it.

of shadows that spun in some forgotten corner, scattering, coalescing, growing into mockeries of faces that reached across a starkly bare room, grasping and holding nothing, sighing and noiseless;

of shadows that dropped like nets from rotted rafters, spreading wings but not flying, soaring but not moving, each with a dark face that I thought I should know;

of shadows lurking somewhere in the shadow of shadows—growing, reaching soaring, flying, grasping, holding, patiently waiting, patiently...waiting.

of shadows...of shadows...of a million dark suns that exploded in my face and awakened me to see the morning pour through my window in golden alarm. I sat up gasping and rubbed an arm over my face to rid the room of the nightmare. My skin was chilled and drenched in perspiration, the sheets crumpled at the foot of the bed, my only pillow somehow tossed violently into the room's far corner. I blinked rapidly, wiped my face again and slid off the mattress, padded across the living room to the lav alcove and took a long, extra-long shower.

The water was thunder, and the noise kept me from thinking.

And as I was eating, finally dressed and calmed, the vione chimed and the comunit screen wavered. I slapped at a toggle; the wavering sparked, brightened, became Joanna. She seemed to have had as bad a night as I, worse if the lines in her face were as deep as they looked.

"Good morning," I said, nevertheless, determined to remain cheerful in the hopes it could help her.

"No," she said. "It's raining." Before I could respond, she rubbed a knuckle under one eye and suddenly said, "There's trouble, Simon. I wanted you to know before they came."

"They came? Who came? I mean, who's coming?" I shook my head at my own confusion, thinking Neil had probably decided to use his pink-slip axe. "Jo, what's going on?"

"It's Jonathan Dare, the man you told me about, the one who stopped you on the street."

"How could I forget him," I said sourly. "He threatened to kill me if I so much as changed one more of his commas."

"He's dead."

I choked while gaping, wiped absently at my chin. "Good God, what did he die of?"

"Murder."

"That can't be right, Jo," I protested. "The guy's too damned big! Blessed priest, the man was a giant."

"He's dead."

I blinked stupidly and shook my head. "Okay, tell me everything, and what's all this about someone coming to get me. Who? His friends, Neil...who?"

"The Blues," she said, abruptly looking to something beyond the view of my screen. At first I thought there was someone with her, but when I asked she denied it. "Just a shadow," she said. "I didn't get much sleep and I'm still not seeing straight. Alex called about the news, see—"

"So tell me, for crying out loud, woman!"

She did, and I made no further interruptions. Dare, the one and only Jonathan Dare of the incredible height and the frightening face, had been found in his Key just after dawn this morning. A neighbor, who had supposedly agreed to wake him, called him twice, and when the vione hadn't summoned the author, he contacted the Blues, just in case. The door was broken in, and once inside the Blues found the Key completely wrecked—furniture thrown and shattered and splintered, dark stains on the wall as though there'd been a fire, the window cracked like a manic spider's web. Dare was in the bedroom, lying half under his bed. When they dragged him out, they found little left of him—he'd been flailed until his flesh parted in strips from waist to neck, neck to crown; his jaw had been broken, teeth gone, nose shattered, eyes…gone. What blood hadn't spilled onto the floor was smeared on the walls, splattered on the ceiling. There was no one else in the Key, and no signs of forced entry.

"He was a bastard, Jo," I said when she'd done, "but he sure didn't deserve to go that way."

"Neil told the Blues that too, apparently," she said, "and he also told them the trouble you and Dare had been having."

"Oh great!"

"They just left here, Simon. They want to talk to—"

A knock on the door made me leap on my feet. Joanna's face suddenly drained pale and her eyes were wide when I nervously broke the connection, and turned around.

It was a Blue named Fein, and without many preliminaries, I was brought to his office.

"Well, primarily I'm an editor, change the books around, see, so hopefully they'll sell. They don't sell all that much anymore, of course, but it keeps the business floating for another month. But I'm also a writer, you see, of something Dare called too old-fashioned. I never went to University, so I had to educate myself with what tapes I could watch and what books I could get hold of. I suppose, yes, it's fair to say I let my enthusiasm for the printed word get in the way of production, but I'm also doing this personal research, something totally on my own, about the public's reading habits—what they are, *why* they are, and so forth. That, too, got in the way when I wasn't careful, and I guess I got Dare and my boss angry at me because I made too many errors and delayed things a bit. Dare and I only had a few words, that's right, and to be frank we didn't much get along. He had his ideas and I had mine, but I sure as hell wasn't going to kill him over them. I mean, what would be the sense? There'll be another along to take his place. There always is, though Neil would be the first to admit they're getting harder to find these days. He,

Dare, was popular for a few years, which was far above average, and sooner or later he would have faded away. I certainly don't think I'm jealous of his talent, no, though perhaps a bit envious of the coin that came his way. But there's no chance of my getting any of that, no chance at all, so why would I kill him? And even if I wanted to, have you seen the size of the man? Do you really think someone like me could get him to stay still long enough to do something like *that* to him? Hey, don't apologize about the yawn. I understand. I had a bad night, too. No, I didn't see anything. It must be these lights of yours, they make odd shadows. Is that all, Mr. Fein? Can I go now? My friends are waiting outside and I think they're anxious."

3

By the end of the month I'd been cleared and was free to move around without the ghost of a cop hovering over me in his WatchDog. I hated those things, have since I lived in the Fringe. They were tear-shaped and painted a nonreflective black, and I couldn't help thinking of them as bloated dragonflies waiting for a corpse to feed on during the hottest day of summer.

Morbid, but I couldn't help it; that was my mood. I couldn't get Dare out of my mind, nor did those dreams soothe me. Every other night, now, it seemed, and each time I woke more weary than when I'd gone to sleep. It must have been catching; even Neil seemed more haggard, as well as Alex and Joanna.

Then...another death.

Two days later, yet another.

The day after that a third and a fourth.

One more day, and a fifth found slaughtered.

Authors and publishers, and one maiden editor.

We all grew nervous, saw shadows following us even in sunlight, and finally I decided to get away from the plex, if only to reassure myself that I wasn't a target. Alex and Joanna agreed to go with me, and when the office shut down on the last day of October, we rented a landcar and headed for the outland.

My place, I liked to think…the hills and trees more of me than any part of the city, including the Fringe.

There was a house a woman left me when I was younger and she thought she loved me; it was set on a sharp hillside overlooking a valley that had never been developed. Huge boulders lay above and around it, the closest trees a stand of birch not ten meters from the rear door. It was a weathered grey, with one window to a wall and a small skylight in the slightly peaked roof. Inside, it was a single room twenty meters by twenty, three of the corners screened off for privacy, the center occupied by a large table on which sat my latest manuscript. As Alex and Joanna each went to their beds to unload their bags, I stood by the table and looked down at what I had done, touched it once and shook my head. Then I drifted out onto the back stoop and said hello to the birch.

The air was, finally, permanently chilled, the leaves turning gradually, the sky taking on a sharp, brittle look. A squirrel danced around the birch, a trio of late-leaving birds swooped and vanished into a canopy of gold. I took a deep breath, exhaled slowly and watched the white plume slide coldly from my lips. Ten minutes later I was joined by the others, and we sat and watched and said nothing at all about the sudden feeling of oppression that seemed to float into the clearing.

"Simon," Alex said at last, "I saw that manuscript."

I stiffened, plucked a dead leaf from my shoe and shattered it noisily.

"Ah yes," I said when his silence unnerved me. "'The hills of October are laden with ghosts.' A pretty good first line, if I do say so myself. Don't you think, Alex?"

"No," he said. "Not really. I only read a couple of dozen pages, but it's obvious you haven't learned a thing working with Benson."

"Now wait—"

"That first page is superfluous, and the rest of what I saw could easily be cut by ninety percent."

"Philistine," I said in what I hoped was a joking tone, but when I saw Jo's expression I knew she had read it, too. "All right, so you don't like it. You can't kick a man for trying, can you?"

"No, but I can warn a friend against wasting his time."

I was getting angry, and though the sun was still bright there was a haze over my eyes as though I were looking through a veil made of black lace.

"Simon," Joanna said, "Simon, what did I say to you the other day? Didn't I tell you that if you persisted—"

"But I'm so close!" I insisted. "I think I know—but I only have a feeling, you understand—I think I know what's going on."

"What are you talking about?" Alex said.

I stood to lean against the door, my arms folded tightly across my chest. "I'm still trying to figure it out, see, still trying to make sense of it. What I mean is, you take a man like Dare, or any of the others…what the hell are they trying to prove by writing?"

"Immortality and creds," Joanna said instantly as Alex nodded. "That's the only reason people write, Simon. A little coin, and a book that'll be around after you die."

"No!" I said angrily. "Come on, think a little farther than your beautiful nose, Jo. The coin—well, maybe, but there's not all that much. And the immortality? Can you name me one book, one novel anyone has published that's lasted more than a year? For a year, period? Blessed priest, even library tapes are shredded after eighteen months. That's immortality?"

They were silent. A wind rose, then, and dead leaves were spilled in uneven heaps over the ground. I shivered and looked up to the sky for storm clouds. There were none. Only the wind. And it was getting stronger.

"But what about you?" Alex said suddenly. "That's what *you* want, isn't it? That's why *you* come out here every chance you get, to do that…that writing in there, so that someone will know who *you* are after you're dead?"

"All right, yes," I said. "That's exactly what I want."

"With that book in there?"

"Why not?"

"I told you already, it's too long and it's not right."

"Why?" I wasn't badgering now, I really wanted to know, needed to know, and would feel horrid when I was told…but much better than if I had been told by Neil again. Or Joanna, whose eyes were so deeply sad that I could not look at them.

Alex lifted a hand, then stopped and glanced quickly at the corner of the house, shrugged after a moment and seemed to shake himself into beginning. "It seems to be some kind of ghost story, or a psychological study that makes it seem as if things are happening that we all know couldn't possibly happen. If I read the whole thing, maybe I could get something more, but on that alone, Simon, you're a failure. You're asking too much of a reader to suspend all that University training for the sake of a shock he won't get anyway."

"I read more than he did," Joanna said softly, "and he's right as far as he goes, Simon."

"No," I said. I shoved my hands into my pockets and leaned forward against the wind keening around the house. Then I straightened, pushed open the door and motioned them inside. Following, I glanced behind me, frowning and wondering where the hell the clouds were. Then I slammed the door and took my place at the table, the manuscript scooped protectively into the circle of my arms. "Listen," I said, "do you ever dream?"

"God," said Alex, leaning back in his chair, "if you only knew the dreams I've been having. Would you believe even the doctor I went to is having them?"

"No," I said, "that's not what I meant. I mean, don't you ever daydream? Don't you ever imagine what things would be like if things were different? It's like taking a close look at what we laughingly call reality, say, and giving it just a bit of a shove this way or that, just to see what it would be like."

The vione chimed off in the corner. I ignored it, but Alex shook his head and walked across the bare floor to answer it.

"No," Joanna said, "it can't be done."

"What? Of course it can be done, Jo," I snapped. "You mean to tell me you can't imagine things anymore?"

"Not the way you mean it," she said. "You're asking too much of us...too much of *anyone*, for that matter. Life has changed, people have—"

There was a sharp thud against one wall and we both jumped, spun around and saw claws of a branch scraping against a window. Leaves were pelting the house like hailstones, and the air above the skylight was fragmented darkly. I didn't like it, and Joanna was obviously getting frightened. I didn't blame her. I'd come out here in all kinds of weather and I'd never seen a display like that.

But I shook the feeling off and turned back to our argument. "Jo," I said, resting my hands atop the manuscript, "I'd be a fool and a candidate for a lockup if I tried to say there actually were such things as ghosts and night creatures and things like that. I used to read about them when I was a kid in the Fringe, but the city's too real, Joanna, and I never believed in them. And *that*, I think, is where the key lies. Don't ask me why, or what, not just yet, but I'll get hold of it, damned if I will."

"So what else is new?"

"Look, damnit—"

Alex returned, his footsteps weary, heavy, and he leaned against the table and stared over my head.

"Neil and two others," he said simply. "Editors in that firm on the fifteenth floor."

This time, when I looked through the skylight, there were clouds. Huge, black to grey and ponderously massing over the hills. Bits of twigs had joined the dervish leaves.

Suddenly I wanted the comfortable bulk of the city, and it didn't take much to convince them we should leave. As I locked the door behind me, I took one last look inside and saw the table, and the manuscript, and blinked away hurriedly an uncomfortable image that waterfalls of shadows were drifting to the floor.

The sky darkened.

The wind rose to maniacal proportions and buffeted the landcar from one side of the road to the other. I parked in front of the office, still fighting that damned wind, and we raced up to our floor where we found Fein waiting, and pale; and I didn't have to ask what Neil's body looked like, or the others.

"Didn't anyone see anything?" I asked, nearly frantic. "Didn't anyone see anything at all?"

Fein shook his head. "It's not right," he said Finally. "Something doesn't feel right." Then he looked squarely at us though we were to be pitied. "Another thing I don't know what you're all going to do come Monday. As soon as the word got out, five of your competitors announced they were closing their doors. For good."

Joanna slumped weakly against me and I slipped a none-too-steady arm around her waist. We were dazed, too shocked for mourning, and though Alex volunteered to return the rented car, he begged off supper with us with a slow and sad shake of his head, a weary wave, and a sigh that could have been a sob.

Jo and I walked. In the wind. Against the dust that blew out of the alleys, the scrabbling litter that fought for our ankles. And the sudden bitter, cold.

"Simon," she said as we approached her Key, "what are we going to do? What are those poor writers going to do? There's nobody now who can afford to take them on. By Monday… Simon, by Monday the whole industry may be dead. It's all falling apart. Damn, it's all falling apart."

I said nothing, only scanned the haggard faces of the peds who fought the wind with us, glanced up once at the sky to the clouds hovering over us. And once inside, I sprawled on her couch while she stood in front of the ovenwall and stared at the menus.

"What's the matter?" I said.

"I don't know. I shouldn't be hungry after all that's happened, but I am, and I don't know what to eat."

"Oh come on, Jo," I said. "Think of something. Just be creative."

You have, as someone supposedly wise once said, a nose on your face that you never even see. Not even in a mirror. You're blinded by your conditioning, by photographs or whatever, by what other people tell you. You never see the true nose, and you never see what's perched on it laughing until, most of the time, it's far too damned late.

I motioned wildly to Joanna to forget about the meal and sit beside me. She looked at me quizzically, obeyed slowly, and I took her hands in mine, grinning.

"I know," I said softly. "Joanna, I know what it's all about now. I have the answer. To everything."

She almost pulled away from me then, but there must have been something in the way I spoke, because she relaxed suddenly, gripped my wrists and linked us. Nodded.

"Tell me, Simon," she said. "For God's sake, tell me."

I hesitated and squinted, a habit of mine when I didn't know how to say what was rolling in my mind. But I tried. I tried.

"Books are read and thrown away these days," I said finally. "It's an economic necessity and a fact of life."

"Agreed," she said, glancing once at the window and shuddering.

I went on—stumbling and stuttering because it was a birth I was midwifing and wanted no part of seeing—to explain that it wasn't simply our population's conditioning that led to this present where plays were not watched but experienced, films became holographic life substitutes, where cinema bowl spectacles have jaded even a youngster's passion for novae and blood. It was more than just conditioning, much more than that. Since the population has been conditioned by its cultural matrix, it had to follow that those who tried to create a people's diversions were also conditioned, all of them having gone through the same educational state, the same pre- and post-school training. They can think for themselves, of course, but what they cannot do is break through the cage that inhibits their imaginations! The imagination that lets them talk to themselves, see things that aren't there, *create* books and plays and…God, whatever else has been lost…create these things out of whole cloth, or even slightly used dreams.

Dare and the others had hated me, not because I was destroying the commercial viability of their material, their work—they hated me because when Neil showed them my first three books, they knew that I could do what they could not: create from a source to which they had no access.

It was this, then, that distressed me, frustrated me, gave me those bouts of horrid, terrifying anger, that made me want to scream when I was alone in my room. Alone. With my imagination.

And the more I talked, the more furious I became, looking for and not finding a single tangible object at which I could direct that rage. Neil was dead. Dare was dead. The others were dying, and I loved Jo too much. My breath came more rapidly, perspiration broke and scattered on my forehead. I made a fist and pressed it to my brow, closed my eyes, and grunted. Nothing happened. Grunted again, and still nothing happened. The rage grew. I tried again. The rage broke into crimson spirals behind my eyes. Once more I tried, waiting for the screaming, until finally it passed and I slumped back on the couch.

"Simon," she said, sliding away from me, "you're…you're not well."

"Insane?" I felt as if I'd run round the country without stopping. I was gasping for air and my lips were trembling.

"No, I didn't mean that. But I've seen you go through this before, in the office."

Something moved in the corner. I didn't look; I knew I would see nothing.

A WatchDog screamed by, and another, and a third.

Someone shouted in the corridor, shouted and was cut off.

"Simon," she said, rising suddenly and backing toward the door. "It was you, wasn't it? Dare, Neil, the others. This thing you have about them—"

"No!" I said, leaning over the back of the couch, one hand outstretched. "Joanna, no, I didn't kill anyone."

"Those fits of yours…you must black out sometimes they're so strong."

"Joanna, please!"

"You can't know what you're doing when you black out."

I shouted her name; she wouldn't stop talking.

"You…you hated them, didn't you, for not publishing that monster of yours. You hated them. Simon…"

I didn't move as she slid open the door and raced into the corridor screaming for help. She pounded on doors until she made her way around to the other side of the building. Then I rose and staggered out to the liftube, stepped in and drifted downward, hearing as I passed each floor people stirring as though uneasy and unable to stay by themselves.

And once outside it was cold, too cold for the sun that was still shining.

4

If Joanna had decided that it was I in some madness who had killed all those people, then I was sure it wouldn't be long before someone like Fein reached the same conclusion. I needed a place to think, then, and headed for my Key, but when I reached the corner of my block I saw that a WatchDog had settled in the middle of the street and Blues were standing deceptively calmly in front of my Keyloft. They were huddled against the wind and blowing into their hands. A crowd was forming. It was a spectacle not to be missed. I stared, holding on to the edge of a building, stared and shook my head slowly as my world began to shatter.

Someone bumped into my back, turned me halfway around, and I began to run, veered at the next corner and headed directly and without hesitation out toward the Fringe. That was where my life was, and the Blues would say that I was from the Fringe, as though that would be explanation enough for my sins. No one would care that I fought my way out, no one would notice that I had circumvented University and made it all the same.

The buildings grew more dull as I ran, the joyhalls not quite as garish, no cinema bowls, no hundreds of well-dressed peds moving from Key to office in an automated stream. I slowed, grabbing tightly at my side, looked up and realized the sun had some time before already set. The Keyloft walls were now dotted with squares of light, the children were gone, the night's peace had arrived.

I slowed. I stopped. I waited for childhood memories to overwhelm me, possess me, produce a tender gentle smile.

They didn't.

I was alone in the Fringe, and a stranger.

I wandered for something like an hour, trying to force myself to be receptive to the ghosts of my past. It was futile, however, and I knew it and I kept trying. With Joanna gone—

A WatchDog shrieked by.

—I didn't think I had anything left. I touched things, I smelled things, I even accidentally wandered onto the street where I had been born and my parents had died. But the Keyloft was gone, replaced by another with a joy hall on the ground and shops to either side and above. It was, as I stared, as though someone had hacked off my left hand, then my right, and left me with stumps to shake hands with my friends.

A WatchDog shrieked by.

Suddenly, a Blue stepped out of a restaurant behind me. He brushed my arm, turned to apologize and stopped, stared, reached into his tunic pocket to pull out a newspic. Of me. And I bolted without thinking. My shoulders hunched, expecting some sort of blow, and I bent over at the waist to make a smaller target. Skidded around a corner, around another, ducked into a doorway and pressed against the wall, gasping, tearing, then spinning out again. Behind me was the city, ahead at the end of the street I could see the buildings break.

I stumbled. Caught myself and stumbled again.

Saw four Blues racing after me, one with his hand pressed close to his face. A sudden feeling of exhilaration washed over me, tempted me to wave at my pursuers and urge them on as though they were the bad guys and I wore the white shirt. That fantasy ended abruptly, however, when a piece of a building shattered away only a handsbreadth from my head, and shards of hot stone pelted my back.

The game was over.

I was mad and I was running.

Less than a minute later breaking past the last of the city and into the outland, through the trees and avoiding the roads, staying beneath the leaves to keep the 'Dogs from spotting me. With any luck at all they would never find me. The advantage here was, I knew where I was going.

Without a timepiece, I had no idea when it was that I finally arrived at the edge of the clearing. But the moon was up, the clouds having fled, and the stars were indifferently cold, like splatters of old ice. I crouched behind a hedge of brush and stared at the grey house, waiting patiently, finally, to see what traps had been laid. I counted slowly and silently to myself until I judged an hour had gone by, rose with one hand bracing myself against a lightning-dead oak, and stopped when the back door opened and Joanna stepped out.

The wind had died, and there was silence.

When I moved out of hiding and walked slowly across the clearing, she started, reached behind her and pulled Alex out to stand by her. They watched me carefully, not moving, only once glancing at each other as though they had known I'd been there all along. The leaves beneath my feet already had a sheath of frost and they snapped when I walked, a cannonade of dying, until I came up to the stoop and waited. I thought nothing. I only stared at them until Alex, his arms too loose at his sides, cleared his throat. I moved back a pace, another, then reached up and brushed a hand through my hair, stroked my cheek once and nodded.

"Joanna called me," Alex explained unnecessarily.

"And the Blues?" I said, bitterly and without remorse.

"Simon, please," Joanna said, one hand reaching out, dropping back. "Please, Simon."

"It seems to me I said that to you, Jo, a little while ago and you ran away from me."

"You frightened me, Simon. You...you weren't the same."

"Yes, I was," I said. "You just haven't recognized me."

"I finished that book," Alex said, diverting my attention. He half-turned toward the door, changed his mind and faced me again. "You were very angry when you wrote it, weren't you?"

It was my turn to move away, and I did, stalking halfway across the clearing before putting my hands on my hips and letting my gaze climb the black shadow-wall of the trees to the icestars in the sky. I heard Alex step down to the ground, his footsteps crackling like walking fire. I wouldn't look at him, though, and he had to come around in front of me to meet my eyes.

"It's angry," he said again. "So full of frustration and hate, Simon! Lord, I didn't know you had all that in you, I just didn't know. Why did you write it? A form of exorcism?"

"The hate's still there, Alex. Ask Joanna. She saw how I handle it now."

"She told me. It isn't safe, Simon, that kind of repression isn't safe. You'll explode one of these days, unless you get yourself some expert help. It isn't right for someone to behave that way, to carry all that inside them."

"The Fringe," I began, but his hand waved me silent.

"Simon, you've used that as an excuse since the first day I met you. You're not the only one who's made it into Prime or close to it from the Fringe. And you won't be the last. Joanna told me everything you said to her tonight, and reluctantly I have to agree with her that you've actually stumbled onto something that just may be important. But you're going about it all the wrong way."

"I did not kill any of those men, Alex," I said, each word flung like a stone into his face. "I did not kill them, I have never killed anyone, and…" I took a deep breath to calm myself, blew it out slowly, and felt my legs beginning to tremble, my arms stiffen. Then a sudden, brief gust of wind knocked a shadow away from his face and I nearly fell onto my back when I saw his expression. "You hate me, too," I said quietly.

"No," he said, his palms out as though I were about to strike him.

"You do," I insisted. "Damnit, Alex, I can see it!"

I lifted a fist over my head and he winced, half crouched, but did not move away. The fist stayed, rigid, then returned slowly to my side as I berated myself for the idiocy I had committed. All those things I had told Joanna, that beautiful sociological theory that explained away in the simplest of terms a malignancy that had struck to the hearts of our people…*wrong*. Wrong because I thought it was the end, and it was not. They hated me now, and I knew why because neither Joanna nor Alex had ever had dreams of putting words between covers. It wasn't the fact that I had the tap to imagination. No, damnit, and I spun around on my heels, nearly groaning aloud in my stupidity and self-pity. No, it wasn't that at all.

And it was not paranoia.

It was a foul form of sophistication, an evil they had created themselves to replace the evils their ancestors believed. They had constructed pedestals to lift themselves above the level of savages, pedestals that brought them Philayork and hovercats, the Colony Domes and a now-building starship; joyhalls, viones, WatchDogs, comunits; they had laid planking from pedestal to pedestal to cover the past and keep their eyes focused upward, but they had forgotten that there were still spaces beneath that flooring, spaces that grew shadows, that grew nightmares, that hid suns.

And I had torn up that covering, and the shadows had surged.

"Simon, are you all right?"

I had shown them nightmares.

"Simon?"

I had shown them dreams.

"Simon!"

I had somehow become atavistic and had shown them themselves.

Glittering savages on a cityplex street.

Anger. Fury. Rage. I squeezed my eyes shut and my head twisted from side to side, my lips opening and closing, my hands into fists. I might have made them more human, more caring, more aware of what they were so they could transcend and grow, but they hated me for it instead of being grateful and wanting to learn, they hated me and were afraid of me and I hated them in turn. My arms became rigid, my feet drifted apart until I reached up for the sky and balanced myself by grasping for the black.

And I screamed.

And I screamed.

And I screamed.

And...I wept.

They had hidden themselves and their legends in a dark and small closet (*I don't believe it, science has proved it can't happen, and even if it could I wouldn't believe*), bolted the door and pronounced themselves cured by turning on a sun-bright lamp to show the truth of their lies.

I slumped to the ground and rocked, crooning, on my buttocks. Alex dropped beside me and put his hands on my shoulders, gently shaking me and calling my name softly. I know he thought I was having a fit, retreating loudly and madly behind a screen of my dreams. He was worried, and I heard him call out to Joanna, the call suddenly choked off as his hands stopped their touching. I opened my eyes, then, blinking, then scrambling to my feet and running back toward the house. Alex was standing upright, his arms pinned to his sides, a roping of shadow twisting around his chest and his legs. Within the shadow were sparks, of green, of red, of colors I knew had no names. And from out of the forest on the back of the wind came others, hundreds, thousands that I cut off from view when I slammed the door behind me.

The room was empty.

I heard an engine sputter into a roar and raced to the front window in time to see a darkness drift out of the trees and settle, in time to hear Joanna scream.

And when it was done the shadowbeasts left and I raced from the house to beat them to the city.

Stopped when I neared it and saw the glow in the sky that glowed with a scream.

Joanna was right. Alex was right.

I had killed them, killed them all, my frustrations and anger somehow becoming lungs to give the dead legends a chance to take life.

And no one will believe it. They'll stay on their pedestals until the absolute end, their eyes always skyward, denying the savage and the nightmares he has.

Meanwhile I run.

And it has come to me in my running that those shadows I've spawned will return to their maker. All of them. Every one. And I can see now the need for a pedestal fortress, for the legends and lies are shields that we bear, legends and lies the armor that we wear.

Gone. All gone.

Like the house in the clearing when I stumble out of the woods, hands and arms and face and neck bleeding, stopping to see a monstrous black pillar where my manuscript had been. The white cage of the birch is the only color left. Joanna is…somewhere; Alex is…somewhen; and the only chance I think I have is to tell

*all that darkness that I was wrong, I don't believe, no matter how many façades
have been shattered in the city I am still of the future…and I do not believe.*

 It's the one chance I have as I run for the birch the one chance I have
 but the white has gone grey
 and the shadows are moving

I used to teach English. I used to teach Julius Caesar. I love that damned play, despite the mangling I and my students subjected it to, and despite the fact that it was the cause of my eventual retirement from the profession. When this story was first published in Fantasy and Science Fiction, the editor, Ed Ferman, suggested that the prologue was too intrusive, that it caused the reader to take too much time to get into the story. I don't know why, but at the time I agreed, and since I could find no other place to put its theme, it was left out entirely—much to my regret when critics quite rightly pointed out that I had cheated the reader by pulling rabbits out of hats by the time the ending rolled around. This, then, is by way of apology, and saying I should have known better. The prologue returns, as originally written.

Caesar, Now Be Still

So help me God, I'll kill him—an incantation of the weak against the supposed strong, an attempt at conjuring a spell where no magic exists, power where there is a vacuum, light without source in the full black of midnight. What it really means is: please, Someone, make me mad enough to be blind to reason. Mad. A double-shadowed word that banishes sanity no matter how it's used. And to be both at the same time, knowing neither one or the other, has only a single indication—that the ghost, if you will, of the Roman who would have been king still walks the battlefield. His enemies have died, and are still dying, and we can only pray that at the moment we hear him he is looking for someone else, on the other side of the hill. Where he can't be seen.

In the park at Oxrun Station there is a broad field that partially climbs the slope of what generosity can only call a hill, and to the right of the field beyond a screen of poplar and hickory, birch and elm is a pond. It's a small pond and clean, inhabited throughout most of the year primarily by a stray family of ducks that have never found their way clear to live anywhere else and by small children who negotiate the sometimes steep and slippery banks with an ease all adults covet and none dare try in the sight of any others. The cooling, squirming mud, the spiders that skate in darts and dashes across the unruffled surface, the bees that hover impatiently over the lily pad blossoms white and yellow are only a few parts of the whole, but parts those who have been tainted by maturity and the world avoid with a guilty squeamishness seldom admitted in the full light of the sun.

Myself, I prefer the gnarled humped roots of a storm-battered oak on the western, lowest bank. There, when the weather and the inclination are right, I take my lunch and watch the ducks and the children until the coming cold prods the former into reluctant migration and the latter are transformed from the near-naked to the near-smothered in coats and scarves and bright woolen caps pulled low and tight over ears and eyes. When all that happens, I surrender my solitude and stay in the *Station Herald* office, just off Mainland Road, a narrow highway that passes Oxrun Station north and south. I put my feet in a bottom desk drawer, loosen my tie with a most effective dramatic sigh, and leave bread crumbs on the blotter, or the papers thereon.

It was just into February by a handful of days, then, when I was preparing to take just such a break from the rigors of working on a weekly newspaper. And I was alone. The editor, Abraham Elderby, was hiding somewhere with an Oxrun councilman; the only other reporter, Peter Baines, was burning in the Florida sun, and our two workhorse secretaries, Harriet and Flo, had taken themselves to the luncheonette several blocks away to get away from my pungent, and morbid, wit. It was only luck, then, that I stayed behind, because not five minutes into a cup of coffee and ham sandwich, Liz strode into the office and stood stiffly on the other side of the low wooden railing that served as a warning, and a symbol, to whatever public happened to drop by. I knew her too well to miss the fact that she had been crying. Her makeup was on the far side of perfect for such a lousy day in an already lousy month, and the way her hands grabbed at the air by her waist, I knew she was hoping it could be someone's neck.

"Hey, reporter," she said, her smile so forced I thought it would shatter, "how about taking me out to lunch?"

I glanced at the desk ahead of me, the two to my left, and tried to look apologetic. "I really should stick around and mind the shop, you know." But I was already kicking the drawer shut and stuffing my sandwich back into its familiar brown paper bag. As I did, I glanced over my shoulder to the back where Elderby's glass-walled office allowed him to play the watchdog whenever he bothered to show up. Since it was empty, and since I was champing, I grabbed for my topcoat and hat and took Liz's elbow before she bolted. She said nothing when I opened the door for her, and we were uncomfortably silent during the time it took us to walk down to the Chancellor Inn and our favorite hideout on the second floor of the converted farmhouse. Downstairs was a bar, restaurant and disco generally subdued during the middle of the day; upstairs was thickly carpeted and dimly lighted, with high-backed wooden booths lined in red leather scattered over the floor in a deliberately irregular pattern. They were large enough only for two in the room we chose, yet not so tight that knees brushed. Artemus Hall, the proprietor for at least a thousand years by my reckoning, greeted us with a sharp nod and took us immediately to a corner by the fieldstone fireplace where we shed our coats, ordered drinks and waited until the waitress had served and left with a grace that would put a cat to shame.

I lit a cigarette, handed it to Liz and waited patiently while she stared at the beamed ceiling, the fire, an invisible point directly over my head. She was neither buxom nor tall, and on that afternoon wore a severe tweed suit-and-skirt that matched perfectly her mood. Her glasses were dull, almost spinsterish, and she hadn't run a comb through her close-cut brown hair. I've never heard anyone call her beautiful, but then no one sees her the way I do—I find no faults in the way she looks.

"He's going to fire me," she said finally, when I refused to make light and refused to look sad.

"No, he won't," I said. "Mike hasn't the nerve."

She worked for Michael Yardley Jarrow, a lawyer whose office defines the word pretension. He was successful with the rich (who make up most of the families within and without the Station's sprawling limits) and moderately so with the rest of us who did not live in the small estates on the other side of the park. As such, then, he was automatically important—important enough to maintain a solid seat on the village council, a directorship at one of the banks, and a few dozen other things that kept him in silks and quiet elegance. He was also one of my oldest and most exasperating friends.

"I fouled up another brief," she said, brooking no arguments from a just-thirty and weary reporter. "He needed it for court this morning and I blew it. He almost slugged me he was so mad."

"Not Mike," I said, disbelieving. "The last time he hit someone was in grade school, and the kid belted him back so badly his teeth still haven't come in straight."

"Damnit, Simon, why do you insist on defending him?"

I opened my mouth to protest, saw the tears struggling to fade without falling, and cleared my throat instead. I thought I was trying to be rational and calming; obviously, I wasn't even in the same ballpark where Liz was playing.

"How come you blew it?" I said then. "Tired? You look it."

She held onto her glass tightly. Sipped. Swallowed. Stared at the fire again. "I didn't get much sleep," she admitted reluctantly. "That prowler was back. I stayed on the couch most of the night."

I didn't say anything, the most tactful thing I'd done in a week. She'd been bothered, off and on for a month or so, by someone she claimed was waiting outside her apartment door. The trouble was, each time she had the nerve to open it, no one was there, no sign, no…nothing. Elderby had complained of somewhat the same thing one day a week before, but I thought nothing of it until Forbes Cunningham was found dead in the park three days ago. Cunningham was, by all accounts, a miserable crank of a man who owned the most prosperous jewelry emporium in the village, one it was said Cartier would drool over. Sam Windsor, the police chief, let me see the body. Shriveled, hunched, as though he were a balloon and all the air had been sucked out through an undetectable hole. Once the word got around—and in Oxrun, where petty theft was the most heinous crime, word travels unbelievably fast—Liz became sure she was the next target. Nothing would dissuade her. Not even my staying over one night to prove to her she was letting her imagination work overtime and with triple pay.

"Did you call Sam?" I asked.

She shrugged. Liz wouldn't call the fire department if her apartment were worse than a furnace. Fiercely independent, and a woman determined to overcome her lack of formal education and climb to the top of her chosen heap with only the slightest assistance from anyone. Including myself.

"All right," I said. "We forget that part. Tell you what, I'll talk to Mike for you, okay? Come on, Liz, okay?"

She sniffed, grabbed a handkerchief from her purse and blew her nose. Acquiescence, then, and something Liz hated. She was, at times, too much her own woman, I thought, and often her pride inflated to the point of choking her. So she blew her nose. Sort of a private signal, and I relaxed.

Then she said she was hungry, and the storm, for the moment, was over.

For Liz. Not for me. After I had walked her back to her office and had trotted back to mine, I heard a faint grumbling whine filtering from the back room. I looked up and saw Elderby pawing at the intercom, glaring at me all the while and biting at his lips. I nodded and shot my cuffs as I headed back toward him, wondering what advertiser had complained this time, which councilman had whispered unkind words into his shell-like ear. He was like an apple baked too long and stuck atop a beanpole nibbled at through too many summers by ravenous vermin. His clothes were hung, not draped, and his left hand stayed at his throat, pulling at the wattles that quivered whenever he spoke.

"Simon, where the hell have you been?"

"Lunch," I said, my innocence role falling automatically into place.

"You were to stay in the office. You were to wait until one of the girls returned."

"A friend of mine—"

"I nearly lost an account because of that bit of selfishness."

"—was in trouble, and I wasn't about to turn her out."

"You're not listening to me."

"You, too."

He stopped and stared at me while his right hand fumbled at a humidor to draw out a cigar no Cuban would be caught dead with; he lit it, blew the smoke toward my face and squinted. He was nervous, I could see it through the mask he liked to wear, but whatever sympathy he might have evoked was easily dissipated by his manner, and that whining voice of his.

"Damnit, Simon, are you in trouble again?"

The reference to my not-so-pious youth annoyed me, but I ignored it for the smoldering I saw beneath his expression. He went on, then, for nearly ten minutes, explaining as though I were a cub what my duties were and how I was to perform them with maximum efficiency, where my loyalties lay, and the location of my desk, not to mention the threats of unemployment fogged in words of seven syllables. At another time in another place I would have stalked out with righteous indignation cloaked about me, but I was irretrievably over thirty, reasonably secure; and with the marketplace becoming more and more jammed with hawkers much younger than I, I could take no chances on the temper of an old man.

There was also Liz.

And finally there was Oxrun Station. The village, the hills around it, the farmland, the...to say peace would be inadequate, to say unique would be clichéd; to say home, however, says everything.

So I listened, nodded contritely, and when it was over, returned to my desk to work on the follow-up article on Forbes Cunningham. The coroner's inquest determined that the age of the man, the weather, and the amount of time he'd been exposed led to the condition of the discovered body. No explanation of why he was in the park, at night, in January, in the first place; that was the police's problem. Now it was February, and people forget. And my job was to make sure that they didn't. The article itself, then, carried nothing new. It was a filler, something to keep the oddity floating around the backs of folks' minds on page eight while the rest of Oxrun went about its business. If anything else ever came up, the transition back to page one would be painless, and years from now people would remember (or misremember) it always being there, for weeks on end, the scandal of the year, of the century.

When it was done, I considered asking Elderby about his prowler. Perhaps there was something in it, a link, Liz and Abraham and…whoever else might be affected. Afflicted. Whatever.

I turned around to stare through the glass wall at my boss. He was fiddling with the Venetian blinds that cut him off from the world I lived in, saw me looking and pointed at the clock. Five. The bars were opened. The inmates were free. I glanced at the girls, working silently on something or other at Harriet's desk, shrugged and bid them a good night. They grunted. I laughed. Prowlers, Cunninghams, and angry advertisers: nothing changed, nothing changed.

I walked east two blocks to Fox Road, turned right another block, and I was at the corner of Fox and High, ascending the steps of a smallish Victorian much like the other homes in this part of the village. It belonged to the Smarts, a long-retired couple who had replaced their children with boarders. My rooms were on the top floor, complete with gabled study and slanted roof over the bedroom/sitting room, and a wind that howled when it thrust in from the north. I poked my head into the downstairs living room to see if anyone was about, then rushed up to change my clothes, wash, sit in an armchair rescued from one of Mrs. Smarts's spring clean-up campaigns. Because of my job I was permitted a phone of my own, and as soon as I was settled I called Mike, got his wife Grace (a fine and rising lawyer in her own right) and asked to be connected with the man himself. Grace hesitated for a moment, something that puzzled me, then did as I asked before I could question her.

"Simon, damnit, I'm working."

"Sure, Mike," I said, "but you'll never get to be President if you kill yourself first."

"Ha. Funny. So what's new? We still pokering Saturday night?"

I thought of the money I had lost at his cards over the years, and told him I would. "But now I want to talk to you about Liz, all right? You've got her scared to death, Mike. And, if you don't mind me saying so, you were rather tactless about it."

He was silent for several seconds, another puzzle, but I had no time to search for layers of interpretation. "Listen, Simon," he said at last, "Liz is a nice girl. She works hard, works fairly well, but…hell, she doesn't seem to fit, Simon. She's not what you call your typical law-office type, if you know what I mean."

It was my turn, then, to keep a moment's peace, shuffling through my stereotypes to see if I could come up with a law-office type. When I failed to do so, he bridled.

"Simon, I know you and Liz are…involved, but I'm going to let her go at the end of the month. Between you and me, of course. She'll find another job, don't worry, but…damnit, Simon, why are you acting like her husband?"

I almost laughed at his consternation, grunted instead, muttered a few words about the coming card game and rang off. I stared at the flowered wallpaper, at the corners, at the chipped desk of drawers where my life was stored. Then I slipped back into my coat and scarf and left the house, walking until I reached the park and passed through the huge iron gates to the winding paths that laced it. I followed one to the top of the hill. I didn't want my oak just then; it was too much bound with summer days and children's laughter. What I wanted, when I left the path and made my way through the trees and shrubs to the open, was the aloof icepick of stars, the single grey cloud that smoked lazily beneath the moon, the lights of the village below and beyond me. I stood with my hands in my pockets, staring down the gentle slope that flattened into a playing field. The pond was to my left, but I still did not go there. Here and there, I could make out a chimney reaching whitely for the black above it. Cars with chains rattled distantly.

I had a brief, disturbing sense of not being alone, but it passed as quickly as it had come.

I looked, then, for omens.

I muttered speeches under my breath, scolding Liz and showing her a part of my shoulder for her cheek and the security it would promise if she would only cut loose one strand of her career and save some of her energy for me.

The feeling again, and I glanced back at the trees, at the black shadow-wall.

I paced through the snow less than an inch deep and looked at the marks I had left. You're following me, I told myself, and before I could respond, found myself standing at the edge of the pond in spite of my intentions. The ice was dark, unpleasantly so, and when I looked down at my feet I blinked rapidly. A face. Blurred and staring. I blinked again, and it was gone. For a third time, then, that not-alone sensation, and I hurried around the perimeter of the ice and through the trees to the fence. There was nothing there, I knew, and told myself it was the slush of February, the dreary grey days that stalked the end of winter.

Stalked.

I shuddered at the word and went home.

On Thursday, two days later, I had just approved the last of Harriet's and Flo's paste-ups for the weekly edition, was pawing through some records of other bodies found in the park (four in the past eight years, all from out of town), when the door slammed open and Mike thundered in, slapping aside the gate in the railing, not stopping until he was standing in front of my desk. Except for a singular lack of hair on his body from the neck up, he was totally ursine, so much so in fact that in high school and college his nicknames were, respectively and predictably, Smokey and Grizzly; I used neither, I knew the man underneath. He was glaring at me in a manner too recently familiar for me to ignore, and his hands were poised over the oblong metal shade of my desk lamp as if he were ready to snap it in half. I didn't bother to smile. I only sat back in my chair and waited. While he opened his mouth, closed it again, swallowed and brushed his hands against his coat front, his sleeves. A forefinger rubbed against the side of his nose. He was steadying himself, and I did not like the sudden pit that had replaced my stomach.

"I had always assumed," he said finally, "that whatever we talk about, between ourselves, is a matter of confidence."

I frowned, and that seemed to make him madder.

"If I had known you were going to blow it, Simon. I would have kept my mouth shut. But you're my friend. I thought you had at least a little discretion."

"Mike," I said, palms to my chest, "I haven't the slightest idea what the hell you're talking about."

"You told Liz I was going to fire her."

"I most certainly did not."

Flo, working at the file cabinets, suddenly decided to visit the ladies' room. Harriet hunched herself over some papers on her desk. From where I sat I could see they were blank; she read them anyway. Carefully.

"She came in this morning, Simon, and told me...she came in and said that since I was going to let her go anyway, she was going to do me one better and quit. She threw—*threw, Simon*—a folder at my face and walked out. Damnit, I thought I could depend on you. I was hoping Liz and I could work out an amicable parting agreement so she wouldn't behave this way. You blew it, Simon. Damnit, you blew it!"

"Michael, in the first place I did not say anything to her except that I would talk to you when I had the chance. Which was going to be Saturday night at the game. In—"

"Forget it. I don't want you at my table."

"—the second place," and now my hands dropped into my lap, "even had I done it, it was my business to do so since you were going to can her anyway. And in the third damned place," I was on my feet, my palms resting on the desk, my face less than a foot from his, "what do you care? If she's not your type, as you said, why the hell are you so bothered?"

"Because she'll talk," he said tightly. "Look, I've had little enough sleep these days, what with people sneaking around the house and scaring Grace half to death. I don't need the aggravation of a stupid angry woman blabbing half-truths around town. Who knows what people will listen to her?"

I closed my eyes as though that would deafen me, opened them again and sagged back into my seat. "Mike, you're not being rational. Lord, you can't be that insecure, not after all you've done, not after all this time."

"She'll talk, make up stories, lurid—"

"Stop it, Mike!" I snapped, slamming a hand on the armrest. "Liz isn't like that, and if nothing else, you should know that. She's mad, she quit, so get yourself another girl and forget it."

"She'll talk, Simon, and at this stage of my career, and Grace's, I won't have it."

"Oh Lord, I don't believe it. The next thing you'll be telling me, this town isn't big enough for the two of you."

"It isn't," he said. "And it's no thanks to you and your damned big mouth."

"I told you once I did not say anything. She knew it two days ago. I wonder why."

It was a staring match, then, until he jammed his hat back on his head and strode out. I was stunned into immobility, I could not allow myself to believe he was as confused as he seemed and could not understand why I was the brunt of his explosion. It wasn't rational, but then it wasn't a rational situation. And when the intercom crackled out my name angrily, I swept aside the papers on my desk and kicked back the chair. Then I spun around and pointed a finger at Harriet.

"Not a word," I said. "Not a goddamned word."

Prowlers and tantrums, I thought as I walked back to Elderby's sanctum and stood on the threshold; I really don't need any of this at all.

Elderby stood with hands clasped behind his back, staring out a curtained window at the tiny parking lot behind the building. He did not turn around when I cleared my throat.

"I warned you not to conduct your personal affairs on my time, Simon," he said. "I warned you. That is your business, on your time."

"Mr. Elderby, I didn't invite Michael in here. He—"

"Mr. Jarrow is a very important man in this town and in the state. It will not do either of us any good to have him mad at the paper."

"For God's sake, he's not mad at the paper, he's mad at me!"

"Mad at you and mad at the paper is the same thing. I'm going to, have to think about making changes around here, perhaps. For the good of everyone."

I watched his fingers entwined nervously, frowned and shook my head. Everyone was nuts, I thought; what the hell's happening around here?

"Mr. Elderby," I said, placating and thinking of no checks coming in, "this is a weekly village newspaper. It is not *The New York Times.* You've got me and Peter and the girls. That's all, Mr. Elderby."

"I'm well aware of that," he answered, turning to face me with a neutral smile. "I am well aware of our position vis-à-vis the metropolitan dailies."

"Good, then what the hell—"

"But it will not stop me from being known, Simon, from having the influence I deserve."

"—are you talking about? Mike and I have argued before and we'll argue again. There's—"

"I will not be thwarted, Simon."

"—no big deal here, Mr. Elderby. No big deal."

"All right, then," he said blandly. "Smooth it over. I saw his face. This was not a little spat."

"Mr. Elderby..." I shut up.

"And the next time you disrupt your work for something like this, you won't be coming back to it. Do you understand me, Simon? You've upset the women, and they won't be worth a damn for the rest of the day. I'm upset, and I can't work for what I want when I'm upset. And you're upset and are now less than useless. Go home. Get drunk. I don't give a damn what you do, but don't come back here until I can have harmony in my kingdom, is that understood?"

I shrugged. I knew the strength of the enemy and my own resources. So I backed out, my hand on the doorknob. Before I could close the door, however, he lifted a folder from his desk and pointed it at me. "This article on the Cunningham thing, by the way... I pulled it. It stinks. And this memo about connections between him and those others over the past ten years? People die, Simon. Some in winter, some in summer. When Peter gets back I'll let him handle it."

I slammed the door.

Glared at Flo and Harriet huddled by the water cooler and walked out of the office, one arm still struggling to get into its coat sleeve.

Wandered.

Was not surprised when I found myself back at the pond where I searched for some trace of summer when everyone liked everyone else and the only worries I had were of filling the hours when I wasn't working, and courting, and sleeping, and dreaming.

The ice was dark, the ice was black, with mounds of snow turned to ice along the shallows, rough ridges where skates had thrown up shavings that had frozen where they'd sprayed. I shrugged off impatiently the feeling that something was hovering beyond me in the grey light, instead imagined myself in conversations with Mike, with Elderby, conversations that ended with verbal slashings, physical beatings, and myself committing the most monstrous acts against the life that animated them. I would move through one, finish and return to refine and polish, like a playwright laboring over the climactic confrontation between general and subordinate, emperor and vizier, lover and lover. And at each killing, in slow motion and mute, I grew more calm; and at each killing, I felt more ashamed.

I decided to straighten things out once and for all; I would talk to Liz, talk to Mike, they would part friends and keep me around for one more try. But by the time I had reached that conclusion, my face was stiff with cold, my ears had gone numb, my eyes heavy with an inordinate desire to lie down and take a nap.

I almost did.

Almost; and hurried back to partake of a bowl of Mrs. Smarts's beef broth. When I thought I might finally get warm again, I rushed upstairs and called Liz. No answer. Called Mike. No answer. Grinned at my fine intentions and read a book until I fell asleep in my chair.

The following morning the Venetian blinds were drawn at Elderby's glass wall. Harriet was preening in front of a mirror propped on her desk. I perched on the edge of her desk and jerked my thumb toward the back.

"Hey," I said, "what's the idea?"

"He's afraid," she said, patting at her hair and smiling. "Says someone tried to break into his house last night. He thinks he was followed to work, too. Spent most of the time with Sam Windsor before he came here, demanding, if you will, around the clock police protection."

"You're kidding."

"Hey, would I kid you, Simon?"

She grinned, and I grinned back. I went to my desk and tried to call Mike, was told by his receptionist that he was not accepting any calls that day. When I prodded, and because she knew me through Liz, she told me he was awaiting instructions from Sam Windsor.

I didn't ask for what.

I stared at the receiver instead, and for the briefest of moments felt that not-alone sensation again. Suddenly, I raced from the office without telling Harriet where I was going. Without a car it took me twenty minutes to reach a colonial-styled two-story apartment building that housed fifteen small units. I looked up to the top left corner and saw that Liz's curtains were drawn. They shouldn't have been. In the lobby I tried to get her to answer the buzz that would unlock the main door, tried the back entrance, and it too was locked. There was an urgency I could not define, and I began to make the rounds of the places I thought she might be, including the pond she had shared with me on not a few warm spring nights. Then I went where she had no place being, trying to convince myself that she wouldn't leave Oxrun without at least a note for my eyes only.

I found her at the Chancellor Inn, upstairs in our booth, and I slid in silently, saying nothing when she ordered a larger-than-usual drink, the third, by the glasses that stood empty in front of her.

"You were at Mike's," I said simply, thinking she was also at Elderby's last night, her anger spilling over to encompass my own private fight.

"I wanted to do something," she said in a small, quiet voice. "And I couldn't think of doing anything but beating them, killing them even… I don't know." Her eyes were frightened, the lines etched from them like a web behind which she cowered. "Simon am I crazy?"

"Silly," I said. "Just a little silly is all. I was mad, too, but I walked it off." I told her of my pantomimes in the park, and by the time I was done, she was smiling. Weakly, but smiling.

"You scared them out of their wits, you know." I said with a grin that banished condemnation.

"How did I do that?"

"By…by whatever you did last night, dope," I said, lifting my glass in a silent toast. "Elderby's hiding in his office, and so is Mike. They're both trying to wheedle live-in cops from Sam."

"God almighty," she whispered and finished half her drink. "All I did was walk past the house a few… Elderby? I wasn't there, Simon."

I almost let it pass, so intent on nudging her back to the Liz I wanted, but when the remark struck home, I made her repeat it, my doubt all too clear. "Come on, Liz, this is me, okay? What did you do, rap at their windows, throw some rocks at the door? What? Come on, I promise I won't print a thing."

I was wrong and too eager. I could see her wrapping her armor back on, strapping on her sword and marking off the combat zone. "I told you what I did and where I was, Simon. And for your information, I told it all to Sam this afternoon when he called me. Seems your "friend" told him about the folder thing and wanted me investigated or something."

"Dumb," I muttered.

"I don't care," she said, startling me because I expected agreement. "Simon, I'm not going to be held down. Not by Jarrow, not by anyone." She didn't have to say whom that "anyone" included; it was evident by the way she turned abruptly to look at the fire. "Sam doesn't think I'm the housebreaker, anyway," she said after a log had cracked into a pyre of sparks. "He believed me when I told him about my own little sneak thief."

"Again? Liz, damnit—" I sputtered into silence, came close to pouting because she hadn't called on me for the hero's protection, but I did manage to get her to stay with me through dinner, which we scarcely tasted, and wrangled an invitation back to her place for what I hoped would be a reconciliation of sorts. I was sitting on the couch watching her pour the coffee when suddenly she stiffened, and some of the liquid slopped onto the carpet. I opened my mouth to ask if she were all right…and grabbed at the edge of the cushion.

The pond. The park. The presence.

It was back, and all the more unnerving because it was obvious Liz sensed it, too. A draught iced around my ankles. I would have sworn I heard a sigh sifting through the door.

February, I thought; it does things to people.

Liz rose, but I stopped her with a wave and threw back the bolt, snapped open the door and lunged into the corridor.

It was empty. Dim lights only, creating rather than dispelling the shadows.

And it was silent, all the more because of the murmurings of families who lived behind the other doors.

I turned, and she was standing in the middle of the room, hugging herself, her fingers massaging her biceps.

"A prank," I suggested.

"You felt it," she said. "It's real, then. My God, Simon, I didn't want it to be so real."

I walked to the sideboard to her telephone and dialed Elderby's number; I don't know why—a hunch perhaps, or something inside telling me things I did not want to hear. After eighteen rings, I broke the connection and tried for Mike. Grace answered, with an urgency that almost threw me.

"Hey," I said lightly, "what's up, Gracie? Can I talk to the man, or is he in conference?"

"Simon, get off the line! We're waiting for the police—" She was cut off abruptly, and it wasn't until I'd replaced the receiver that I realized I had been hearing in the background the first climbing wail of a man…screaming.

Liz stared at the door.

I stared at the telephone, frantically trying to make sense of what was happening. I didn't hear what I thought I heard, I told myself; I didn't hear it. It wasn't Mike.

But it was, and I snapped out of the stupor I'd fallen into and grabbed for my coat, Liz's arm, and bolted from the apartment. It seemed like hours before the elevator came—wondering why in hell I hadn't used the stairs—but it was close to that before I was able to get her car to work. She seldom used it, I more than her since I didn't have one of my own, and it stalled four times when I tried to race to the police station. Four times. And not once did Liz ask me a question, prod my thoughts, offer me something more than the silence more cold than the air that fogged the windshield.

When I finally parked at the curb, she took my arm and looked at me steadily. I shuddered; there was nothing in her eyes.

"Simon," she said, "I'm sorry. God, I'm sorry. We could have had it, you know. We could have had it."

"Later, Liz," I said, patting her hand and pulling her from the car. "We'll talk more later. Come on."

I pushed through the double doors, mostly a milky translucent glass, and hurried across the green-tiled waiting area to the low desk that squatted, much like my own, behind a wooden railing. A radio dispatcher was working his mike at the far wall, harried and cursing when static-filled responses filled the large room. Fred Borg was the man on duty at the desk, and he almost but not quite grinned when he saw and recognized me. I asked for Sam, was told he'd been summoned but hadn't come in yet.

"Look, Fred," I said. "I was just on the phone with Mike Jarrow. Something's wrong out there, I don't know what. I was talking with his wife when we were cut off. I think I heard someone yelling in the background."

Screaming.

"How long ago?"

I looked to the round clock on the wall over the dispatcher's head. "Twenty minutes, maybe. I had car trouble."

He rubbed a hand through what was left of his hair and slammed a pen into its holder. "Forget it, then," he said wearily. "Look, Simon…damnit, man, why the hell did you have to come here? Now, of all times?"

"Hey, Fred," I said, leaning closer and staring, "come on, Fred, what?"

He sniffed, looked down at his log book, then up and away to the white globes of light suspended on dark chains from the faintly green ceiling.

"Ah, God," I said, grabbed for a wooden chair and slumped into it. "Damn." And when I finally looked around to tell Liz what Fred's silence had told me, she was gone. The doors were open, and letting in the cold.

———

I wanted to go after her, but I couldn't. My legs wouldn't work and my weight had grown too great. I would go to the apartment later and explain, perhaps comfort and work things out. Right now, however, I had shock to fight through and mourning to work on. I was so close, I thought; Liz was right in my hand.

I told Fred, then, to check on Elderby. I was told they already had. Everyone, in fact, who had reported a prowler that Sam had been disposed to pass off as a prank.

Half an hour later the patrols were back in for a quick debriefing, and I didn't like what I heard. Mike had been found in the shower, the water wrinkling his skin until he'd seemed to have aged a hundred years; Grace was on the front yard, half-buried in a bank of snow. Elderby was in his bed, an unused rifle at his side.

Everyone assumed that since I was the only reporter left to cover things, I'd stick around for all the details. I didn't. I left and headed for Liz's apartment, needing her then and wanting to know what it was we could have had, and now could not. But when I got there, she was gone, and suddenly I was frightened and furious at myself for allowing my mind to forget her even for an instant. I borrowed her landlord's car and drove the streets aimlessly, searching for signs of her, spoors, a trace in the air, and saw her car in the middle of the road in front of the park.

Like a madman I ran through the entrance and angled to my right, cutting across the lower field and into the stand of trees. It was dark, too dark, and too often I fell over things invisible, my hands snapping out to catch me, skidding on the snow-frozen ground and burning from the contact. A low branch caught me on the hip and I was spun into a bush more thorn than twig. I cried out and ran again, ignoring the stinging on my face, the shallow gasp of my lungs. And when I broke into the open. I held on to my oak for support and stared. Knowing then what it was all about.

She was already standing in the center of the pond, looking down at the ice, looking up, looking down. She wore no coat, no gloves, and it was then that I felt the presence again, heavier now and more threatening, spiraling up from the ice with a faintly crimson glow that allowed me to see everything through a helpless squint. She was looking down again, to where I had seen that face. The death mask beneath the ice, eyeless and grim.

I called out but she didn't, or couldn't, turn round; and I cried out when the first small flakes drifted down from the black.

If I were a scholar I could quote and expound upon the wisdoms willed to us by the masters not always lamented, wisdoms covering ambition's thrust, ambition's force, and the accompanying curse that goes with the territory. But…none of us believe in curses or epigrams or quotes from the masters. Not any more. We've withdrawn into a shell not of sophistication born of learning, but of fear born of knowing. Fear that we will be found out and destroyed, or exposed, if one is much different than the other.

And the man who would have been a king had demurred and so lost a kingdom, brutally and bloodily; but the ambition, *not the justice*, of his, for want of a better word, life-force keeps him wandering. Caesar, clearing that endless battlefield not of his murderers, for they had done that themselves, but of his rivals. At least that's the way it was in Oxrun that night in February and on all those other nights when some men dared dream of things not theirs. And those who had allowed themselves to be open to the weapons of anger and hatred combined into cornered rage had been weakened to the point of vulnerability.

All of them.

And when their ambitions were drained…

So I stood and I watched.

There was nothing I could do for my Liz right now. She knew, had known all along, and had resigned herself to the embrace of the figure that seemed to have grown from a single crimson flake, gathering others about it until it lifted from the midnight ice and loomed man-tall, man angry, man ambitious. If she had time to scream before he kissed her, I did not hear it—the wind did it for her; if she had time to look at me once before the end, I did not see it—the snow lashed at my face unbowed and staring.

No one will believe it, however; it's too…well, take my word for it, no one will believe it, not even the important visitors I'll be meeting at the train whenever I can.

But that's not the worst part, that's not what turns my summers into December, my dawns to sunsets, my pond to dust.

The worst part is that I'm safe from it all. I know it. And *he* knows it. No matter what the pretension that filters into my work, I am an ordinary man and will be nothing more.

I am no threat to anyone, least of all him.

I'm alone in the dark, in the snow, in the park.

It's over, then, Caesar, at least for now. Be still, and let me go home.

I have work to do.

Not that it matters.

White Wolf Calling

Snow: suspended white water humping over hidden rocks, slashed by a slick black road that edged around the stumped mountains and swept deserted between a pair of low, peaked houses that served as unassuming sentinels at the mouth of the valley; drifting, not diving to sheath needled green arms that bent and held in multiples of thousands, spotting indifferently the tarmac walk that tongued from the half-moon porch of the house on the right. A snowman with stunted arms and holes for eyes squatted awkwardly beside a solitary spruce, watching nothing and making uneasy the brown-bundled man who stood by the mailbox. He leaned heavily against a broad-mouthed shovel, staring at the home opposite, turning his red-capped head to look beyond it to the forest that wavered through the sailing crystals up the slope to blend before the summit into the grey-white air.

No wind. Breathing only as he listened to the sunset, strained to hear the summons of the wolf.

"Mars?"

The shovel skittered from his stiff hand, banged against the walk and angered him with its rifle volley clatter.

"You think you have the power to move that house with just your eyes?"

Turning, he bent to retrieve the shovel, waving his free hand to indicate he had heard, and did not approve. Not so many decades before, he had begun calling his wife Venus because of her shortening of his own name to laughingly deify him; hers was Samantha, but his Venus she was. On the porch now, with crimson cheeks and her back reed-fragile, she folded her arms against the cold, waiting as he took a frustrated poke at the soiled snow the village plow had left to harass his cleaning. The mount was almost ice, and he glared at his gloves as if to blame them before hurrying to the house.

"Get inside, you dope, before you catch your death."

"I haven't seen the wolf, Venus. I'll probably live forever."

"Quit your smiling, Mars. That isn't funny at all. Get inside."

"You go on ahead. I'm almost done."

"I'm stubborn, Mars Tanner. I like to watch you killing yourself while that shiny new snowblower I gave you for Christmas lies rotting in the garage."

He pinched at her nose, tugged a lock of hair. "I may not be as young as I used to be, kid, but I can still handle anything that comes out of the sky."

She made a face and thumped him on the back as he went through the door, then rushed down the darkened hallway into the sweet-smelling kitchen before the warm stinging yanked at his parchment face and dried his lips.

"Tea?"

"No, thanks."

"Coffee?"

He cocked his head and raised an eyebrow. "Every time you ask, and every time I have to tell you, dummy, that coffee gives me gas. When are the boys coming back?"

"If they're sober, they'll be back in time for supper, as always," she said, taking his cap and stiffly new coat to hang by the wood-fed stove. "Some boys. They're almost forty, you know."

"In age, maybe, but their heads are at least two dozen years behind."

Venus tugged at the strings of her apron, letting the blue and yellow cloth tighten around her waist before she wriggled to settle it into place. Her hair was bunned grey, narrowing her face, sharpening her nose to a pale robin's beak. Only her chin remained youthfully rounded, even when she was mad.

"I don't like the way you make fun of them, Mars. They've come to hard times, in case you've forgotten the accident. It wasn't easy for them, losing both their wives as suddenly as that." She stared at him standing by the refrigerator. "Two daughters-in-law, and no grandchildren. It hasn't been easy for me, either."

"Those so-called women, and I'm sorry to say it, thought the boys had money, Venus. They took one look at our property here, didn't think anything at all about how land is cheap in this part of the state, and they talked themselves into believing we were rich. And neither Carter or Jonathan did anything to discourage them. Those women were too young and too damned impatient, and neither of my sons had brains enough to handle them."

Suddenly annoyed with himself for speaking when he should have been thinking, Mars poked aside the curtains on the back door and glared at the first staggered row of pine at the end of the yard he had cleared himself during their first summer in the valley. Seeing nothing, more angry because he thought he might, he sat at the table and dry-washed his hands. Venus moved behind him, rested her cheek against his still-thick hair and sighed just loud enough for him to hear. Knowing she would soon begin to caution him about little Tommy across the road, he shifted uneasily and cleared his throat.

"In to town today, I heard Pierson talking at the barbershop."

"It's about time you got a haircut," she said, sitting, one boned hand shaking unconsciously across her face in remembrance of a time when her hair was black and hung in gleaming ripples in front of one eye. "You're beginning to look like a sheep dog. Doesn't look like a very good one, though. Even without my glasses I can see it doesn't look like a very good one."

"That's because I didn't get one. I was to the hardware store looking up a new hammer when Pierson called me in for a chat. He says, and you know how Pierson is when he says anything, he told me fat McKenzie saw the wolf last week, just before his car smacked into the telephone pole."

"He was drinking. The newspaper said so. And that mechanic had done something to the steering. You think they had a trial for nothing?"

"McKenzie was scared. He told me."

"Of what, for heaven's sake? That mechanic? Mac owed that man a fortune for gambling, and practically everyone in town heard them fighting one time or another. My God, Mars, Mac outweighed him by a hundred pounds. If he was scared of anything, it was of having to pay the man and have nothing left for his wine. You know he always drank. I knew him for thirty-five years and can't remember the day he was last sober. Even on his wedding night when he married that Cranford woman."

Mars grinned. "You were there, I suppose?"

"Mars!"

"I wouldn't be surprised. You do get around, you know."

She feigned a roundhouse slap, he mimed a ducking wince, and they laughed, forgetting for the moment what McKenzie had seen.

"I'm going to take Tommy out to the cabin tomorrow to help me with the wood."

Venus wiped at the smiling tears in her eyes and shook her head. "That boy's not good for you, Mars. He's not your son, you know, and I doubt that the Dovnys will approve of your trying to make him."

"Oh, for Pete's sake, Venus, his father's never home, and his mother's flat on her back because of that skiing accident that busted her back. He happens to like my company, and I happen to like his. And with no one else his age around close to play with, we get along just fine."

"Well..."

"We can take care of ourselves, dear, don't worry. If I see the wolf, I'll spit in its eye."

Venus tried to smile, rose instead and bustled meaninglessly at the stove where supper was already steaming in three huge black pots.

Neither of them admitted believing there was a snow wolf in the mountains, had never even heard of such a green-eyed creature until the Dovnys's purchase of the land opposite them where they had constructed the house Mars hated because it spoiled his rocking chair view. He had met the Slavic father only once, at a Board of Education luncheon two years before at the village school. The man's English had been formal, as if memorized from a grammar book, but he charmed and was charming, and Mars had become friends with the blond-banged son when he had straightened a runner on the little boy's sled. The boy was the one who had told him and the village about the white wolf.

"Oh, I get it," Mars had said as he pulled boy and sled up a slope behind the house. "You're talking about one of those werewolf things. I've seen them a lot on television, on those horror show festivals."

The boy frowned bewilderment until Mars had explained, then shook his head and squinted to think harder. "No, the wolf only comes when someone is to die. It's not a person."

"Funny, but I never heard of that until you came around. How does it work? Is it kind of a family tradition? Maybe a Czech folk story, something like that?"

The boy had shrugged.

"Have a chocolate bar?"

The boy nodded and stuck it in his pocket.

Mars had completely forgotten that day until Samson O'Brien claimed he had shot at a wolf bigger than any he'd seen in his life. He was jeered when he failed to produce a pelt, or the tracks when he led a group of men to the site of the hunt. A week to the day later, his wife knifed him in the back when she learned he had been seeing the daughter of the mayor.

"Mars, are you trying to hypnotize yourself, or has my company gone stale after all these years?"

He blinked, tried a boyish grin before shaking his head. "Sorry," he said, leaning back in his chair. "I was thinking."

"Well, stop it. The boys are home. I heard them on the stairs."

"You want me to go up?"

"What for?"

He shrugged. "Talk to them. See what their plans are. God knows there isn't any paying work around here."

"We won't be around that long, Pop," and Mars grimaced when he turned so abruptly he twisted his side.

The sons were twins, dark-haired, taller than their parents and heavier about the chest and waist. Carter was the younger by three minutes, but his face was shadowed with lines and puffs; Jonathan was the same as he had been at thirty, except for the eyes that seemed perpetually half-closed.

"I wasn't trying to ease you out," Mars said, almost pouting, while they noisily took their places at the table.

"I know, Pop," Carter said.

"Of course he knows," Jonathan said, not bothering to disguise a slighting sneer. "He knows everything, don't you, Carter boy? Even took Pop's advice and knew enough to put the girls on that goddamned, beat-up excuse for a train."

"That's enough!" Venus said, slapping plates down in front of them. "The past is past, and I won't have that kind of talk in my house. You two have got to get back on your feet again, and soon. Your father's too proud to admit it, and too good to say it, but we can't have you around here indefinitely. It's too much of a strain."

"I know," Carter said, rising to help ladle the soup. "Just need a little readjusting, that's all. Besides, my leave's up in a week and I'll have to be getting back to camp."

"My goodness," Jonathan said, "does even a captain have to run like a buck private? Something else I didn't know. When are you going to make major, by the way? Ever?"

"Go to hell," Carter said.

"Language, brother," Jonathan said, scooping chunks of butter onto steaming slices of homemade bread.

"That's enough from the both of you," Mars said. "Your mother's right, as always. My pension can't handle everything. We love you both, but soon you've got to make a move. I'm talking especially to you, Jon. Your brother at least has a check coming in."

"Pop." Carter said before his twin could snap again, "why don't you sell the house? Maybe move to one of those retirement places. I know you love it here and all, but for crying out loud, the physical upkeep alone is going to do you in one of these days."

"I'll buy the place," Jonathan said, suddenly solicitous.

"Neither of you will," Venus said, taking her seat. "We've been here since you were born, and I'm not about to leave it now. Say grace. Mars, before I lose my appetite."

And dinner passed into evening as the snow greyed, crusted, and was littered with snapping fallen branches weakened by ice. Fireplace flames shadowed the living room in spite of the lamps, and Mars stood at a window, listening to his shattered family playing at playing cards, listening later, as he wandered the house looking for sleep, to whispers: the house itself, talking down to dawn through the mouth of the furnace, the pops of cooling wood in the fireplace, the creaks of boards searching for a comfortable place to shy away from the rising wind; the wind, riding the back of the snow, drifting powder over the road, pushing against thin glass, humming to itself in wires strung through the air, once to a crescendo covering hushed words; the words, snapping, biting, accusing, and prodding the weaknesses of the old man in vain attempts at deadly prophecy, husking laughter when one suggested the other do Mars the fatal blow.

Standing in the hallway, Mars shivered at the door of his sons' room, pleading for a prayer, sucking back the trembling that directed him to break down the barrier and cast them out.

He thought of Tommy, the surrogate son, and cursed his lack of wisdom that had made him a failure.

In his own bed again, wondering, he listened to the wind, heard faintly the cry of the dead calling for death.

And in the morning, after he had seen the brothers off to the village to notch another day at the tavern bar, after picking up after himself in bedroom and bath, he stood in the back yard and waited as Tommy ran awkwardly through the snow to him, dragging a sled still shining with varnish. Mars smiled, adjusted the peaked cap that covered the long blond hair, pinched the rounded cheek with his glove and led the boy into the woods, up the slope to a narrow plateau where freshly cut stumps pockmarked the ground.

A makeshift shed euphemistically called a cabin stood bleakly at the far end of the clearing. It was missing a front wall, served as a storage area for the logs Mars cut twice each winter. Tommy scrambled from stump to stump, climbing, daring Mars to spill him into the snow. The old man smiled, encouraged the boy to play on his own while he pulled a tarpaulin from a handmade toboggan and began loading the split wood, strapping each layer from front to back, finished with the canvas strapped side to side.

It was noon, and he was sweating, gasping, but not yet ready to give in to the aching that stretched his muscles and pounded through his lungs. He pointed out to the boy the peak where three hunters had lain wounded when a local man had gone berserk one evening in the tavern, escaped from the sheriff and had done some hunting of his own. They had endured the freezing night unprotected except for their clothes, only one surviving to testify at the trial, dying shortly after in the county hospital.

"They saw the wolf," Tommy said solemnly, and Mars laughed, cuffed him on the back of the head.

"You never did tell me how that works," he said, deliberately light.

Tommy rubbed a black mitten across his nose and sniffed. "I told you. The wolf comes when somebody's to die."

"But no one's been killed, much less even scratched, round here in a hundred years. By a wolf, that is."

Tommy looked up into the old man's face. "The wolf doesn't do it, silly. Father says the wolf… I don't know. It just comes. I don't know what it eats, but it causes, not does."

"You know, maybe I should get to know your father better," Mars said, taking hold of the unraveling grey rope that was tied to the ends of the sled's steering bar. He waved the boy on, and they moved up past the cabin. "I haven't seen him in nearly two years to talk to properly. I hope he doesn't think I'm unfriendly. I just never got around to it somehow."

"He works in the city," the boy said proudly. "He comes home on weekends and sleeps most of the time. He's very tired."

Mars nodded.

"Mommy's sick all the time."

"I know, son. I heard about it in the village."

"She can't sit up like us. Her back hurts all the time."

"I know, son."

Tommy jumped off the sled, and Mars sighed gratitude as they trudged in tandem toward the run they had made the week before.

"You know something, Mr. Tanner, I think my father's trying to scare me with the wolf story. He said it comes all the way from our home in…in…" He stumbled silently, mouthing the name and trying to give it voice. Mars had learned early not to help him. Czechoslovakia was the boy's private problem. One of these days, Mars thought, he'll pronounce it right and we'll have a damn big party.

The snow crackled beneath them as they turned around, hissed like scraping glass when Mars lay on the sled, Tommy climbed onto his back, and they raced down to the clearing.

Grinning and shouting, Mars sideswiped a log and spilled them both into a wave of snow that seeped down their necks like traces of ice. Lying with his face up, Mars squinted at the impossibly bright clouds, widened his eyes as a shadow darkened them and saw the laughing boy hugging his face.

"Mars, I think I need you."

"My God," Mars said and clasped the boy to him, closing his eyes to keep them from emptying, opening them to see the wolf.

It was white to its tail, with glittering beads of snow and ice clinging softly to its unmatted fur, swinging as it moved silently around the edge of the clearing. Breath in turbulent rivers of misted grey snorted from its nostrils while it turned around and faced them, its ears upright, its head slightly cocked. It stalked, slowly, and Mars rocked, still chuckling in his throat, keeping the boy's face pressed to his chest. The white wolf circled, and Mars twisted on his buttocks to keep the animal from getting behind him. Snow flecked from the sky, veiling but not hiding the green eyes that were deep close to black in the creature's magnificent head.

A ghost or a god? Mars thought as he pulled his legs from underneath him and struggled to stand without releasing Tommy.

"Hey," the boy said. "You're hurting me."

"Maybe," Mars whispered, "but you're tough. You can take it."

"Sure," Tommy said and squeezed harder, laughing.

The wolf backed away when Mars steadied himself, watched as man and boy sidled toward the toboggan. It bobbed its head once, whipped its tail and trotted off without looking back. Tommy began coughing.

"You got a cold?"

"Same one I had last week."

"Come on," Mars said, swallowing to keep his voice level, "I'll get some warm soup into your craw."

"What does that mean?"

"It's a foreign word, son. Foreign to you, that is."

"I know a lot of foreign words, too."

"Good. Maybe someday you can teach them to me."

"When, Mars?"

"I don't know. Someday. Soon, I guess."

With the runners freshly waxed and the slope working with him. Mars had little trouble hauling the load of lumber down to the house. Tommy pushed from behind, calling out every few feet to be sure Mars knew he was helping. And when they parted, Venus handing him a pot of stew to bring to his mother, Tommy waved, stepped into the road and was nearly struck by the car that raced out of the village and into the driveway.

"Goddamnit, you idiot," Mars shouted at Carter. "Why the hell can't you watch where you're going?"

Carter heaved his bulk out of the car and stumbled past silently, muttering nothings and leaving a waft of mixed beer and liquor.

Mars grabbed him by the shoulder and yanked him around. "Where's Jonathan?"

Carter shrugged, shook the hand off and staggered into the house, brushing past Venus without taking off his coat.

Cursing, then, his own thoughtlessness, Mars spun around, but Tommy was already on the first step of his own porch. He turned and waved, and Mars wanted to call out. He lifted a hand instead and sagged into the kitchen. Despite Venus's proddings, he remained silent throughout the evening meal, wondering what would have happened if Tommy had seen the green-eyed specter. It was a miracle he hadn't, and

Mars was moved once to laugh at his suspicions of the divine. That he was frightened he wouldn't admit, not even to himself.

Jonathan was returned by two of Mars's friends just before midnight, and the three of them carried the unconscious son into the bedroom, making little attempt to keep their voices low since Carter was already asleep and would not awaken until his stomach decided it was time to empty.

The fireplace, then, and the aroma of burning pine while Venus went to work on some knitting of hers: a scarf she had started the winter before but hadn't the patience to finish when its perfection eluded her clumsy fingers.

"What is it, Mars?"

He looked away from the fire.

Thinking: *McKenzie.*

"I saw the white wolf today."

"You didn't." She set the yam at her side and leaned forward with her arms resting trembling on her thighs.

A bubble of sap boiled.

"Bigger than life and twice as heavy. Damnedest thing I ever saw in my life."

"Why didn't you say anything?"

"We didn't believe there was such a thing, remember?"

"You saw it," she said. "It must be so. You never did have much imagination, Mars."

Thinking: *three men bleeding.*

"I think it was trying to get the boy to look at it."

Venus hummed nervously, then left her armchair for the sofa and curled her legs beneath her as she rested against Mars's unmoving arm. "Now you are imagining."

"You just said I never did, but maybe you're right, I don't know. I was thinking, though, that this thing, whatever it is, was never around before the Dovny people came."

"You saying maybe they brought it with them? A pet of some kind?"

Mars didn't know. From the time he had returned to the house from the clearing, he had been seeing movement in the corners of his eyes that escaped when he turned his head, white movement speckled green.

"O'Brien," he said without realizing he had spoken aloud. "Hush that talk," she said, gliding a hand against his mouth until he kissed it and carefully placed it between his own. "All those men were just bums, flops, failures, and I don't mourn their passing. And that wolf is just a wolf and had nothing to do with them."

Sleet began exploding like glass against the house.

"One of these days it'll move out to the city."

"Into the city?" She laughed, gasping, incredulous. "Come on, Mars Tanner, can you really see that beast walking the streets of a big town? With no one doing anything but staring or running scared? In a city, Mars?"

He thought: as he had left the clearing with Tommy, one backward glance had been sufficient to note that the snow where the wolf had been pacing was clean. There were no depressions to indicate an animal of that size had walked a warning.

"Mars, you're frightened, aren't you."

He watched the sparks like fire rain raise up into the chimney. "Venus," he said, "we've done bad by our children. One we drove into the army, the other we just drove. I don't think we ever really knew how to be parents."

"We did the best we could."

It was a tired argument, one that usually left them not speaking for hours.

"I should have cared more, I guess, been more ambitious, but the store was good enough for me."

"They went to school, Mars. They learned things.

Yeah," he said, scratching his stubbled jaw, "and blamed me for not doing the same."

A commotion on the steps forestalled her answer, caused her to straighten as if her sons would have been affronted by their parents' intimacy.

They came down into the foyer carrying suitcases and already wearing their overcoats. As Mars strode angrily toward them, Carter lifted a hand. "Don't say it, Pop, but we have to go. It's no good here, and you were right yesterday."

"The dear captain's going to get me something at the PX," Jonathan said.

"But why now?"

"Listen, Pop, there's no sense in our making it any harder on any of us. Some folks got the touch to do things right, and some don't. We don't."

"What's the matter with your eyes?"

"I been drinking a lot, in case you hadn't noticed. Just let us go quietly, and maybe one of us will write when things get settled. When we get the time."

Venus remained on the sofa, tilting her cheek to her sons' kisses, brief and without even momentary affection. And they were out the door before Mars could think of an appropriate farewell to forty years.

"Samantha," he said, his back to the room, "don't ever let anyone tell you that I didn't love you."

Suddenly there were shouts and Carter came running back inside.

"Your rifle, Pop, where is it? Never mind," and he snatched at the weapon cradled in the wall rack in the hall. Mars hurried to the door, but Carter brushed past him, answering with a wordless shout the urgings of his brother.

"God," he said, stopping long enough to pull a box of cartridges from a breakfront and stuff the magazine. "You should see that animal, Pop. Biggest damn thing in the world."

"Oh, my Christ!" Mars said and ran into the kitchen, grabbed his coat and slapped on his hat. Venus he pushed back into a chair as she tried to follow, and with a muttered "Samantha" rushed outside, nearly colliding with his sons who were standing on the edge of the porch. Jonathan had the rifle to his shoulder, sighting, waiting until Mars saw the white wolf trot unconcernedly from behind the spruce in the center of the yard. His son fired; the bright star flared from the barrel, and a puff shattered from the snowman's head. The three men descended to the walk when it was obvious Jonathan had missed.

"Never could shoot worth a damn," Carter said, grabbing for the stock, being pushed roughly aside.

"That will make a hell of a coat," Jonathan said, stalking now as the wolf padded from the yard to the slippery road. Immediately, lights in the Dovny house blinked on sporadically until the grounds were lighted with squares of pale sun. The front door opened and Tommy stepped out.

Mars watched the progress of the wolf, unable to speak, dizzy from the cold that lanced at his face in droplets of sleet. Tommy called out, waving, and began to climb down from his porch. Jonathan swung the rifle and fired again.

"The boy!" Mars shouted. "Goddamnit, Jon, watch the boy!"

"Shut up, Pop," one of them said.

Tommy had reached the bottom of the steps, was angling across the front of the house when the wolf broke into a run toward the corner nearest him. Tommy sprinted after it, and Mars, unthinking, ran across the road toward him.

Someone shouted and the wolf halted, grey now beyond the light.

Tommy clapped his hands and shouted encouragement as Jonathan moved to the center of the road and took aim.

The wolf moved, placing the boy between it and the rifle.

Mars, arms spread and mouth open, flung himself into the air.

Jonathan fired.

And in the silence echoing from flake to flake as sleet turned to snow, Mars sprawled on the ground, twisting his head from side to side as if searching for a door into a room without pain. He gasped as Tommy roughly rolled him onto his back, heard the careless shriek of tires as a car skidded, straightened and bulleted toward the village. They'll never make the turn at the railroad, he thought.

Distantly, he heard Venus screaming.

Into the snow he opened his eyes and saw Tommy kneeling beside him.

"You never ate the chocolate I gave you," he said through the sparks that wouldn't leave him be. "Probably threw away the stew, too." He arched his back and gasped. "Don't suppose I could get a second chance, could I? I could do better."

Tommy shook his head. His left arm nestled in the ruff around the neck of a white wolf. His right hand stroked the head of another. He bent his face closer to peer into Mars's face, and Mars saw the glimmering green in his eyes, feeding on his failure before he died.

"Daddy's home," the boy said. "You said you wanted to meet him."

Finding the right title for a story is a pain in the ass. Sometimes a title comes full-blown, without a story attached and I write it down in my journal. Sometimes it comes while I'm working, and sometimes (God help me) I have to stare at the finished piece and grunt myself something to put at the head of the page. When I'm stuck like that I usually do one of two things: pick up a book of poetry (Frost, Cummings, and anyone else I can think of), or pick up my Shakespeare. And in that volume of his collected plays and sonnets I discovered, for me, a remarkable thing—that it was possible to use characters' last lines for my titles. I've done it four or five times now, and they've saved me more than once from tossing my IBM out the window.

Also, equally relevant here, is the story of my first firing. I've mentioned I was a teacher once. True. After I left the Army, I moved to a new town, to a place reputedly even more liberal than the one I'd left. Not true. And three years later, after a continuing battle with my department chairman over my handling of Julius Caesar and other things. I was fired. That night I sat down and wrote "The Rest Is Silence" and killed the sonofabitch.

The Rest Is Silence

1

Beware of dreamers: *that would be my epitaph if I could have a grave to go to when I die. But all there is now is a rambling, shrinking house, and a fog that wisps away my words as I speak. I have committed suicide (unaware) and have been murdered for it (all too aware); but if I have to shift the unbearable blame for this madness elsewhere, it has to go to Julius Caesar, late of Rome and the Elizabethan stage. After all, if he hadn't gotten himself so famously killed,*

141

Shakespeare would have never written a play about it nor would I have had to teach it. Yet he did, and I did, so here we are. And now I know all too well just where that is.

After the fact, events have a diabolical way of falling into place that makes a curse of hindsight and hell for the present. Case in point: a Wednesday in October and a perfectly ordinary English Department meeting. Chandler Jolliet, the commandingly tall chairman, was quietly and efficiently razoring our confidence in our collective abilities. Apparently a virgin member of our troupe had decided not to concentrate on *Julius Caesar's* examination of power, but rather on the in-depth characterization of the conspirators, Brutus in particular. God forbid that we should deviate from the chartered lanes of the courses of study, but this youngster, fresh from college with stars in his eyes, had taken it upon himself to do just that, and we were all suffering for it. Jolliet's sycophants and friends were murmuring and nodding; and the rest of us, who had endured this brand of tirade before, were daydreaming, planning our Christmas vacations and plotting assassinations of our own. And when the hour-and-a-half tantrum was over, we nodded our heads in sage obeisance and shuffled out, as slaves must have done before the overseer's whip. In the hall, however, the culprit, Marty Schubert, cornered me and Valerie Stern to press his case.

"I don't understand," he said. "What's so holy about *Caesar* that I can't talk about something new for a change? I'm not saying Jollie's way is better or worse, but for God's sake, what the hell does he have against me? What did I do that he hates me?"

"Not a thing," Val said, guiding him gently by the arm away from Jolliet's open office door. "It's just his way of breaking you in." She looked back at me and smiled. "Eddie's been through it. So have I. You just have to grin and bear it."

"Why?" he demanded as anguish and anger gathered in his features like thunderclouds.

"Because we need the jobs, Marty." I said, not liking the sound of my voice, so recently like his, so recently crushed. "There are too many teachers and not enough jobs. Val, me, and a few others, we've been around much too long to go hunting for other positions. Who'd hire us when they could have newcomers at half the salary? The only thing we can do is play the game, Sam. Play the game and hope he has a heart attack, or a lingering case of diarrhea."

Marty stared, not quite sure if I were serious. Finally he decided I wasn't and laughed. But his cheeks were still flushed and his eyes glinting, as if he'd been repeatedly slapped. We signed out in silence, and in the parking lot Val and I watched him slump to his car and drive slowly away. Val, her eyes hidden by uncut bangs as black as my mood, shook her head. "He's a smart kid, Eddie. It's a shame to see the old bastard do him in like that."

I could only shrug, and she accepted that as a sign of the times under which we lived. We parted, silently, and drove home much faster than I'd intended, for there was nothing for me there. The apartment was still the hospital-white, bare-floored cell I'd resigned myself to when I finally realized there was no place else for me to go. I wasn't clever enough to quit and enter business, nor was I ambitious enough to climb out of the classroom into administration. Sometimes I entertained the spirit of Mr. Chips and envisioned thousands of ex-students tearfully waving good-bye at my retirement. A farce for all that: I could barely remember the names of kids I'd taught the year before, much less those I'd challenged in my virgin year.

It rained that night, if I recall correctly. My unlisted telephone continued collecting dust. The end of a perfect day. And the world kept spinning.

The following morning, however, with the sun barely risen, the telephone scared the hell out of me by working.

"Eddie?"

"Marty, that you?" I was still asleep. I must have been, or his actor's deep voice would have identified him immediately.

"Eddie, listen, I can't go back. Not after what he's done to me."

That woke me up. "Whoa, son, hang on a minute. Don't let that creep get to you like that."

"I'm sorry, Eddie, but I can't do it. I understand your position, really, and I'm not kidding, but I've been thinking it over. In fact, I haven't slept all night. I just can't go back and face him. Would you do me a favor and stop over on your way in? You can take my books and stuff in with you. My resignation, too."

Since I was still rather foggy, all I did was mumble an agreement, take a shower and fix myself some instant breakfast. I made a quick call to the school, telling the secretary I might be a little late, car trouble, and hung up before she could get too nosy. On the way to Marty's rented duplex, I kept the window rolled down to wake me up. I was worried. Marty was one of the brightest, most dedicated teachers I had known, and somehow I had to keep him with us. If for no other reason than he actually liked the kids he worked with, and they, in turn, held him in enormous respect.

He opened his front door immediately when I knocked. He was dressed for work, but unshaven, and his breath as he welcomed me told me what he'd been thinking with. He was sober, though, and solemnly waved me to a chair.

"Marty, listen—"

"I know, I know, Ed. I'm cutting my career out from under me, right? Nobody's going to hire a teacher who quit before Christmas for reasons like mine, right? You want me to last out the year, find another school and then tell him to shove it. Right?"

All I could do was nod, and he laughed at my confusion and the wind spilling from my best noble speech. To my surprise, he nodded, too.

"Well, you are right. I've been sitting here watching the sun and the clock, and I've decided to do just that. I'm going to smile if it kills me, then do what I want when he's not looking. Maybe," he added, grinning, "I can help drive him to that early retirement you guys are always talking about."

"I wish you all the luck in the world," I said, returning the grin, though more relieved that he was still with us than responding to his humor.

"But listen, Eddie," he said. "I'll tell you one thing: I'm not going to take that kind of abuse in public again. And neither is anyone else." And for a frightening moment, his anger returned.

"Sure thing. Whatever you say, Marty," I said, standing quickly. "Just play it safe for a while, will you? See which way the wind blows. I doubt that Jollie's after your hide. He just doesn't like original thinkers, you know what I mean?"

"I think we'd better get going, don't you? The education of our nation's children lies perilously within our hands."

"Yea, and verily," I said. "Onward. I'll meet you there. I think you'd better shave."

"Brutus was right, though," Marty said as he held open the door for me. "We all stand against the spirit of Caesar, but unfortunately, the spirit doesn't bleed."

"Come again?" But the door was shut before I could get an answer. And I didn't remember his remark until after Thanksgiving, when my own classes were destroying Shakespeare's poetry. When the lines Marty had paraphrased came up in the discussion, I became unaccountably nervous, and I kept seeing Jollie draped in a toga. When I passed the fantasy on to those I could trust not to run immediately to the boss, they laughed, and soon enough, Jolliet became Caesar, and Marty was an instant celebrity for inspiring the analogy.

What a blow it was, then, when we received a party invitation from the old man.

2

I was sitting in my classroom, commiserating with Val over an impossible malcontent who was disrupting her classes, when our department bird watcher and sapling look-alike, Wendy Buchwall, scurried in waving a pink slip of paper. "You're not going to believe this," she said, "but we've been invited to a costume ball."

"You're right," I said. "I don't believe it. Who's passing that insane idea around. It sounds like Guidance is on a new kick."

"No, him," she said, holding the paper in front of my glasses just long enough for me to make out Jolliet's pompous scrawl.

"Him?"

"The Man, Val."

"You're kidding. Cut it out. It isn't funny."

Wendy, obviously still unbelieving herself, handed her the invitation, and we sat for a quiet moment wondering if we'd stumbled into an alternate universe that delighted in perversity.

"It figures," Val said finally. "A Shakespearean ball, yet."

"That's ridiculous," I said when Wendy handed the paper to me. I read it, blinked and hoped it would go away. "Hey, this thing is on the Friday over Christmas vacation. Brother, he sure knows how to ruin a holiday."

Wendy perched on the edge of my desk and shook her head. "There is absolutely no way I am going to drag my husband to such a farce. He'll divorce me. He'll have good reason."

"Dream on," Val said. "Unfortunately, I don't see how you can gracefully get out of it. Unless you're dying."

"Says who?"

"Says tenure, dear. We three unholies are bucking for that lovely piece of security. We're stuck. And," she added as Wendy turned to her, "if I remember correctly, we all advised Marty to play the game. What's he going to think of us if we don't go along? We, honey, are on the same team."

Wendy stuck out her tongue and pouted, kicking her heels against the metal side of my desk until I was more than tempted to dump her onto the floor. But Val, as usual, was right. The three of us had drifted into this valley high school at the same time, each running from a city faculty horrific in its brutality. All of us had at least ten years behind us, and it was a wonder that we were hired at all. Now we were facing the final step—no tenure this time and it was back to housekeeping for Wendy, a library for Val, and God only knew what for me. It was times like this that made me want to strangle the wag who said, "Them's that can't, teach."

I began doodling on the desk blotter. A noose first. When I drew in a stick man, I couldn't decide who it was.

"I don't want to go," Wendy near whispered, sadly now.

"No choice," Val said. "No goddamned choice."

"It's the principle of the thing," I said, suddenly angry. "I don't know why the hell we let that man push us around like this. Christ, we're like children as far as he's concerned."

"Principle," said Val in her maddeningly calm way, "does not put bread on the table."

And silence. I remembered when I had been as idealistic as Marty Schubert, and mourned myself those days. I began to see just why he had reasons for hating me, and I wondered if, in fact, he had. Right then, it suddenly mattered very much. Not only did I care that he understood what I was doing and why I didn't fight the world as he did, I was also a little frightened. For the last two weeks, pranksters of a most unfunny lot had been dumping mutilated fowl on our doorsteps. Mine (two barn owls) were missing their hearts, Wendy's and Val's their entrails. Jolliet, too, had been similarly victimized, and although we had been passing the incidents off on some kid who was too eager to delve into the literal meanings of the occult in Shakespeare's more gruesome moments, I couldn't help thinking of Marty, his rage, and those tears in his eyes.

"My God," I finally shouted, getting out of my chair and tossing the pencil into the wastebasket. "Whose damnable idea was this in the first place?"

"Mine."

I looked up and Marty came in, hands clasped in front of him like a marching priest. Wendy jumped off the desk and punched him twice on the arm, hard. He laughed and ducked playfully away from her further attack. Val threw an eraser at him, and I stalked around until I slumped against the chalkboard and glared at him. "Traitor," I said.

Marty smiled innocently. "I thought you wanted me to go along with him."

"Oh, brother," I said. "That was the general idea, yes, but did you have to go for assistant god? A Shakespearean ball? Jesus, Marty, couldn't you have done better?"

He glanced around at the three of us, shrugged and appropriated my chair. Immediately he sat, his feet were crossed on the desk's top, scattering several papers. "But Willy is his favorite man. All I did was kind of ease him around until he fell into it himself. He, uh, really didn't care for it at first. It took a lot of talking." He smiled again, but this time there was no mirth, and I knew he was lying. Jolliet would have died before going through a year, a goddamned day with Lear, Hamlet and all the rest of the bloody crew. Marty, for his own reasons, knew exactly what he was doing. I didn't know if the women caught on, but I didn't like it and abruptly lost the will to banter any more. The game had turned sour; I wanted to spit.

"I wish you hadn't done it," I said.

Marty shrugged his indifference to my opinion.

Val, meanwhile, was mimicking an ultrasensuous walk up and down an aisle, tossing kisses to the pale green walls. "I'm not ashamed to say that Cleopatra would suit me just fine."

"You'll make an asp of yourself," I said.

"You'll go to hell for that," she said and blew me a kiss, a real one, and I couldn't help but admit to myself that she could easily slay my bachelorhood dragon.

"Too obvious," Wendy said, off on a track of her own. "Why not beat the bastard at his own game and go as the conspirators? Who knows, maybe the Ides of March'll come early this season."

"That's the spirit," Marty said, abandoning my chair and heading for the door, a little too quickly. "I might be Marc Antony."

"But he was a double-crosser," Wendy said.

"Yeah," he answered. "How about that?"

After he'd gone, I picked up a piece of chalk and began scribbling what I could remember of the "Friends, Romans, countrymen" speech on the blackboard. It helped me not to think.

A few minutes later, Val picked up her coat and purse and took Wendy by the arm. "Come on, bird girl," she said. "Let's hit the road. Eddie, if all you've got is your famous TV dinners, drop around. I'll see what the larder has hidden from payday."

I stopped writing and nodded without committing myself. Then I listened to their heels tracing a unison beat down the hall. Outside my window I could hear a snowball fight. From the back of the school came the muffled shouts of an afternoon basketball game, the cadence pounding of feet responding to a cheer. "I still don't like it," I said to the empty chairs.

3

The Christmas break arrived none too soon for my rapidly decaying nerves. Though there had been no repetition of the practical jokes that had stained my doorstep, Marty's increasingly foul temper had strained our not-too-deep friendship. More and more he sniped at me for surrendering my ideals, would then immediately laugh as if to salve the wounds he knew he was inflicting. And there was fury in the dust he raised when he left school each night.

Since I was without a family, and Val had headed for an aunt's, I treated myself, on Christmas Day, to a gluttonous delight at a nearby restaurant that deserved a better fate than being buried in the hills. The more I ordered, the better the service was; and when the meal finally ended, I was actually laughing with the waitress. It was a good, rare feeling, and I drove home slowly in order to preserve it. There had been a snowfall two days before, and the lawns and fields had not yet been all trampled by children and snowmobiles. The snow had hardened, filmed with thin ice and contoured smooth like unbroken clouds. I grinned; I whistled; and when the telephone rang just as I was hanging up my overcoat, I even said "hello" instead of the usual "yeah?"

"Marty here, Ed. I just wanted to wish you a merry, and all that. Also, I have a friendly reminder of this Friday's gay festivities."

The measure of my good will weathered even this miserable reminder of that costume affair. "Bless you, Tiny Tim," I said. "Having a good day?"

"So-so. I'm at my, uh, uncle's place now. Where the party's going to be, you know? Strange old guy, but he's teaching me a few things, and I'll put up with anything for a free meal. Can't complain. You?"

"Just great, just great. But as long as you brought it up, what are you going as?"

"Huh?"

"Oh, come on. The extravaganza, my boy. What ingenious rig have you devised, or is it a secret?"

"Oh, that. Nothing special. Since everyone seems on a Caesar kick —"

"I wonder why," I muttered.

" —I thought I would just grab a sheet and go as the soothsayer."

He laughed, but somehow I failed to see the joke. For all the scheming he had done, I thought the least he'd go as was the Poet himself. A soothsayer just didn't seem to fit the occasion. I told him I was thinking of Macbeth, but he didn't seem to care. As soon as he learned I was still going, he chatted meaninglessly for a while, then rang off, leaving me with an absolutely preposterous image of him wandering the halls of this uncle's house trailing a permanent-press sheet beneath Japanese sandals and whispering "Beware the Ides of January" into everyone's ears. The image, unbidden, was immediately replaced with one equally unwelcome: of a figure in immaculate white posturing on a rounded dais while all the English Department sprawled at his cloven feet and drank hemlock laced with sulfur. The man's face was in clouds, and I couldn't tell if it were Marty or Jolliet. I held the picture as long as I could, working to eliminate its inexplicably obscene horror by trying to think of an appropriate theme for it. But the only song I could come up with was "After the Ball," in dirge time.

For the rest of the day I had the feeling that, while some entertained the ghost of Christmas Future, I was hosting the Scrooge of Hellsmas Past.

Quickly I grabbed a bottle from my private, not-very-select stock and sloshed out three quarters of a glass, most of which I finished before I'd lost my nerve. At the same time, I delved into my puny knowledge of Freud and attempted to fashion an explanation for the vision, if vision it were; but I was interrupted, gratefully, by the telephone. This time it was Wendy, slightly drunk and wishing slurred season's greetings for nearly five minutes before apologizing and hanging up. I hadn't even had the chance to say hello.

I had dreams after that, better forgotten, and finally came the night, the Friday evening when not even the Second Coming would have cheered me up. Feeling as ridiculous as I ever had, I climbed into my car, decked out in the closest approximation of Shakespearean Italian the local theatrical costumer could dredge up. If anyone asked, I would be Romeo, or Petruchio, or perhaps even Iago; at any rate, no one was going to get the same answer twice, and I didn't really care. For the moment all I worried about was being stopped by a local policeman and having to explain, while taking a drunkometer test, why I was dressed in tights, a scarf and a red-plumed hat.

It wasn't until I reached the house and was getting out of the car that I saw the still-red heart of a bird lying on the seat next to me. I gagged, tossed it away and leaned against the car hood, trying hard to breathe. I told myself to turn right around and go on home. But I spotted Val's car and decided I'd better stick around, although I wasn't sure why.

Originally, the house had been a development ranch which successive owners had bastardized by splicing on additions so often that it sprawled idiotically over a full acre, if not more. I'd passed it often and had never known who'd lived there, but I wasn't surprised to learn that it was Marty's uncle's. Somehow it seemed to fit. At least, however, he'd tried to even things off a bit by enclosing two inner courtyards, one behind the other, with a roof of glass, thus providing his guests with green grass and roof-high shrubbery to hide in while the snow fell and turned the sky white. This I discovered not two minutes after I'd rung the doorbell and had been admitted to a living-room-cum-foyer by a woman I didn't recognize and who apparently didn't know that harem girls seldom appeared at the Globe. She was, however, friendly, and immediately guided me to the first garden, where most of my fellow sufferers were rapidly draining the first of seemingly endless punch bowls.

Val, true to her threat, was Cleopatra, so much so that I began at once to make plans for later. Wendy and her husband struggled valiantly, and lost, as Bottom and Titania. The others were dressed as I was or were tripping over homemade togas. The masks we wore seemed less to hide than scream our identities, and what laughter there was seemed false.

I squirmed and was uncomfortable, and welcomed Val's offering of a drink with a smile and a kiss just this side of rape. She grinned.

"Down, whoever you are. We've only just begun to play."

"But Madame Egypt," I protested, sitting gingerly on a plaster, gingerly because the tights I was wearing were that and more. "This is too much. What are we supposed to do, sit around and drink all night? For that I could have gone to a bar."

Val coiled beside me, hugging my arm, and we watched as the newcomers were ushered in, grabbed by Wendy and hustled away with filled glasses before we could identify them. I blinked and shook my head. "I didn't know we had this many in the department."

She laughed, making quite sure I noticed she was not about to let go of my arm. "You should see the back patio. Courtyard. Whatever. I guess Marty told Jollie he could have anyone he wanted. It's amazing. I didn't think he knew that many people."

"Speaking of which, where is mine host? It'd be just like him not to come."

"Oh, he's around. He looks like a drip-dry bed with all his sheets. But Eddie, his beard, his face...it looks too real." I frowned and was about to get an elaboration when Wendy staggered over and punched me viciously on the arm. For the first time in months I was in no mood for her imitation heavyweight, and I think I would have hit her back if her husband, Dan, hadn't followed her over. I shook his hand without standing as we passed the usual acquaintances-who-don't-really-know-each-other's greetings.

"Where is the creep?" he growled, and I could see, even with his ass's head, that he wasn't kidding. I looked to Wendy who smiled dryly and waved a hand toward the roof. "I told him about Jollie and Marty. And us."

"Bastard," Dan muttered belligerently. "Men like him shouldn't be allowed to work."

"Smart guy," I said to his wife, but she wasn't listening, staring instead at the glass over our heads.

The snow, which had started nearly an hour before I'd left, was powder, and a slight wind was skating it across the glass in swirls and nebulae, which made me think of watching herds of antelope stampeding before a pursuing helicopter. I sensed Val watching me, and I grinned and said without looking at her, "Beautiful. Stare at it long enough and you'll forget where you are." There were scratches in the glass, and snow caught and held there, then quickly escaped to be replaced and replaced again. Suddenly Val tugged at my arm. I looked down, with the odd feeling that I was actually looking up, and then saw Marty enter from the glass-walled breezeway that divided the two courtyards. I was going to laugh at the preposterous sight, but something about the ancient way he walked stopped me. He nodded at each guest, but passed them as if they were statuary, stalking rather than winding his way toward us. When he arrived, however, he was smiling, his greyed head bobbing as he looked quickly around.

"Beware—"

"—the Ides of January," I interrupted, and was surprised at the glare he shot at me.

"How'd you know I was going to say that," he said, his voice matching his made-up age.

I shrugged. "ESP. Besides, it suits you."

The glare shifted reluctantly to a frown, to a bland smile. "Oh, well, nobody was laughing anyway. How do you like the ball?"

"Where's the music and dancing?" Val wanted to know. "How can you have a ball without an orchestra, or even a radio? I'm disappointed in you, Marty boy, really I am."

Marty said nothing. He only resumed his bobbing. "Don't worry. Everything's all right. All these people are for show anyway. They'll be gone soon, and then the real party begins. By the way, have you seen our fearless leader?"

We shook our heads, and he grinned, yellow and brown-black.

"Caesar," he said without elaboration.

"Why not?" Val said.

"That," I said, "is the most disgusting thing I've ever heard. The man can't be serious, he just can't be. And before I forget, old man, I found a bird's heart in my car tonight. I don't suppose you know anything about it."

"So did I," Val said. "Wendy, too." She tried smiling, but I saw the way she swallowed convulsively. Fully angry now, I turned back to Marty, but he stopped me with a feeble wave.

"Don't worry about it. Bad joke. Like Jollie's costume."

I wanted to pursue that "bad joke" of his, certain now that he was the one who'd been deviling us, but Val must have known what I was thinking because she placed a gentle finger on my lips and mouthed "Caesar." "Him? What about him? You know, if you tell me he's wearing a plastic laurel wreath, I'll vomit, if you'll pardon the vulgarity."

"No," Marty said. "It's real. He said it took him two hours to get it right. He didn't want to use any string. Authenticity, he said."

I had a comment, several of them, but suddenly there was a crackling, ripping flash of lightning, followed hard by a deafening explosion of thunder. The entire house quieted, and a couple of women shrieked. Only a few times before had I ever witnessed such a phenomenon, and each time, the feeling of watching snow falling while thunder and lightning played out of season was as close to staring dead on into an open grave as I'd like to get. There was an encore as eerie as the first, but this served to shatter the silence and everyone began talking at once, the noise rapidly regaining its former level until, without realizing it, I found myself listening to some canned music. Quite accidentally, I discovered the speakers hidden within the huge, junglelike thickets of forsythia that lined the garden's perimeter and served to screen most of the house from those in the center. Curious it was, and impulsively, I grabbed Val's hand.

"Come on," I said. "There's something I want to see."

"Hey, wait a minute," Marty said. "Don't you want to see Jollie?"

"No, thanks," I said, "that can wait, if you don't mind."

Marty frowned until he appeared to make a decision. "Oh, well, you can see him later, I guess. It won't make any difference. Where are you going?"

I pointed. "The other courtyard."

"Oh. Well, look, try not to wander around the house, okay? Even with a single floor, all those additions make it too easy to get lost." He laughed. "I ought to know. I came through the back door once, and it took me two hours to get to the front. You know, when I told my uncle about this party, I thought he—"

"Marty," I said, not altogether politely, "you have other guests. Val and I'll talk to you later on, after you've done the host bit. I'm sure you wouldn't want to offend anyone."

"Now what was that supposed to mean?" I could see it then, the reason why he looked so old, weighted, weary—the rage was still there, and no longer merely directed at Jolliet. The old saying "If looks could kill" came disturbingly to mind, and I involuntarily stepped back.

"I didn't mean anything," I said. "Forget it. Come on, Val." And once into the corridor, I pulled her close to me, felt her shivering. "Sorry, love, but I have a feeling I'm not exactly in the spirit of things."

"Relax, Eddie," she said as I guided her into the back garden. "I think I'm going to develop a splitting headache in a few minutes. In fact, as soon as Jollie sees us and we smile a little."

"I have this odd feeling I'm going to have to be chivalrous. Coincidence."

We laughed quietly as we stepped onto the grass and looked around. Except for a slightly denser crowd, there seemed to be no difference between the two party areas. Then I noticed the red and purple streamers, and the red balloons dangling from string taped to the glass roof. If the idea was to make the room more festive, it failed miserably. All it did was make a pleasant garden look tawdry.

"Notice something?" I asked.

"What?"

"Except for spaces cleared for doors, you can't see into the house from here. And vice versa, I imagine. I wonder why someone would bother to make a place like this if you couldn't see it unless you were in it?"

Val stepped in front of me then, crossing her arms over her barely covered chest. "Why don't you really relax a little, Ed? Try to enjoy. Worry about something else besides the architecture. Like my dry throat, for instance."

I stared dumbly for a moment. And I wondered. None of this—the bizarre party, the birds' hearts and entrails, the people who now seemed to be leaving—none of it affected her. As I led her to the refreshment table, I began to think I was far too susceptible to atmosphere, especially when it seemed to be of my own creation.

"You're so cheerful," Val said suddenly. "I don't think I can stand it."

"Try," I said, nearly choking on a swallow of cheap whiskey. "And if you want entertainment, turn around and blink rapidly before it goes away." As she did, I added, "Jesus Christ, I never thought I'd live to see the day."

4

Both of us indulged for a moment in the cinematic cliché of allowing our mouths to drop open. Entering the garden through a door in the back was Jolliet, all six-plus feet of him so elegantly swathed in a toga laced with purple that he actually commanded a slight bow. His longish brown hair was combed straight back and held by a laurel wreath twined with some kind of gold metallic thread. Big in a suit, he was huge in that costume, and no one, least of all myself, laughed. For some reason, we didn't dare.

"My God," Val said weakly. "That's spooky."

"It's downright unnatural," I said sourly. I had expected to find the man a supreme source for derision, and he had double-crossed me. I became furious and poured myself another drink while Val waved and sent him striding regally toward us. The still-thinning crowd parted wordlessly, and when he stood before us, he took Val's hand and bowed over it, his lips barely brushing her skin.

"Caesar," she said, easing her voice up from her throat in a way I'd never heard before.

"My dearest Cleo," he said, ignoring me, but not her cleavage. "Egypt misses you, I've no doubt. The serendipity of your countenance entices me. Would you care to join me in a devilish concoction I invented myself?"

Val laughed and gently disengaged her hand while holding up her still-full glass with the other. "I have one, thanks. Romeo, here, makes a good servant."

"Thanks," I said, extending my hand to my boss, who barely touched it.

"Grand celebration, isn't it, Eddie? I really believe the old man would have been delighted to be here."

The "old man" was Shakespeare. The way Jolliet talked about him, I've often thought they were roommates in boarding school.

"Marty's done a fine job," I admitted. "And if you don't mind me asking, where in God's name did you get that costume? You could have been born in it."

"I've often wished I had, Eddie."

"Surely not as Caesar," Val said. "Your life would have been shortened considerably."

Jolliet smiled wickedly. "Not mine."

All I could say was, "Oh." Then, "Did you ever find out who's been playing those jokes?"

Immediately he stiffened. "I'm sorry, Ed, but I'm afraid I cannot call that a joke, especially when I discovered the severed head of an owl in my automobile this evening. No, not a joke. Some misbegotten prankster, perhaps. More likely someone deathly afraid of facing me himself, and therefore he uses less direct, less committed means of expressing his displeasure. You, possibly?"

"Not me," I said, laughing. "That's too original for me."

"Hardly original. Ed. The disemboweled chicken, the owls, are straight out of the so-called occult literature available in any shoddy paperback. The child obviously has problems and has decided to use me as a focus of his aberration."

"That so," I muttered into my glass, not bothering to note that the "old man" himself was not above employing the so-called occult. The conversation, continuing with Val while I sulked, might have been funny to someone unused to his instant analyses, but having been subjected to them several times myself, I was definitely not amused. And during a pause, I said, "How do you figure it's a kid? One of your students?"

He waved an arm and a yard of cloth, gathering both Val and me into a circle of apparent great confidence. "My students? Absolutely not, Eddie. They know better. I've taught them better. They all have come to realize the value of reason, and this is hardly the act of a reasonable man. No, I rather think it's the result of an overimaginative mind that somehow feels I've wronged it. As much as I dislike those things, however, I must admit I'm intrigued. I can't wait for the next manifestation."

"Oh?" I said. "Very interesting, really. I'll hope you let us know what happens next. I really hadn't looked at it your way before."

Jolliet nodded, smiling too much like a shark to please me. "Of course I will. Glad to see your interest. We should talk about this sometime. I'd like to hear what you think about these occult things. *Rosemary's Baby*, and such."

"Great," I said. "It's a date."

Someone called his name, then, and when he looked up, it was Marty, beckoning from the doorway. "Ah, excuse me, Eddie, Val, Marty has a surprise for me. A contest or something, I imagine. I'll talk to you later."

When he disappeared through the rear door, Val snatched away my empty glass and slammed it onto the table. "I hope you'll let us know what happens next," she mimicked. "I really hadn't seen it that way. Oh, brother, Eddie," And she rolled her eyes skyward.

Doing my best to imitate her slinking walk, I sidled up to her and grabbed her hand. "Oh, Caesar, baby," I said as huskily as I could. "Oh, Caesar, darling."

We stared at each other for a long second, and we didn't laugh.

The music grew, then, as did the voices, the laughter and not a few high-pitched shrieks. People were moving as if in a quiet panic from garden to garden. I looked for Wendy and Dan and saw only sequined masks and faces like raccoons. I found myself staring at mouths, since eyes were forbidden to me, and their grotesque writhings made me dizzy. I started to curse the whiskey and looked feebly around for a chair. The room had become perceptibly colder, the snow fell more heavily and seemed now to be freezing on the glass roof despite the warmth beneath. I shook off an impression that the house was beginning to move, ignored another ghostly display of thunder, and watched as the people began to leave, with none replacing them. Val, unaware of my gathering nightmare, hugged my arm and whispered something about Wendy and Dan. I nodded mutely and, when she left, renewed my friendship with Miniver Cheevy, cursing the fates and drinking.

Through a slowly descending curtain, then, I lost vision of the rest of the evening. I wandered. I drank. I shook off a woman in a harem costume who wanted to see what my codpiece was hiding. I tried to vomit, and couldn't.

I do remember standing at a window and watching the snow fall.

I do remember standing by a speaker and listening to muted trombones.

And when next I opened my eyes and could see without falling, I was in a bed in a hideously dark-blue bedroom. A single light burned on a wrought-iron night table. I struggled to sit up, then waited for dizziness to pass. There was a constant pounding at the back of my head, and my mouth was dry to rasping.

And still the house was silent.

In a foolish moment, I searched the bed for my hat, realized what I was doing and laughed, stopping immediately when my throat burned.

Carefully, I pushed myself off the bed onto my feet and, using the walls for support until I was sure I wouldn't fall, I made my way to a dimly lighted hallway. Ruefully remembering Marty's warning about too much unguided wandering, I left the door open and walked to the nearest corner. I could hear snatches of mournful music, and I tried to locate its direction. When it became obvious I was losing it, I headed back the other way, staring without seeing the paintings on the dark-papered walls. None of them were striking enough to recall individually, except for their color: night. I cannot even now remember seeing one brush-stroked sun or noon-drenched meadow. I'm sure there were no people, no animals, no houses. Just…night.

I've since tried to locate that hallway again to verify these vague impressions. But I'm unable to.

Maybe later.

But I doubt it.

And then, quite by accident, I found a corridor I knew led to the gardens. Immediately I began to hurry, uneasily imagining some humiliating scene when Marty and Jolliet discovered I'd missed a fair portion of the party. It was all I needed to end a perfect evening.

But the gardens were empty, the tables, refreshments, folding chairs gone. The balloons were broken, the streamers shredded and hanging loosely. I called out for Val, half expecting my voice to echo. Then I called for Marty. Wendy. Even Dan. But when there was no response, I went into the front room where I'd met the harem girl. It was a small room, heavily paneled in walnut with an ugly moose's head perched over the front window. After a quick look around, I opened the door, shuddered at the shock of the cold and looked out. There was snow yet, and an oddly gathering fog. I could see, just this side of that wall-like mist, a couple of cars, including my own, still in the drive; so at least I wasn't alone. Under the circumstances, that was the greatest comfort I'd known in ages.

But when Marty snuck up behind me and whispered, "Beware the Ides of winter," I immediately lost everything I'd drunk onto the front stoop. Marty became solicitous at once and helped me back into the house.

"Now that was a stupid thing to do," I snapped, yanking my arm from his grip. "What the hell are you trying to do?"

"Shut up," he said, glaring. "We're waiting for you in the back garden."

"Oh, now wait a minute," I said, one hand to the wall to aid my abruptly uncooperative legs. "As soon as I can, I'm leaving, fella. This bullshit has gone on long enough."

Marty only stood there. I shook my head in a vain effort to clear it, then rubbed my face vigorously.

"If Val is still here," I said, "tell her to come out if she still needs a ride."

Marty shook his head. "The back garden. Come on, Eddie, you're holding up the works."

"What the hell are you babbling about?" I demanded, but he had already turned to leave. At the door he switched off the lights and looked back at me. Right then I was tempted to leave, even without my coat, but curiosity more than his heavy-handed manner made me follow him.

Through the first, still-empty garden. And the second.

"All right, all right, Mr. Barrymore, where is everyone?"

"I said the back garden," Marty said without turning around. "The back garden."

5

I was too frustrated and confused to be apprehensive about the way Marty spoke to me, and I had to hurry to catch up with him as he made a sharp left through the rear exit and strode rapidly along a corridor that felt as if it had been carpeted in velvet. Another turn, and yet another before we stood in front of a glass wall streaked with dust and through which I could see what at first I refused to believe.

Here the house was two stories high, and in the courtyard framed by walls of stone were Val, Wendy and Dan, Jolliet and a man I'd never seen before. They were sitting on the sparse grass, but far from comfortably. As soon as Val spotted me, she ran into my arms before I realized they were open to receive her. Dan was dazed, his plaster ass's head broken on the ground beside him, his wife huddled in the protection of his arm.

And Jollie. I saw then that he wasn't sitting at all. He was propped up against a white stone bench, and there was more than purple on his toga. There was blood, drying like rust, pooling at his twisted legs. In his left hand he clutched the laurel wreath.

Before reason returned and all the scene's implications penetrated my own daze, I said, "I'm ashamed of you, Marty. That's hardly original."

Val, not understanding, gave a cry like a struck bird and backed away to stare at me, horrified. And while she did, I admitted to myself that I wasn't sorry. That he was dead, it grieved me because he was human and deserved better, but because he was Jolliet, I felt nothing but morbid curiosity.

Marty, meanwhile, had come around to face me, grinning. Beneath the beard his teeth seemed yellow-aged, and his eyes only echoed his grin. That look, more than anything else, snapped me awake, and I turned away to find a telephone. Marty snapped something I didn't quite catch, and the old man placed himself in front of the door. He was shorter than I, and easily forty years beyond me, but I checked myself and stared at him. Val, who had slumped wearily to the ground where she'd been standing, said, "That's the uncle, Eddie."

I nodded; he nodded back. And suddenly I began to laugh. Ludicrous: a murdered man, five teachers and an eccentric. And still I laughed. The hero's image I'd had of myself in fantasies that had lifted me from my more than prosaic life shattered like a twisted mirror with all the pieces shredding my eyes. I turned back to Marty, gagging now at the sight of Jollie's blood. He gestured and I sat, heavily. Val crawled slowly over to me, and we huddled, reflections of Wendy and Dan. I think I said "It's going to be all right" a few times, but neither Val nor I were listening or believing. One of us was shivering.

At last Marty seemed to tire of watching us and dragged a folding chair from behind a bush. The old man stayed where he was.

"You're going to die, you know," Marty said. "But not like that," and he nodded toward Jollie's body. "It's not the way you want to, is it? Do you like uncle's place, by the way? He used to be an illusionist; that's why the house seems bigger than it really is. He doesn't talk; so don't ask him any questions. The snow's coming down a bit more than earlier. Bad driving, not that you'll care."

"Okay, pal," I said, tired of his rambling. "Just get to the point and stop this...this...whatever."

"Why, Eddie, you're frightened."

"No kidding."

At that moment, Dan came out of his stupor, and Wendy began crying. When Marty saw it, he waved a hand at his uncle, who hurried crablike to the Buchwails and stood over them. Dan scowled, Wendy tried to crawl behind him, but the old man only looked until Dan eased himself to his feet and pulled Wendy up beside him. The former illusionist must have also been a mesmerist because they didn't speak, didn't see us, only followed the old man out of the garden.

"Where are they going?" Val asked, straightening and pulling out of my arms.

"To hell," Marty said flatly.

"And what are you, an angel?" I said.

He laughed. "Oh, my God, no. Is that what you're thinking? That this is the end of the world and I'm Gabriel in drag? Oh, Christ, Eddie, no wonder you've never gotten anywhere."

"Then where are they going?" Val repeated, her matter-of-fact tone the only sane thing in the world at the time.

"Nowhere," Marty said. "Nowhere at all." And he grinned, and that grin was rapidly fraying my nerves, or what was left of them.

"So what do we do now?"

"Wait."

That did it. His damnable calm and refusal to let us in on his cosmic plans infuriated me to the edge and over. I jumped to my feet before he could raise a hand to stop me. Head down, I struck him dead on the chest, my hands scrabbling for his neck. We fell off the chair and were separated when the ground struck us. Quickly I got to my feet, but not soon enough. Marty was waiting, swinging. There was no pain at first, nor did some magical part of my brain tell me I didn't know how to fight. I just stood there, trying to hit him while he pounded me to my knees. When sensation came, tears came and I fell to my side, sobbing, aching and utterly humiliated. There was salt in my mouth and one eye was closing. Val cradled my head and murmured nothings until my agony extended beyond the physical. I pressed my face into her breasts and continued to sob.

"You all played the game, you see," I could hear Marty saying, his disgust no longer hiding. "Too afraid to be even the slightest bit idealistic outside your own private ravings. You rationalized your powerlessness against a single man until you actually believed it. You convinced yourselves that you could do nothing but teach, and marked that damned school as the ends of your lines. Tell me something, Eddie: how many new teachers have you wiped out in the past three years? And how many at the school before that? And the one before that? How many teachers have you murdered?"

"Go to hell," Val said. "And leave him alone."

"Oh, I intend to do just that, Miss Stern."

"All right, then, you've made your point, little man. Now how about letting us go?"

"I'll think about it."

"What's to think about? You've murdered a man, and I doubt you'll get away with it. You've destroyed Eddie here, and you've made me harder than I thought I could be. What more do you want?"

Marty righted his chair and sat, crossing his arms over his chest while I rolled over and pushed myself up. I knew I was hurt, but whatever pain there was had dulled to a permanent, background throbbing easy to ignore. And while he was busy tormenting Val, I finally realized what had happened, what was going to happen, and I knew I wasn't man enough to fight it, or even explain it to Val. She was right. I was finished.

Marty, the soothsayer, had taken to himself the standard of the dreamers against the realities of the world. He had ranted more than we had, raged and railed until he had literally accumulated for himself a massive vortex of powered righteous indignation. Gully Jimson, Don Quixote and every dream of perfection and transformation twisted around him until he could, finally, strike back. Once. That was all he needed. And he paid, dearly.

"That man," I finally said, not stronger but more sure. "Nickels to dimes he's not your uncle."

Val looked quizzically at me; Marty smiled, genuine respect and grateful humor revived in his eyes.

"You know," he said, and I nodded. "This battle is very tiring, you see. He tried it when he was twenty-six. You'd never believe it, but he's thirty-four now. I met him last summer and thought he was crazy until he explained how it could be done and showed me a newspaper clipping of an unsolved disappearance. When that department meeting was over, I knew I could do it but was undecided until just before you came over to pick up my resignation. I wasn't mad enough until I saw you. He won't live much longer, though. It takes a lot out of you."

"Then why bother?"

"Because sooner or later—"

"What are you two talking about?" Val demanded.

She was frightened now, her shell pierced and peeling. Marty reached for her shoulder to comfort her, but she twisted away, shuddering.

"Sooner or later what?" I pursued. "All us cynics and realists will be gone, and the world will become a better place to live? The dreamers will march, the sunrise will come, and all God's children will be free at last to roam among the flowers?" I trembled, wanting to yell, feeling more like weeping. "When this is over, you'll be as aged as your friend, and just as useless. Don't you think you'll do more good by inculcating your students than destroying your so-called enemies?"

"What enemies?" Val said. "Eddie, this isn't funny at all. Please help me."

I reached out and took her hand, softly, and turned back to Marty. "I'm sorry to say there are more of us than there are of you."

"Bastard," he said.

At that, Val leapt to her feet, her face streaked and shining. She was naked now, and her exposure belied the clothes that covered her. "I want to go home, and damn both of you," she said. "Marty, damn you, let me out of here."

Marty looked at me, then behind me. The old-young man shuffled in, stood silently by the door while I wondered how many he had banished in his pitiful moment of glory.

"Take her out," Marty said.

The old man nodded, and Val, after a wild, almost feral stare at me, hurried after him. I made no move to stop her, called no reassuring words after her. I had been vampirized, and could only wait.

Marty stood, then, and slowly followed them. I turned on the ground. I thought of jumping and killing him, but dismissed it. Marty would die sooner than he thought, and would live to regret it. His friend must have learned how to harness and focus that rage/power from others before him; Marty had obviously learned it from him, and I suppose now that it must take a special kind of fury that only dreamers can muster. But why he didn't learn, why he didn't take the warning of the after effects, I still don't know. I don't even know if that other man had been a teacher, a preacher or a young-and-coming politician. Not that it matters.

And I have to admit he did try to warn us with those Shakespearean omens, to remind us of the Prince's caution not to take lightly that which we do not know.

"The house is yours," Marty said. "Take care of it, while it lasts."

"Hey, mind if I ask you something? How many places like this one are there?"

"As many as there are people like me. And him."

"Do we all get a house?"

"No. Some just walk. Others float. One or two fly. It's ail the same, Eddie. It's all the same."

And he left, and I rose to my feet and staggered around until my legs decided they'd work for a while longer. I explored and found food, though I didn't think I'd need it. I decided this must be a thing…a something about time and space displacement, a nondimensional locus of a dreamer's rage. There's probably an empty field now where the house was. And as long as Marty lived, I knew I'd be here. And when he died, the hold on the house and me, and all the others, would be gone; and thus would I die.

I did wonder, though, who had the worst of this nightmare. Marty, I often thought, because he could only call upon this power once and is even now trapped in the world of the living to watch his dreams shred like so much yellowing cloth. Of course, I've also collapsed in self-pity, repenting my cynicism and wordliness to all the walls of his house, promising the sky and apple pie. But never for long.

If I am doomed to be a cynic, then he is doomed to be a romantic. What comes after, I don't like to consider. If it's more of the same...

And the end cometh. Marty is dying. The lights begin to fail room by room, and there is cold. Outside, where there is nothing but fog, the light turns black. I have a radio that had somehow — thanks, Marty, for that anyway — kept me in touch with the musical world, but the bands fade one by one. I can find only a single station now, and I wonder if Val can hear it, floating, walking, encased in her own fog, and dying. I still twiddle around until I can finally catch it, then hold the radio close to my ear and listen as if it were the laugh, of little children. But all I can hear is "After the Ball."

The rest, dear Hamlet, is silence.

Strange how the littlest of things and people can dig their hooks into your mind. One summer afternoon I was working in my study when I heard the neighborhood children playing outside. There were four of them. The three eldest were teasing the youngest (a girl about six) unmercifully, screaming "A bee's gonna sting you!" and running away, laughing. She would cry, they would return to console her, and start it all over again.

I also have this file of pictures I cut out of photography magazines. Some because they're beautiful, others because they're weird, and others because I know, instinctively, there's a story in there somewhere. So, years after the above incident, I was stuck for an idea and pulled out the file. I saw a picture of a small boy in a suit and a little girl holding a bouquet of daisies. They were standing on the other side of a porch door whose center, wide panel was glass. I don't know why, but a connection was made, and it wasn't long before I found myself on Hawthorne Street again.

When All the Children Call My Name

1

Poe asked the question: *Is all that we see or seem but a dream within a dream?*

No. But I wish it was.

And in the meantime, in the waiting…another drink, another cigarette—one follows the other like sip and swallow as I look out over the porch to the fence, and the gate. In darkness.

In memories.

It used to be, this time of year, a season of excitement for me, when my skin tingled and my blood sped its youth—when you knew how much better it felt to go from cold to warm than hot to cool. Fireplaces and hearths and a warm soothing brandy meant something then, and mufflers and blankets fresh from the attic trunk and the soft easy comfort of a grumbling furnace. It all meant something then, just as it all means something now; but the difference between something and something is a years-long crossing, and if I could only find a detour I might have missed, maybe then I could go to bed.

I retired from the force nearly five years ago, long before the age when my uniform and waistline would label me dinosaur. I wanted to travel, to experience, to obey the cliché of doing that which I had never done before it was too late, and remember it with fondness. So I did, and I did, and when I returned to the village nothing had changed that I could see, and there were no deaths that surprised me.

Last spring it was, then, when I was offered a part-time job as a guard/confessor/patcher of wounds in a small playground on the far side of town.

It was a dastardly move old Greshton made. He knew I'd be chafing as soon as I grew tired of bending over the roses that thorned and the apple trees that bore fruit despite my clumsiness and the delusion that I knew what I was doing.

"Kit," he said not two weeks after I'd returned, "I'll be honest with you. Nobody wants to do it for the money we're offering."

"Well, I wouldn't either, Marve," I said, "except that I might run against you next fall and I'll need your vote."

He laughed, a single explosion of sound that threatened to clear his desk of its clutter. Then he tugged at an earlobe, pushed a hand through the wisps of hair clinging defiantly to the memory of their fullness. He'll make that gesture when he finally loses it all, I thought, and every time he does he'll look surprised when his fingers don't find anything.

I reached over to pluck a cigar from his humidor and stuck it into my jacket pocket. "But I'll take it, Marve, as long as I don't have to wear a uniform."

"Well, I don't know about that," he hedged. "There are regulations, you know. And even if you are an old friend, we can't go making exceptions. The younger ones might not understand. Why, the Park Commissioner—"

"Hell," I said, "you're the Park Commissioner, and the Sanitation Commissioner, and the—"

"All right, all right," he said. "But carry something with you, okay?"

I frowned, puzzled. "What do you mean, something? What do you think's going to happen out there, a riot because the swings break down, for crying out loud?"

Marve pulled off his glasses and rubbed them vigorously against his shirt. "Big kids," he said, blinking through his myopia as if he resented my independence of artificial lenses. "They like to come around and bother the little ones. You know what they're like, Kit. Carry something in your pocket, just in case."

I would have argued, but the morning was fading and I had an appointment. I agreed to find something menacing, and harmless, and we shook hands as we always did, in silence. But as I left the office, a trick of shadows that had no business being where they were halved his age to an ambitious thirty. It was a disturbing moment because I seldom remembered how old we were, always overlooked the added fold beneath the eye, the turkey-wrinkle under the chin. Not that Marve and I kidded ourselves—with his sixty and my fifty-five—but neither did we spend our evenings in regretful lament. He was too busy being mayor and all the rest of it in a town just the right size for people like us, too busy watching his grandchildren grow and leave and return in the pages of hastily written letters.

And me, I was too busy planning my campaign.

Why is it, I wondered as I hurried outside, that men always seem to look at women as objects of a military campaign? As if they were instinctively the enemy, and we the brash young majors who would storm them into submission.

Ridiculous posturing, I thought as I stepped into the Franklin Inn. And yet I paused to allow my eyes adjustment as they scanned the faces of the luncheon customers: a throwback reaction to the days of my beat when I was the Wichita marshal seeking trouble and danger in the local saloon.

Immediately I realized what I was doing, however, I grinned and shook my head, moved hurriedly to the backwall booth where Catherine was waiting.

Though she was the first one I'd called after my return three weeks before, I hadn't had the nerve to see her until now. Slender, dark-haired still, aware that an inch of pancake no matter how artfully applied to a fifty-year-old face was always an inch of pancake. I'd been gone for nearly two years, and the measure of my fear of finding things changed sent my glance instantly to her left hand. Ringless. To her faintly red lips. Smiling. She half rose and I gallantly waved her down, snapped my fingers for a waitress and ordered our drinks without consultation.

"Is that the way they do it in France?" she said. She took a cigarette from her purse, screwed it into an amber filter and waited for me to light it. Not impatient. Bemused, because she knew it annoyed me when her match flared before mine.

"France, Belgium, Italia—they're all the same to me," I said in mock boredom.

"And the women," she said.

"Scrawny, busty, no hips and no sense of humor."

She pouted her sympathy. "Oh, poor Kit, he couldn't pick one up, could he? You mean to say they weren't impressed by your policeman's record? Your exploits in the colonies?"

"More by the size of my traveler's checks," I said. "And I suppose you were similarly besieged? Dansworth pounding on your door, Falkner chasing you around your desk, Greshton cheating on his wife and holding secret trysts in a luxury motel?"

She nodded, and blew smoke into my face. "Take that, dirty old man."

"Dirty, yes," I said, and left the other unspoken. A finger reached out and traced a cross on the back of my hand. The waitress set down our order and, with a smile of recognition when I spoke to her by name, hurried off to leave us wrapped in the dim light, the dark wood, the quiet conversations that drifted without touching us. We were silent, and said much; we ate as though there could be no further intimacy. Wine, then, and we toasted.

"And how are things at the paper?" I asked. "The weekly scandals keeping you busy?"

She shrugged. Being secretary and jack-of-all-trades to the editor of a small-town newssheet, she once told me, wasn't nearly as glamorous as being a hooker, but definitely more promising than hushing kids in a library.

"Well, I myself have a new job," I said when she couldn't offer me gossip. "I just saw Marve and he thought I'd make a great Chief of Police."

"You're kidding."

"Yeah," I said, and grinned. "Actually, he wants me to babysit a playground."

"You don't mean the one on Hawthorne Street?"

"That's right! How'd you know that was the one?"

She fussed with the ashes of her cigarette, took a nervous puff and sent the smoke toward her lap. "Well, a lucky guess. It's the only one I know of not watched by a school guard." She faked a smile and brushed a strand of hair back behind one ear. "Aren't you superstitious?"

"About what, a playground?"

"For God's sake, Kit, haven't you talked to anyone since you got back? Didn't Marve tell you?"

I blinked stupidly and shook my head.

"Just around the time you came back," she said, "one of the kids was murdered there."

"Here? Murder?" My voice rose and I coughed to cover my embarrassment. Our community wasn't pristine, but murder was something usually relegated to old maids' nightmares.

"A young boy, fifteen. He was found by his mother."

"Jesus," I whispered. "How?"

"I don't know. Nobody's talked. Chief Dansworth had the mother and the body out of there before anyone knew what had happened. All he gave the paper was a statement."

My first reaction was suspicious disbelief. In all the time I'd worked for him, Danny had never held anything back from anyone with a vested interest in police work. That he was refusing cooperation with Falkner's admittedly minor newspaper seemed not only out of character, it was just plain wrong. But he did it, and was doing it, and Falkner was apparently willing to wait. It must have been a particularly brutal slaying, however, because not even the coroner was willing to discuss the condition of the body.

"Dumb," I said finally. "Danny knows better than to act that way. Maybe if I went—"

Catherine smiled tolerant encouragement, like a pat on the head. "It's over," she said. "The family's moved to New England and, as far as I can tell, your former cellmates are only going through the motions, praying for a miracle. You, on the other hand, are going back on the front lines, and you'd better get in shape." She stared pointedly at my stomach, which, while not quite barreled yet, was at last hinting in that direction.

"No problem," I said, slapping my chest and flexing my biceps. "I can still handle any kid who wants to test my reputation. But now I know why Marve wants me to carry something."

"Something?" she said. "What's that mean?"

"For Marve, it could mean anything from a tank to a derringer."

I could see she wanted to second the motion, but I forestalled her by rising and holding her coat while she slipped into it. We walked, then, until it was time for her to return to the office, and at our parting she made me promise to call her that night. And every night, though she wouldn't say it.

Nice girl, I thought as I headed for home; and I must have been smiling because people kept giving me the oddest looks as they passed me.

2

I wasn't supposed to start work until the weekend was over, but a light Sunday rain turned the hours into years and I fled the house before I began screaming. I walked, to renew my acquaintance with the neighborhood, my old beat, the stores downtown. And though I didn't know precisely what to expect, I was rather disappointed that nothing drastic had altered. A few new houses here and there, two shops replaced by two others—but otherwise I could have just slept for two weeks for all that the traveling did to make things different.

Disappointed, then, but oddly pleased that I had no more culture shocks to absorb as I slipped back into my living.

And not surprisingly, I ended up on Hawthorne Street.

The playground was small, a couple of acres on a corner, surrounded by a twelve-foot cyclone fence, bordered by woodland on the two sides not touched by streets. In its center were a half-dozen oaks so rich in their foliage the green looked like cloud, and their shadows midnight. At the base of the trees the earth had been undisturbed except to admit a concrete bench, but the rest of the area had been paved over with a blacktop supposedly softer to land on; somehow, though, a skinned knee tinged with dirt was more natural than a torn elbow with bits of black clinging to it. Progress, I thought, and turned my attention to the far-rear corner and the swings and slides, jungle gyms and seesaws; they had been painted recently and mocked the sun in their gaiety, and seemed rather pathetic without children clambering all over them. The remainder of the area was open. For baseball, I supposed, and touch and those screaming games of tag that jar your nerves and make you want to join rather than leave them.

Then I stepped closer to the fence.

There was a lone sliding board beyond the swings, one of many but the only one that faced directly into the corner. Mats of some kind had been fastened to the fence, battered now by the weather and the kids who charged down the metal slope and slammed into their protection. Some mother's idea, no doubt, to keep her fragile son from jamming his head between the links. I grinned, turned for home, and saw four children walking quickly toward me.

Now, two years is a millennium when children are growing, but I didn't need help recognizing these; and they knew me right away. The eldest was Darlene the redhead, followed like an entourage by Miffy the brunette, Tim the freckled and finally, lagging as usual and vociferous about it, Stevie—who spent more time biting people's legs than his meals. They were glad to see me, and I them—they'd been regular features on my beat since the day each had been born. We grew up together, so to speak, and they were laughing when they ran up to hug me.

Now, dammit, I thought as I crouched to receive them, leaned back against the fence to consider the smiles and the grins and the giggles they gave me—now, dammit, I'm home!

"How do you like our place?" Darlene said. As scrawny as the others, if it hadn't been for her Celtic green eyes I would have sworn she was a boy.

"Your place?" I said. "That's funny, but I thought everyone could use it."

"Anybody can," Tim said from behind his freckles. "If we let them."

"Oh, now that's really big of you," I said, poking at Steve, who was eyeing my thigh. "And I suppose you charge a fee, right? Come on, now, I know you better. You make the little kids give you pennies, right?"

"Not me," Steve said.

"You they wouldn't dare touch or you'd eat them for lunch," I laughed, and he darted behind Miffy's back, peered around her and grinned with his thumb in his mouth.

"How come you're here?" asked Darlene.

"Who, me? Well, I like the swings."

"You're too big," Miffy said, and pushed at my arm.

"Well, maybe. Actually, I'm going to be working here starting tomorrow."

"You can't work here," said Tim. "There's nothing to do."

"Sure there is. I'm going to beat you guys up when you get into trouble."

"Are you going to be a cop again?" Miffy asked, wide-eyed and tugging at Darlene's elbow. "Are you going to arrest people?"

"Only if they try to steal from you," I said. "Nope, just keep an eye on things is all. Like I used to."

"But Mr. Craig, how—"

A faint shouting distracted us. I rose, stiffly, and looked through the oak stand to a group of boys no older than seventeen scaling the fence. The first one to reach the ground began tossing a football into the air, laughing and waving at his friends. Dressed as I was in civilian clothes, I didn't think any orders of mine to vacate the place would be appreciated, much less obeyed, so I only watched until I knew I'd recognize them again if I saw them on the street.

On the street.

Come on, Christopher, I scolded myself; you're no more a policeman now than the sun is the moon.

It was a bad feeling. Like looking over your shoulder and finding a fine-edged knife protruding from your spine.

I hunched my shoulders and turned to leave, stopped when I saw Darlene and the others leaning against the fence. If looks could kill, I thought.

"You kids interested in some ice cream or something?"

They declined without looking up. I shrugged and tried to console them by explaining that things like this invasion wouldn't happen again while I was on the job. "They have their own places to mess with, don't worry. When they see I'm back they won't bother you, okay?"

They said nothing.

"Okay?"

"Okay," said Darlene, took Stevie by the hand and led them all away. I watched as they rounded the corner, keeping close to the fence, then vanished beyond the trees. I stayed for a few minutes longer to watch the game, feeling my muscles tense and relax as passes were caught, end runs were made, touchdowns sent them into screaming hysterics. Their language wasn't the language I remembered using at their age, but then nothing is the same when you outgrow a playground.

Finally, stomach growling, I left for the roast I had simmering in the oven. Something about the group disturbed me, but I didn't realize what it was until I had cleaned up after eating. There had been five of the boys, and for some inexplicable and unpleasant reason, I knew without proof that they were incomplete. I wish I'd known why then, but one of the boys was missing.

And when I mentioned it, laughingly, to Marve a few days later, he nodded thoughtfully. And not without some guilt.

"Gary George," he said. "He was part of that long-haired mob."

"Was?"

"I thought you knew already. He was killed a few weeks ago, right there in the playground."

I kicked myself for forgetting what Catherine had told me, but when I pressed him for more details he was evasive and told me it was over and done. One of those small-town tragedies that never seem to be solved.

"But how is the job?" he said. "Not too difficult for your feet, I hope."

"If you're subtly and cleverly asking me if I'm still in shape to keep standing all day, then don't worry. I'm doing just fine. Besides, I use the bench a lot. Read, and it's right where I can see everything that's going on."

"No problems?"

"Come on, Marve, what the hell kind of problems could I have? Look, this whole job is featherbedding and you know it. There are more mothers there than kids. More carriages than I've seen in my whole life. Listen, those women can outscream the whole damned police department when it comes to spotting a kid even thinking about doing something wrong."

"All right, all right," he said. "Don't get excited."

I wasn't, and I told him so, and we finished our dinner, had a few more drinks and went back to his house to get drunk on the sofa.

Just like the old days.

When one of us was young.

3

So passed July and August and the first three weeks of September.

Catherine and I saw each other several times a week, usually for dinner and a drive to the movies. It was a drifting game we were playing, and a purposeful one—the widow and the widower still clinging to their pride. Sooner or later we'd steady the current and stop at Marve's office so he could say the words. Sooner or later. In the meantime, however, we drifted and gossiped and remembered with lessening pain the way it had been with spouses long gone.

That playground, on the other hand, was becoming a trial.

Not because of the sullen summer heat that defied even the shade, slowed tag to a walk, made slides and swings unbearable to touch.

And not because of the others who shattered the humidity with shrill warning shrieks.

The kids, led by Darlene and Tim, accepted me rapidly, and once in a while I joined in their sport. They were often, as kids have a habit of being, cruel to each other and laughing friends five minutes later. Unbrainwashed by the adult scheme of things, they played in what I'd

176

often thought to be the real world, as opposed to those playlets we acted in each day. But they were never cruel to me, not even unintentionally. They brought me cones when that ice-cream man jangled his infernal bells twice a day; they told me stories of their playmates and their birthdays and their visiting aunts; and once Miffy brought wrapped in a napkin a piece of a cake her mother had made.

We did fine.

It was the teenagers who consistently threw rocks into our pond.

Greshton's Law, tacit but enforced, warned the older kids to keep to the schoolyards, which always opened from mid-morning to past dark. But the friends of the late Gary George refused to acknowledge the mayor's warnings, my threats, even the occasional passing of a mobile patrol. They persisted in swaggering through the gates each morning, confronting me with muttered taunts and generally hanging on just long enough for my stomach to cry out for antacids before taking a swipe at a Miffy or Steve and racing off.

When El Daniels ran away from home the group became four; and worse: belligerent. And one September Saturday they bowled over at least a dozen of my little people before running out of reach.

The following week, however, I saw them sneaking over the fence by the slide's corner. One had caught his jeans on a jagged shard of metal, and I ran over to grab his leg and yank him down. The others raced back into the woods, but this one I had and I wouldn't let go.

"All right, Davey," I said, holding his arm and walking him back to my bench. "Let's have a seat and a talk."

"Ain't nothing to talk about."

"Davey," I said, trying and failing to make his eyes meet mine, "when I was a cop and your house was along my patrol, you were a pretty good kid. You never gave anyone trouble, ever. So what in hell is going on around here? You know the rules. Why are you wasting your time hassling a bunch of kids just out of diapers?"

Despite Marve's description, Davey didn't have long hair. It was tightly curled and nearly covered his ears, but it stayed clear of his shoulders and gleamed with constant washing. He was a slight boy, fighting to grow a mustache and losing, determined that the tighter his shirts the more attractive he would be to the opposite sex. He was proud, but I had never known him to be arrogant.

"You know about Gary, right?"

Only it took him several minutes to speak to me. First he stared at the children gathered around the corner slide; then he worked at his hands for a while before brushing nervously at his hair. I knew it wasn't me. Black going grey, pudgy after a summer's good eating, dressed in comfortable old clothes that fit me loosely; imposing I wasn't, so I knew it wasn't me.

"You know about Gary, right?"

I nodded.

"You heard about El, too?"

"Sure I did, but what do they—"

He jerked his head toward the children. Playing jacks. Catch. On the swings. No one used that corner slide, but I had grown used to that. I think it was because of the mats—it took all the fun out of getting hurt.

"They did it."

"Davey, dammit—"

"Well, they did, Mr. Craig, honest! I wouldn't lie to you."

"Oh, sure they did." Already he was beginning to annoy me. "And after they murdered poor Gary, they kidnapped El and took him to their hideout in the hills, right? Come off it, Davey!"

He stood, his face lifted to catch the leaves' fragmentary shadows. "They don't like us, Mr. Craig, and—"

"Well, I don't blame them. After what you guys do to them, what do you want, an invitation to a party?"

"You don't understand."

"Oh, get the hell out of here," I said, waving him away in disgust. "You're as bad as they are. And stay away from here, you understand?" I called after him. "Stay where you belong and don't bother us any more."

He ran, not looking back, and when I glanced over to the children they were laughing, and applauding. I grinned, rose in a half-bow and went back to my book I kept under the bench. But I wasn't able to concentrate. Davey, no matter how he'd changed since I had last seen him, was not the kind of boy who delighted in tormenting children. I had no answer, but I didn't like it.

The following morning, then, I was the first to arrive, and after unlocking the gates and propping them open, I toured the inside perimeter searching for lost shoes, socks, buttons, whatever the children and the mothers had left behind. When I reached the slide, however, I stopped and grabbed at the railing that bordered the rusted steps. At the foot of the curved metal slope was Eliot Daniels. His head was resting against the slide's lip, and as I walked slowly around to kneel before him, I saw that his eyes were opened. And staring. And his mouth was agape in a silent, terrified scream. I was no medical expert, but I knew without checking that the young boy was dead; and I knew, just knew, that this was the way they had discovered Gary George.

Footsteps snapped my head up.

Darlene was approaching me timidly, a puzzled smile on her baby-fat face. I rose quickly, nearly ran to her side and turned her around with a hand at her waist. "We're going to open late today, dear," I said. "Do me a favor and tell the others, will you? Tell them…well, just tell them we'll be opening late."

I didn't stay to watch where she ran after she left me; I hurried immediately to the nearest call box and phoned in the report. Mechanically. As if I'd never left the force and I was still wearing the blue. No one questioned me after I'd identified myself; it was enough for someone to recognize my voice. Five minutes later, a patrol car and ambulance had screeched through the gates and I told Dansworth all I knew with a minimum of conjecture. He smiled when I'd done, patted my arm and told me the playground would be closed for the rest of the day.

He knew I would hover. He knew I would dance around the fringe of the investigators, making a nuisance of myself, pretending it was twenty years ago and nothing had changed. He knew it, and he didn't tell me to get lost. Only that the playground would be closed for the rest of the day.

For that I was grateful. More so when I stood on the sidewalk and my skin suddenly grew cold, my stomach lurched, perspiration soaked through my shirt. I should have gone straight home to bed and a brandy, or straight to a bar and a beer, or straight to Marve's office. Instead, I went hunting for Catherine and, finding her, dragged her from the office and into the Inn. I told her what had happened, and after she had gone through the motions of calming me, comforting my soul, she ordered us stiff drinks and a meal I knew I couldn't eat.

But I drank, and I ate, and an hour or so later we were outside and walking.

"Those poor kids," I said for what must have been the fifth or sixth time. "Damn, this is going to tear them up."

"I know what you mean," she said, her hand tucked around my elbow and squeezing when I couldn't contain a shudder. "Once is bad enough, but twice...they'll be having nightmares for a year. Especially that little one. What's his name...Steve?"

"No," I said, "not them. I mean El's friends, Davey and the others." I told her about the talk with Davey the afternoon before. "They're really scared, Cath, they really are. Now they're going to think that place is jinxed or something, and they're not going to be able to stand it, you know. It's a blow to their manhood, whatever they think that is. They're going to get worse, I know it. They're going to bother those children until someone gets hurt, and then they'll be in real trouble. Cop trouble."

"Kit, I think you're exaggerating."

"Yeah, well, you should have seen Davey. He hates those little kids, Cath, he hates them so much...well, what can I say? Marve was right. I'm going to have to carry something around with me from now on."

She stopped and pulled me up short. "What do you mean? A gun?"

"No," I said, moving us on again, not liking her expression.

"I still have my nightstick stowed away someplace."

"That's barbaric, Kit! You can't mean that."

"I don't know if I do or not. Yes. Yes, I do. I don't want any of them, big kids or little, getting hurt. I don't want another El Daniels in my playground."

She stopped again, this time letting go of my arm and standing back a pace. "*Your* playground? Kit, what's the matter with you? It's not your playground, and it's not your beat. That's over, Kit, over. You're not a cop any more, and those kids...if you try something, they could hurt you badly."

"No, they won't."

"Dammit, Kit, you're stupidly stubborn. Stop playing the role, will you, please? Will you grow up? Now! Before it's too late."

She left me then, standing in the middle of the block with my hands clenched in my pockets. I watched her go and I didn't try to follow. I was trembling, not because of what I had seen, but because if my hands had been free I would have struck her.

4

I walked on aimlessly, staring at but not seeing the old and well-kept houses, the lawns still green, the trees only hinting at the colors to come. I stopped at a drug store and bought a pack of cigarettes. I sat for a while on a bus-stop bench and watched the traffic waver in the dusk, then vanish behind headlights. I walked again, where the sidewalks were alternately black and gray, where the September warmth was lost in October's chill.

I considered going to Marve to drown my sorrows. But if Catherine hadn't understood, he certainly wouldn't. He was a grandfather and didn't believe that people could be surrogates. Either you were or you weren't was his belief; and if I was playing any kind of a role at all, it was being a cop.

But I wasn't.

I'm not quite that stupid. Sentimental, perhaps, over the years I'd spent working my beat, but I hope I'm intelligent enough to realize when it's all over and the door's closed behind me.

No. What I was trying to do, what I had done in my playground, was make myself available to the children for comfort. There were the mothers, of course, and the babysitters and the occasional father—but then there's the old man not quite so old who always has a place on his knee, an ear cocked, a joke, a stick of gum, the small things forgotten and so delightfully needed.

When I looked up to see where I was going, I found myself predictably at the playground gates. It was dark inside, and the nearest streetlight had been out for days. I reached out to brush at the cold damp fence, and heard voices. Distant. Almost like the afterthought of a wind.

181

I squinted and tried to see through the dark to the other side. A muffled laugh, a stifled giggle, and I was into the woods and making away along the fence as quietly as I could. Twigs and thorns stabbed at my ankles, sliced my hands, but when I reached the mats I could make out a small group of children standing around the slide.

I couldn't believe it. I would have sworn it was Davey and his friends preparing some kind of destructive revenge; but it was Darlene and Tim and a half-dozen others. They were staring up at Stevie, who sat on the slide's platform, waved once and pushed himself down. I tensed, waiting for the thud of his body, and frowning when I heard and felt nothing. I peered closer, and Tim was readying himself for the earthward trip. Steve was gone. I decided then that the best thing I could do was sneak back through the woods and find a telephone to call their parents. I don't know why I didn't call out myself, why I didn't scold them, scare them, send them running for whatever hidden exit they had. I don't know why, but I didn't.

And Tim swooped down the slide, reached the end, slipped off…and vanished.

Not into the shadows. Not into the darkness. He vanished. Into something not there.

So did Darlene. And Miffy. And each of the others.

Down the slide, off the slide, and…somewhere.

I was alone. And it was silent. A breeze caught one of the canvas-seat swings and twisted it. A ghost-thing that sent me careening out of the woods, down the street and into my home, where I stood in front of the living-room fireplace and stared at the flames. Of course, I thought, I hadn't seen what my eyes were looking at; and I began to wonder if playing the part of a playground father included playing the part of a senile old man.

There was a table by the front window, and I turned around to reach for the decanter of brandy I kept in its center. As I did, I looked through the pane and out to the picket fence that bordered my lawn. Darlene was standing there, her hand on the gate latch. She was staring at the house. I ran quickly to the door, but by the time I had reached the lawn she was gone, her footsteps faint and fading under the nightblack trees.

Now I've done it, I thought. Now I've unwittingly intruded on one of their secret games. I'm done for. No more jokes, no more comforts. They'd have nothing to do with me now, nothing more ever.

I slept badly, then, and awoke only when Marve called me to tell me I was late and was I planning to quit. I grumbled an excuse—something to do with my drinking—and forced myself through a cloud of depression to the bench under the trees, where I took out my book, prepared for a day of loneliness.

Five minutes later I looked up to see myself surrounded by a gaggle of children. Grinning. Miffy giggling.

I opened my mouth to speak to them, to find some way to apologize and excuse my actions of the night before. I was ready, but suddenly they stiffened and backed away. A motion on my left, and I saw Davey walking toward me, two boys waiting by the gates and trying to look inconspicuous. I sighed loudly and leaned back to wait.

"Afternoon, Davey," I said coolly.

"Mr. Craig," he said, almost comic in his formality. Then, before I could stop him, his face reddened and he shouted something unintelligible at the children. They didn't move. He snatched at Steve's arm, yanked him close and turned to me. "Ask them," he demanded. "Ask them what they did with Chuck!"

"Chuck? Davey, let that boy go immediately!" I rose and slapped his hand loose. Stevie didn't run away; he only sauntered back to his friends and they moved in a pack toward the swings. "Now, what's this all about, dammit?"

Davey shoved his hands in his windbreaker pockets and wasted a few seconds scanning the overcast sky. I saw with a start, then, that anger and something else had combined to produce tears he didn't want falling. He swallowed several times, then ducked his head to gaze at the ground. "Chuck," he said. "He's run away from home. Just like El."

"Davey—"

"I was there!" he insisted. "I was sleeping over, right? I thought I heard this noise outside, so I got up and went to the window. That one," and he pointed to Darlene, "was standing in the back yard. Chuck was there, too, talking to her. I ran downstairs, but they were gone before I got there. I must have run around that block a hundred times, Mr. Craig, and I couldn't find them. I woke his folks, but they only called the police. They didn't believe nothing about the kid. They wouldn't listen." He looked up, and the tears fell. "They done something, Mr. Craig, and if somebody doesn't help Chuck soon…there's only three of us left, Mr. Craig. It don't make no difference now what we do. God, you got to do something."

Before I could say anything, he raced to the gates and away, the other two following closer than shadows.

I must be getting old, I thought; I don't understand a damned thing that's going on around here. But Davey, for all his fool faults, had frightened himself into something bordering on hysteria. He probably knew Chuck had been in some kind of trouble—a girl, drugs, something like that—and when he ran away, Davey used a dream as his excuse. But I couldn't help thinking of my own dream that night; the kids and the slide and Darlene on the lawn. I knew it was weariness and a drink or two that made me see what I thought I saw, but it disturbed me nevertheless, made me walk slowly over to where the children were playing.

"Darlene," I said, "Davey tells me you were at his friend's house last night."

She only smiled and pulled at her braids. "Not me, Mr. Craig," she said when I repeated my not-quite-question. "I have to be in bed right after supper."

"Me, too," Stevie said, clinging to my leg, then sliding down to sit on my foot. "Me sleep, too."

"Good for you, Stevie," I said.

"Mr. Craig?"

"What is it, Darlene?"

They were all around me now, and I couldn't help a glance at the slide, the mats, the hole that wasn't there.

"We…" And she looked to the others, who were smiling broadly and trying not to laugh. I've seen that look before, when the children want to be solemn, want you to know that what they're going to say is important and yet they're embarrassed. Usually, they run away shrieking, immediately twisting the compliment into a game.

"We like you, Mr. Craig."

I was startled. Though I didn't know what to expect, that was definitely not it. Miffy took my right hand and rested it briefly against her cheek. And so did the others, one by one until I found it hard to swallow and the light blurred at the edges of my vision.

"We really like you, Mr. Craig."

The years I had weighted my shoulders. I knelt, then, and Stevie scrambled silently onto my lap.

"Would you please visit us sometime? Sometime soon?"

I would have been pleased to see their homes, but I knew from what Marve had once told me that their parents were beginning to resent the influence I had over their offspring.

"Will you let them get us?" Tim said, pointing vaguely toward the gates.

"No," I managed to say through Stevie's insistent hugging. "Don't worry, kids. I won't let them hurt you."

They broke, quietly, and after a moment I realized I had been dismissed. And glad I was, because one more word would have had me bawling like a baby. It was a good feeling, a needed feeling, and it should have had me cloud-walking for the rest of the day, but I couldn't help thinking about Davey and his friends; they were so terrified now they'd be moved to do anything, and I was tempted to call their parents to warn them. Tempted, but I did nothing. It would only be meddling again, or so they would think. And if they complained loudly enough, Marve would be forced to take my playground from me.

I didn't want that.

But the following morning, Chuck was at the foot of the slide. Staring.

And people began to talk.

5

The disintegration was slow. A child here, a family there, but within a week or so after Chuck's death the playground was practically deserted and even the comfort of my little friends couldn't stop me from seeing that proverbial handwriting.

Catherine told me, finally, while we were at dinner. Told me about the whispers, and the letters. "You should hear them, Kit, and read those things. It's disgraceful the way they're behaving."

"What can it hurt as long as they don't come out to lynch me?"

She puffed on her cigarette angrily, her face momentarily obscured by the smoke. When she waved it away impatiently, her bracelets jangled, the only harsh sound in the dim quiet of the Inn. Then she reached across the table and took both my hands in hers. "Kit, it's getting dangerous for you. I hear things in the office, I really do, and there's talk that you did it. All of it. Can you believe it?"

"Ah," I said. "Just because Gary was killed just around the time I came back, huh? I must have learned some foul, dark sins while tramping across foreign soil."

"I know it's coincidence, Kit—"

"Well, of course it is, dammit!"

"—but they don't know it. Marve called me today and asked me how you were feeling."

That hurt, more than if she had accused me directly. "What's his damned problem, huh? Can't he call me? He has to go through you, is that it? Hasn't got the damned guts to face—"

"I said you were a little tired is all. I said there was nothing seriously wrong with you." The "is there," however, was as clear as if she had said it.

I bridled, immediately paid the check and took Catherine home. In silence. In anger. Wondering what the hell I had done that would make my own town turn against me like that. But all it took, obviously, was one frightened mother, one angry father....

I ran to the playground, ducked into the woods and climbed the fence back by the mats. When I was over, I had to sit on one of the swings to calm my lungs, to wipe the perspiration from my face and palms. And when I was sure I could stand without my legs trembling, I went to the slide and walked slowly around it, touching it, pressing against it, standing at its foot and sighting along its length to the top, and to the mats not three feet from the end. They met in the corner, black slabs against the night, and I blinked slowly when I imagined I saw a hazed shimmering, a distortion of vision not quite circular. I rubbed a knuckle into my eyes and knelt on the ground in front of it. Reached out my hand.

And it vanished.

Into cold/warmth, a feeling of winter/summer, sunlight and clouds.

I yanked my hand back, scrubbed it against my side and ran. Clambered over the gates. And ran.

Again I had had too much to drink. I know it.

But I can't help thinking:

About coming up undetected on a child in a room, listening to him talk seemingly to himself. There might be a doll, or a shadow on the wall, or a favorite stuffed animal, toy truck, tin soldier. There would be a scowl when he was interrupted.

About watching a child chasing himself in the yard, shrieking with delight—and that instant frown when an adult comes by.

About children sitting on the ground, solemnly and intently staring at a tuft of grass, an anthill, a sliver of bark.

Kid stuff.

But my hand vanished.

Suppose, then, there's a world—no, not *a* world, *the* world, where reality lies uncovered, to which children unaffected yet by us and our deceptions can escape. To remember, to know what it's like and return with resentment for what they are becoming.

Suppose, just suppose, they really get angry. With a kid named Gary, or Eliot, or Chuck. Suppose they invite Gary, Eliot, Chuck to visit their world. Suppose they drop them down the slide and watch them vanish, rush in after them and haul out their bodies.

Why bodies?

Because despite their youth, Gary and the rest are already blinded; and the light they are exposed to frightened them to death.

We like you, Mr. Craig.

I don't believe this for a minute, of course. Not a word. Not a thought.

We really like you, Mr. Craig.

But I don't think I'm going to look out my window any more.

Would you please visit us sometime? Sometime soon?

That way I won't see Darlene at the gate, the others beside her. Miffy with a bouquet of flowers in her hand; Stevie sucking his thumb; Tim with his baseball cap pulled down over his eyes. I'm their friend, I know, but what they don't know is that friendships can hurt more than enmity can.

And if I don't see them, maybe I won't hear them. Maybe I won't hear Darlene when she calls me out to play.

"When I Grow Up" is the title of a story I had written for Stuart David Schiff, the editor of one of the finest magazines of dark fantasy around, Whispers. When I'd finished it and turned it in, I discovered that I couldn't let go of the idea. I didn't think there was enough to turn it into a novel, but every time I sat down to work on the story I kept coming back to it. I asked myself if it were possible that I needed to explore another facet of the problem presented in Stuart's piece, and two months later I had "Secrets of the Heart." I'd never consciously attempted to write on more than one level before, but it seemed to me the only way I was going to get through this story and have it work. It would be cheating, I think, to identify the levels for you—that's half the fun of reading (this coming from an ex-English teacher, remember). I don't think, however, that I'll try it again. Suffice it to say, it was an exhilarating challenge, about the most exhausting fun I've had in years.

Secrets of the Heart

I'm all alone in the house now, a terrible thing to be when you're used to so many people being around all the time. But the others are gone. A few of them, of course, were able to leave when I changed my mind. A few. And some of them died. A lot of them. It wasn't my fault, though. All I did was show them. Once they understood they all asked me and I showed them. That's when some of them started to leave, and that's when they started to die. It wasn't my fault. I didn't kill them and I didn't make them leave. They asked me. They really did. They…asked me.

The last time there were five of them. They came to the house late at night in the rain. The biggest man, with water all dripping down his big funny hat, smiled at me when I answered the door and he said: "Excuse me, little girl, but would you mind if I used your mother's telephone?

189

We had a slight accident back there around the bend a ways, and I have to get us a tow truck."

My mother always told me never to let strangers into the house, and my father did too, but these people were trying so hard to smile in the rain and shivering and wet and cold. So I let them all in and they stood around in the foyer like little wet puppies while I took the big man back into the kitchen and showed him the telephone on the wall.

"My name is Miriam," I said then. "Your friends aren't very happy."

"George Braddock," the man said, holding out his hand after he took off his glove. We shook hands just like big people do, and he took off his hat to show me his hair, all white and thick, just like a big cat's. "I'm afraid they're rather shaken, Miriam," He said then. "Our car slid off the road into a ditch. We've been driving a long way, I got us lost, and I wasn't really paying much attention to my driving. Let that be a lesson to you." He reached for the phone, then looked over at the stove. "Say, would your mother mind if we brewed up some coffee or tea or something? We sure don't want to catch our death at this late date."

I didn't mind at all. I put on the kettle and took a jar out of the pantry, and while he was talking to someone at a gas station—and he was very, very unhappy at what he was hearing, I could tell—put cups out on the table and went to the front again.

"George says you should come into the kitchen and have coffee or tea or something else that's warm," I said. They didn't seem to want to move right away until a lady yanked off her bright blue kerchief—so much hair, and so bright and yellow!—and said, "Well, I'm not going to wait around for pneumonia, folks. Come on. This is dumb standing around here."

The others, another lady and two men, followed her slowly, smiling at me as they passed and being very careful indeed not to drip too much water on the hall carpet. When they got to the kitchen, they took off their coats and hats and sat down and waited for the water to boil.

"Of all the damn luck," George said, coming away from the phone and sitting with his friends. "The man says there must be a hundred accidents out there today. He can't possibly get out here for a couple of hours, at the earliest. Looks like we're stuck for a while."

"Beautiful," the yellow lady said. "That's just beautiful."

"Oh, come on, Helen, it isn't all that bad. We could be still sitting in the car, you know." He smiled at me standing by the stove. "And at least Miriam here is a gracious hostess. We certainly won't freeze to death."

I wanted to say something then, but I didn't. Instead I just smiled and brushed my hair away from my face. The woman called Helen shrugged and looked like she'd decided it wasn't so bad in here after all, and the other woman, who was a lot older, like George, took a pack of cigarettes from her purse and lit one. When she saw that there weren't any ash trays, she dropped her match on the saucer I gave her.

"Where's your mother, Miriam?" one of the other men said. "Don't tell me you're all alone in this big old house."

"Bill, for Pete's sake, don't start," said Helen, taking a cigarette from the older lady's pack and tapping it on the back of her hand.

"Why don't you leave him alone," the white-haired lady said. Then she turned around in her chair and looked at me. She didn't like children. "I'm Mrs. Braddock. Are you alone, dear?"

"Yes, ma'am," I said. Always be polite: that's the first rule.

"She must work," said Bill, and the other man nodded. Bill was Helen's husband. The other man was a friend. Nobody liked anybody very much. I knew that.

The kettle started to whistle then, and I picked it up and poured the water into the cups. Mrs. George said that she wanted to help me, but I said that I could do it all right; and, besides, it wouldn't be good for her arm to hold the kettle because it was heavy.

"Whatever are you talking about, child?" Mrs. George said, though her smile really wasn't very nice.

"It's the way you hold it," Bill said, pointing. "Anyone can tell your shoulder's bothering you again."

"Nonsense," she said, but she put her hand in her lap and gave me a funny look.

They talked a lot after that, and I kind of walked around the kitchen listening and not listening, and then I went out to the front where I looked through the windows at the road, waiting for the tow truck that was supposed to be coming in a couple of hours. They were very polite people, I guess, but they weren't very nice. I knew that. And I don't like people who aren't very nice.

Then I touched a finger to the windowpane—it was cold and slippery, like ice—and knew that someone was standing behind me. I turned around and it was Bill. He had a funny look on his face and he bent down to push my hair back behind my ear. It felt funny. I shook my head, and it fell back where it belonged. "You should have a barrette," he said, real soft. I stepped away from him and he followed me, grinning now and rubbing one hand over his stomach. "You're afraid of me, huh? I don't see why. I guess it's because we're strangers, right? You don't know me and I don't know you."

"I know you," I said.

He kind of blinked at me then and looked around as if there was someone standing in the corner. Then he straightened, smiled funny at me and went back to the kitchen. Then I saw Helen standing in the doorway to the hall, just looking at me. I smiled and she turned away. Their friend, whose name was Calvin, was looking in all the cupboards for something to eat. George told him it wasn't right he should do that, but Calvin only told him to keep quiet for a change, there's only a kid around and who's going to know the difference anyway for one lousy box of crackers. A moment later he found some cookies, and I guess they weren't really that mad at him because they all drank and ate, and then George got up and came out to where I was standing and said, "Miriam, I've looked over my options here, if you know what I mean, and I think I'd better take a quick walk down the road and see if I can spot the tow truck coming. I certainly don't want to have to impose on you any longer than I have to."

I shook my head.

He frowned at me a little and went to the front door. It wouldn't open. He looked over his shoulder at me. "Why did you lock it?"

I walked away from him into the kitchen. The others weren't looking at me, though, they were looking at George, who walked past them without saying anything and tried the back door that led into the yard where I used to play. He couldn't open it.

"Well, for heaven's sake," Mrs. George said. She made a funny little laugh. "It's just like in the movies."

I didn't think so, but I didn't say a word. I just stood by the stove and watched them getting more and more nervous, though they were trying not to show it, while Mr. George went around trying to open doors and windows. Helen was getting madder and madder finally, and she was glaring at me; Calvin had finished the box of cookies and he was asleep, his head resting on his arms on the table, his mouth open and snoring. Bill wouldn't look at me.

"All right, Miriam, this has gone far enough," Mr. George said. He was standing in the doorway, his hat still in one hand. "What does your father have here, some kind of electronic lock on everything? Well, it doesn't matter. I think you ought to let us go now." He reached for the telephone.

"It doesn't work," I said.

He tried it anyway, because hardly anyone ever believes me when I tell them things. Like the time a long time back when I told my father and my mother that they were always thinking bad things about me because I was their only child and they had me while they were very young and now they were wishing they didn't have me at all. *Prancing around here like you own the goddamned place, like you were some kind of princess, like you own your mother and I lock, stock, and barrel! Well, I'm sick of it, Miriam! And by God, I'm sick as hell of you, damnit!* That's what he said; and though my mother told him to stop saying things like that in front of the child, I knew she was thinking the same thing. I knew that. So I told them that if that's the way they wanted it, then they didn't have to stay in my country anymore. That's when my father spanked me. It was the last thing he did before I decided that being a princess was fun.

That's the second rule.

When Mrs. George, who was smoking again and blowing the smoke up at the ceiling, told her husband to sit down, he did. And I could see that he was trying very hard not to yell at me the way he wanted to. "Now, Miriam," he said, very softly, with a little serious frown that made tracks across his forehead. "Miriam, I—"

"You're in my country now," I told him. "You have to do what I tell you."

That's the last rule.

"Oh, it's a game!" Helen said with a clap of her hands. It was like glass breaking.

"Great," said Bill. "So how do you keep score?"

They all laughed at that except me. I didn't like them making fun of my country, or of me. As a princess, like it says in the books in my father's study, I had to show them that I was the ruler. So I decided that Calvin should stop snoring. Nobody noticed it right away, but they did after a while, and then they pushed me out of the way like I didn't belong there and began making lots of silly noises about finding a doctor and why is his face so horrid looking, and George was yelling that the damned telephone doesn't work, and Helen was crying quietly, and Bill just stood away from them and looked at me.

I didn't like him watching me.

They put Calvin down on the floor, and George tried giving him mouth-to-mouth something, but that didn't work and he was breathing real hard when he finally sat up. Then they carried him into the living room and put him on the couch, and George put his coat over his face. Then he saw me standing in the foyer looking at them, and he said, "Do you mind, young lady? This man is dead."

I knew that.

Then George decided he wasn't going to be nice anymore. He looked out at the storm for a while—shivering once when lightning came down and lit up his face—and then told the others that it looked like they were stuck for the night, if all the options were considered. He looked around a bit and, without even asking me, said they should go upstairs and see if there were any bedrooms they could use.

"But...but what about the child's parents?" Mrs. George said, though I knew she wasn't as calm as she looked. "Good Lord, George, they could walk in at any moment. What would they think?" She looked at Helen, who was pale and trembling. "Don't you see, Helen? They could walk right in on us."

"No," I said, and I could see George believing me. He put his arm around his wife's shoulders and led her to the stairs. Helen followed him, and Bill came last. They went up and I waited for a while, listening to them walking around and turning on all the lights and talking in loud whispers. Pretty soon they were laughing. And pretty soon I could hear Helen making funny high noises and slapping Bill, who was laughing so hard he was nearly choking. It wasn't right, though, that they should be so silly when their friend was dead on my couch. And it wasn't right that they weren't playing the game the way they were supposed to. I guess I should have expected it because none of the others did either, but I always hope that this time was going to be the different time. So I waited until it got real quiet—except for the rain scratching at the house—and then I went to my room, which is next to the kitchen beyond the pantry, and I sat on my bed and thought for a very long time; and when I was done with all my thinking, I decided that I knew all about George and Mrs. George and Bill and Helen.

And once I decided what I knew, I decided not to change my mind.

———————

And the next day it was still raining, though the lightning and the thunder had gone away for a while. Everybody came downstairs and went into the kitchen. I could hear George cursing a lot, but the others were very quiet. They were scared. Bill tried to get out a window in the night, but the glass wouldn't break. They were very scared. And they all almost jumped up to the ceiling when I came out of my room to watch them and see if they'd learned to play the game right.

"Miriam…" George started to say something else, but he looked awfully old all of a sudden and only shook his head. Mrs. George's eyes were very red. Helen hadn't combed her yellow hair. Bill, who was standing by the stove, folded his arms across his chest and said, "I've read about people like you, you know. Telepaths, telekinetics—you do all those things with your mind, right?"

I knew what he was talking about. And he was wrong. Some things not even a book can tell you about.

"Bill—"

"For heaven's sake, Eleanor, don't say 'nonsense' again. We tried everything. It may be crazy, but it's the kid."

"I'm a *princess*," I told him. I was getting very mad.

"Her folks probably ditched her," Helen said, suddenly being very brave when her husband didn't fall down after I'd glared at him.

"No," I said. "They just wouldn't play by the rules."

"Wonderful," Bill said. "So what did you do, banish them from your creepy little kingdom here?"

"No," I said. "I just looked up in one of my books about princesses and queens. Sometimes I'm a fairy princess, you know, and sometimes I'm the Queen of the May. I was the Red Queen that day," and I made a slow chopping move with my left hand.

"Oh my God," said Mrs. George, and suddenly they were all running out of the room, and George was hammering on the door while Helen was throwing things at the windows to break them. Only Bill stayed behind, still standing there, still looking at me.

"Why?" he said. I guess he was very brave.

"Because you're not nice people," I said, walking over so that the table would be between him and me. "You do bad things to little girls like me, your wife gets into accidents all the time because she drinks, Mrs. George takes things from stores when nobody's looking, and —"

"All right, all right," he said. He was pale. His hands kept pushing into his hair. "So what are you going to do, kill us all?"

"I wouldn't do that," I said, really mad that he would think that of his princess. "When you're nice again, you can go."

There was the sound of breaking vases and chair legs snapping and Mrs. George crying loud and high.

"And what about you," Bill said then. "Are you little miss perfect all the time?"

"I'm the princess."

Someone was kicking at the door.

"Does that make killing people nice?" He looked like he was going to kneel down then, but he changed his mind. "Listen, Miriam, we all have secrets of the heart, you know. Some of them are bad, some of them aren't so bad. But like I said, nobody's perfect. Not me. And, Miriam, you aren't either, princess or not."

I frowned, trying not to listen to him, but he said it again and walked out of the room like I wasn't even there. I thought about it as fast as I could. I hurried around the table and saw him look back at me, then reach out for the door. When it opened they all ran out like they were really and truly afraid of me. I didn't mind, though. They would find their car and it would be all right, but a minute later I decided that there would be this really big truck…

I shrugged and went back to my room.

I knew all those words Bill was saying about me, but there was more to it and he didn't know that. He didn't know everything I could do when I thought about it and decided it would be so. And after a while I decided that I wasn't really a princess. I never had been a princess. This house wasn't my country, and the people who came here and weren't nice and didn't leave… I wasn't their ruler. I had broken one of my own rules. That's not nice.

That's my secret of the heart.

So I looked in the mirror and tried to decide how old I was. But I looked the same as I did when my mother and father didn't do what I told them. That was a long time ago. I think there weren't any cars or planes then, but I don't remember. And I'm still the same. My hair never grew and my face never got skinny and I never got tall and…and…so I went into the living room and, like George always said, I tried to review my options, which I think means choices.

I could follow my own rules, of course, and punish myself—but if I did that then I wouldn't *be* any longer, and I didn't want to be dead.

Or I could be very nice all the time and everyone who came to my house would like me after that and no one would have bad things in their heads or hearts about anyone else. That would make things very easy for me.

Or I could go outside and make the whole world my country and be nice and no one would have to worry about anything ever again because I would be…

I don't know if I have any more choices. But I *do* know what I can do—Bill said it was telesomethings, and the books on the shelves say it's magic. He knows he's wrong, of course…now. He knows that a telesomebody can't make something out of the summer air, the autumn wind. I can. So I guess it's magic.

That's nice.

And since the house is empty, I decided it was time to go outside for a change. But when I opened the door and took a good look at my world…well, magic may be a nice word and it may be nice to have it, but all of a sudden I was very sure of one thing—that being nice all the time can be very, very boring.

I *know* that… now.

I am an unabashed, though not fanatical, fan of e e cummings. And whenever I need a lift, a title, or a reading experience to put me in my place, I pick up a collected works and pick a few poems at random. It took me a long time to find the key to his rhythms, the double edges of his language, but when I did, it was indescribable, even for a writer. One of my favorite poems is "Anyone Lived In A Pretty How Town," and I was determined for years to write a story titled "Floating Bells Down." The problem was, after more than a dozen starts, I couldn't find the plot. There was a character there, and an opening sequence, but nothing to link them with, no spark other than my determination to force the title to the story. It languished. Enter Barry Malzberg, who called me in the summer of 1977 and commissioned a story for an anthology he was editing with Ed Ferman, called Graven Images. *He knew I'd been a teacher of drama and asked me to work on a piece about the theater. I said I would, with absolutely no idea at all what I'd do. But it was my first commissioned piece and I was damned if I'd lose the opportunity. I fumbled through my journals, my poetry books, my files…and found "Floating Bells Down." The result, combined with my equal love for Tennessee Williams and "The Glass Menagerie," follows.*

A Glow of Candles, A Unicorn's Eye

There are no gods but those that are muses. You may quote me on that if you are in need of an argument. It's original. One of the few truly original things I have done with my life, in my life, throughout my life, which has been spent in mostly running. Bad grammar that, I suppose. But nevertheless true for the adverb poorly placed.

And how poorly placed have I been.

Not that I am complaining, you understand. I could have, and with cause, some thirty years ago, and for the first thirty-seven I did—though the causes were much more nebulous. But the complaints I have now are of the softer kind, the kind that grows out of loving, and are meant—in loving—not to be heard, not to be taken seriously.

For example, consider my beard. Helena loved it, once she became accustomed to its prickly assaults. But I do not need it anymore. There is no need for the hiding because I have been forgiven my sins—or so it says here on this elegant paper I must carry with me in case the message has been lost—forgiven my trespasses. But I like the stupid beard now. Its lacing of grey lends a certain dignity to a face that is never the same twice in one week. And it helps me to forget what I am beneath the costumes and the makeup and the words that are not mine. Yet it's not a forgetting that is demanded by remorse, nor is it a forgetting necessitated by a deep and agonizing secret.

It is a forgetting of years, to keep me from weeping.

Because the secret is out.

Has been, in fact, since the first evening I presented this prologue— a device not original, but originally apt.

No secret, then.

But I like the beard anyway.

And so did my Helena, whose hair—such hair—was once so wonderfully long.

Attend then—or so says the script I no longer need to guide me—but before you decide where applause is warranted, be sure that you understand, be sure that you know exactly what you are applauding. We are still, after all, and in the last sight of the Law, criminals, you know. I nearly murdered, and she nearly surrendered.

And I think that they will catch up with us at the last. Not because we have escaped and were pardoned. But because we have escaped and have been free.

1

Gordon was alone and friendless....

Well, not really, but at the time there wasn't much that I wanted more. I tried to be careful, however, not to disrupt the taping session by allowing my reinforced skepticism and growing discomfort to put lines in my face where character should be, and where, I prayed constantly, it would stay before the bottom dropped out of this market, too, and I had to return to so-called regular employment to build up my account. To cover myself then, I placed right palm to right cheek in what I had been taught was an overt display of not-quite-hopeless despair coupled subtly with the proper degree of Shakespearean melancholy. Then, working at not flinching, I lowered my buttocks onto the conveniently flat rock behind me and stared at the river. They called it a river. Actually, it was something less than two hundred meters of recycled water not nearly deep enough to drown a gnat.

…his weary but undaunted brain struggling mightily for the miraculous wherewithal to extricate him from his precarious dilemma…

The subvocal narration, buzzing in my left ear so I could follow the cues, raised in me first a gagging sensation, then an impulse to swat at a nonexistent fly. I managed to swallow several times without its showing, then shifted my palm to my chin and supported it by resting my elbow on one knee. I could have brought it off. But my concentration slipped. The fact that I was naked, cold, and resignedly anticipating a drenching from the slate-grey clouds massing efficiently overhead goaded me into a mistake. After five minutes of gazing I could not help but frown instead of assuming the attitude of intense problem-solving on the subconscious level. And when it was done, there was no taking it back…and I knew it without anyone's prompting.

Unfortunately, no one bothered to turn off the tiger.

I heard it, a grumbling that should have come from the clouds. I rose quickly as it stalked into view, a creature so magnificent in the terror that it instilled that I could not take my eyes from its pelt, its face, the waterlike rippling of its muscles at shoulder and haunch.

A dark-feathered bird swept in front of it, but its gaze did not leave me for even the length of a blink.

Slowly, I backed toward the river, crouched, my fingers hooked into pitiful imitations of claws. Everything inside me from heart to stomach had suddenly become weightless and was floating toward my throat, and I felt a curious giddiness that split the air into fluttering dark spots before coalescing into stripes, massive paws, and disdainful curled lips exposing sharp white death.

It should have leaped when it reached the boulder I had been sitting on. And it did. And despite the training, the quiet talks, the assurances of my continuing good health ...despite it all, I screamed.

The tiger struck me full on the chest, its front paws grabbing for a hold, its rear claws reaching to disembowel. I fell as I used the creature's momentum to spin us around, dropping off the edge of the low bank and into the water. There were three rows of fire across my ribs, six more on my shoulder blades, but I held the tiger under, a minute, more, until at last it quieted and I thrust it away from me and staggered back to land. The entire sequence could not have lasted more than three minutes from start to finish, but I felt as though a dozen years had been suddenly added to my life. What there was of it.

I fell, gasping, spitting out water, then rolled onto my back and stared at my hands. They were bloody, and I sat up abruptly, looking around wildly for someone to patch me.

This was not supposed to happen.

I was to be strong, clever, luring the beast to its drowning...but I was not supposed to be clawed.

Immediately, a white-coated tech raced out from behind me and waded into the water with two assistants, the better to lug the simulacrum back to the shop for another repair job and, I imagined, another shot at another sucker like me. A fourth man, his shirt and trousers rumpled and soiled, wandered over to me and slapped in quick succession antiseptic and med-patches onto my injuries. I smiled at him. He scowled. I knew what was bothering him. If I couldn't be cajoled into doing it again, he would have to do some pretty fancy editing to keep the blood from showing. I think he expected me to feel sorry for him. As though it were my fault.

And when he was done, with not a word of condolence, or even of encouragement, I moved stiffly back to my rock and sat, waiting with dripping hair while those clouds waited to soak me until, finally, the artfully gnarled bole of a beautiful oak on the opposite bank split open with a zipperlike tear, and the director stepped out.

"Great," I muttered, and dropped my hands into my lap.

The director paused for a moment as if reorienting himself, sighed, and retrieved a powered megaphone from the rushes on the riverbank. He sniffed, look everywhere but at me, and yanked a crimson beret down hard over an impossibly battered left ear.

"You're Gordon Anderson, right?" The voice should have been godlike, under the circumstances. Unfortunately, it wasn't. It squeaked.

I nodded.

"You okay?"

Bless you, I thought sourly, and nodded.

"Shouldn't have done that."

I didn't know whether he meant me or the tiger.

"Gordon Anderson," he said again, as if tasting it for some hint of its flavor, or for some trace of its poison.

He stared at the sky, sighed once more, and then I realized I was expected to stand up. That I refused to do. The last time I was naked and standing, my female co-star had nearly strangled laughing. It had almost cost me the job, but she had felt sorry for me and blamed it on her lunch.

Besides, those patches weren't new. The antiseptic was weak and I was hurting, badly.

Meanwhile, the squeaking continued.

"Sorry about the animal, but you're supposed to be experienced at this sort of thing, Anderson. That's what they told me at Casting. You're supposed to be experienced. A stage actor, right? You're supposed to know about these things, Anderson, if I know anything about that sort of…living. Am I getting through to you, Anderson? You're supposed to know!"

I could think of little more to do at the moment but nod again. My fingers kept returning to the patches, touching, pressing, wondering how I was supposed to handle the flood sequence without ripping open the bandages and bleeding to death. I would see the Diagmed people afterward, of course, but I had a feeling they could do nothing for me. The healing would be speeded up, but there probably would be scars. And why not?

"You're supposed to be brave, yet frightened, Anderson," the voice piped on, as though my screams hadn't been real enough. "Fearless, yet hinting at grave doubts as to your next plan of action. There is a flood coming, Anderson, a *flood!* Do you have any idea what that means?"

"I'll drown," I said, just loud enough for him to misunderstand.

"I don't think you're right for this job, Anderson, to tell you the truth," the director said after a carefully measured dozen beats of pacing, and waiting for word that the tiger was all right. "You…you are required, you see, to set an example, the perfect example, for the audience—in case you've forgotten. You must radiate courage, determination, and just a *drop* of apprehension. You have trials yet to come, remember, trials that you cannot possibly imagine. And these trials that you cannot possibly imagine are filling you with challenge and trepidation. And, I might add, those children out there who are watching will want to *be with you!* They have to understand not only the vicissitudes of life, but also their symbolic representations in your journey. If they don't, they're only going to get nightmares. Do you follow me, Anderson? I say, do you follow me?"

Whither thou directeth, midget, I thought, then quickly nodded and raised my hands in a virtuoso combination display of supplication (for the continuance of the job), surrender (to the director's artistic authority), and defiance (for the sole benefit of the tapeman who was still running his idiotic machine).

The director grinned.

I clamped my hands firmly on my knees and straightened to my full sitting height.

"That's fine, Anderson. I knew we would be able to communicate once you got to know me a little better. Now, we have about thirty minutes or so before the flood. Why don't you take a short break and prepare yourself? We can run through the close-ups later on, when the flood goes down. Is that all right with you?"

"Whatever you say, boss," I said. And after he had tramped off somewhere to commune with whatever he communed with to make these tapes, I slid off the rock to the carefully trimmed grass, crossed my legs, and folded my hands over my stomach. After a doubtful glance at the sky, I closed my eyes, wrinkled my brow in practiced concentration, and fell asleep.

When I dreamed, it was of a small glass unicorn surrounded by low-burning candles.

———

The flood came precisely on cue—the director wouldn't have had it otherwise—but the finely woven strands of safety line that should have prevented me from being swept away into the next sound stage snapped under the pressure. Luckily, I was out of position and managed to grab on to the director's oak, where they found me tightly gripping the trunk when the waters subsided. When I opened my eyes and they realized I was far more frightened than injured, they let me be. Except for the director, who slapped me on the back, patted me slyly on the left cheek (both of them), and strode bellowing off toward the setting of the next scene—the earthquake.

Slowly, testing one limb at a time, I unwrapped myself from the plastic tree and snatched at the robe one of the crewmen held out for me. After a moment's hard glare at the water and the sky, I stumbled off to the dressing room we all used in common. There was no one inside the long, narrow building when I arrived, and for that one small favor I was eternally grateful. I dried myself as best I could with my hands refusing to close, my arms disobeying the commands from my muddled brain; then I sat in front of my mirror and watched a single drop of water fall from my chin.

I stared at my reflection. Stared at the array of small and large jars, long and short tubes, hairpieces and skin dyes, false-flesh and false eyes. Stared at them all until they blurred into a parody of a rainbow; stared, grunted, and swung my fist into their midst, smashing until all were scattered on the floor.

Stared at the mirror, at the reflection, at the high creased forehead and brown eyes and slightly hooked nose and slightly soft chin. My fist came up to my shoulder. Trembled. I wanted to split open my knuckles on that face in the mirror, and drive cracks through the world that existed behind my back.

But at the moment—and only at the moment—it was all the world I had, and my hand dropped slowly to the table, where it rested on a ragged bit of cloth I used out of habit to wipe off my face.

In the beginning the idea had been a tempting one. Begun by the British and expanded by the Americans, the tapes were the foundation of a dream-induced system through which young people would hopefully be matured without actually suffering through the birth pangs of adolescence. Hospital wards with soft colors, nurses with kind faces, and for two hours and twenty minutes every other day the young were wired and hooked and taped to a machine, which I and others like me, those actors with no place to go, inhabited. We wrestled with tigers, endured floods, endured women and men and disasters personal. It was, as the narration stressed again and again and again—who knows how often?—all very symbolic, and all very real.

Watch! the voice ordered.

Take care, the voice cautioned.

Watch, and take care, and listen, and apply…apply…apply…listen… apply…

A debriefing, then, which lasted for something like an hour. More, if you were new to growing without aging. Less, if you'd been in the system for a year or more.

The first children/adults would not be through the entire program for, the director once told me, at least another ten months. But, if you listened to him carefully and believed his raving, things were moving along just splendidly.

I could see it without much prompting.

Eleven-year-olds with greying hair and wrinkles and a walk that bordered on the burlesque of infirmity.

A girl twelve with the mind of a woman.

A boy ten with the rebellion sponged—exorcised out of him, exorcised and leaving him without dreams of how it had been when he had been…but he never had been…young.

It was, admittedly, exciting. And the nightmares I had about the possible consequences were only just that. So I rationalized whenever I went to the studio. After all, frankly, it was a job. An actor's job. Just about the only one left.

I had been in Lofrisco, wandering about that coast-long cityplex, when Vivian-my-agent called me and brought me back to Philayork. It was *the break*, she told me confidently—the chance for exposure, and the cash, that I needed.

"Listen, Gordy," she'd said, "these kids will know you for the rest of their lives! Not by name, but they'll recognize your face! They'll want to see you on stage—if that's what you're still after—on the comunit channels, the cinema bowls. You'll have it made, you idiot. You can't pass this up."

And, to be honest, I hadn't. But neither had I forgotten the near-empty houses I had played to when I had managed to wheedle permission to leave those joyhall holovid arenas and cinema bowls.

Near empty.

Partially full.

There had been five in which I was an understudy. I didn't much care. It was live, actors and audience, and I drifted from one theater to another waiting for the chance to get in on the action. But they all folded in less than a month, the audiences deserting them long before the last curtain. Drifting in, stalking out, curious more than anything, and no one bothered to wait for the players who slunk from their failures from unlocked stage doors. Several times I tried to ask someone just why he was leaving, but never got an answer that cured the question.

Finally, when I cornered one of the directors and demanded to know why her play was a failure, she only snapped an arm toward the gap that was the stage and shrugged. "I guess we're running out of gimmicks. We need a new one. I don't know. The way things are going, I don't really care."

The Storm's Eye had three dozen sets, and auditorium seats that slowly tilted back to focus audience attention on a holovid simulation of the typhoon threatening the actors on stage.

Great World Yearning had catapults and springboards, trapezes, and a 360-degree stage.

Blessing had four orchestras, three tenors, waterfalls, ceiling storms, a marching band, rehearsals for the audience's instrument parts, and a prominent reviewer who insisted on getting every name in the theater for his comprehensive critique.

Take This Crown had seventy-nine speaking parts and four burnings at the stake.

Where Hath God Raged had a planetarium, an espernarrator, and a colonist from the Moon.

Three playwright/producers had created them all. And when the last one gave up hope, I took the slip marking the deposit to my account and wandered from theater to theater. Something, I knew, had died in both artist and observer. Then, taking the easy way out, I managed to locate and assault with tears and fists all three of the creators one by one. All in darkness, I sought out those so-called playwrights, and after each attack I fled until my lungs burned me to a halt.

My justification at the time was simple: They were murderers, of something I could not yet understand: They had been part of a conspiracy to kill off words.

I wandered, waiting to be caught for my crime, listening for the accusing scream of a WatchDog swooping angrily beneath the Walkways, netting me, lifting me, locking me away.

I had to have been mad to have done it. But there, were no still and small voices directing my attacks, no sudden blind fury that drove me to the call of insanity that guided my hand, only those questions, all beginning with *why?* and the knowledge that the playwrights had been midwives to disaster, had birthed disasters before, and were part and parcel of what I knew was the dying of a dying art.

Yet there was no feeling of catharsis.

I had done it.

Nothing more.

So I sat in front of the dressing-room mirror and thought of the tiger and its claws, and of the tiny director who was forcing me unknowing to remember.

It was a play within a play within a play within a dream.

Like a beautiful thing I had seen once, and from which all I could remember was a tiny, shattered, fragile glass unicorn.

I pushed away from the table and dressed as best I could with the patches pulling at my shoulders and ribs. My fingers fumbled as I snapped my shirt closed. My thighs were elastic as I slipped on my boots.

Sooner or later I would have to tell someone what I had done. There had been nothing on the news and, though I wondered, I kept silent.

But not for long.

Helena.

A studio flyer took me to the entrance of my Key loft and, once inside the lobby, I sagged against the liftube frame and held on. Looking down. Looking up. Rising free, falling free. No need to worry, Gordon, old son, the magics of science will give you faith.

2

I had been born, raised, and eventually cast willingly adrift in Philayork, the largest of the East Coast cityplexes. My father was the owner/manager of a joyhall which, in addition to the usual game rooms, gaming rooms, and stunt rooms, had a small cinema arena. None of the major features played there, but the minor ones were nevertheless sufficient to lure me from spools and tapes, to spend days and hours drifting through the stories that holoed around me. It wasn't the technics that ensnared me, enraptured me, but the men and women who portrayed the characters, and the men and women who paid their small admissions to eavesdrop on the plots.

> ("Marta, over here, hurry! Listen to what this guy is saying about the Count. You listen, Will, I'm trying to find out what happened to the Colonel. We'll meet by the Grand Canyon when I'm done.")

They all knew it was sham and that they could if they wished put their hands through heads and cannon fire and the rings of Saturn or the domes on the Moon. But naturally they wouldn't. They listened, compared notes, reconstructed stories, and returned for what they had missed.

By the time I was in University, I succumbed to a temptation, which was easy enough since I knew most of the plots by rote. I stole time here, sleep there, and several times managed to last through nearly three quarters of a show before anyone realized I wasn't part of the action. The idea that I could be something and someone I wasn't intrigued me. I did research, spent time in regular theaters in the less-visited parts of the city, and changed my emphasis in University without telling my father. When he did find out, and heard my dreams, one of us lost, and I left.

Studied. Learned.

Discovered agents and sold myself to Vivian. Who laughed at my studies. (*"My God, Gordy, nobody needs a script on the stage anymore; who told you you needed to learn how to memorize?"*) She took me quite literally in hand and showed me what show business was, outside of the school.

For eighteen years, then, I managed a fairly steady and obviously unspectacular living playing that man over there in the corner talking to the beautiful blonde, and that wounded trooper crawling through the Martian sandstorm, and that body, and that face, and…and. Until, between takes, I found myself wandering back into theaters that had stages and audiences and waterfalls and…and…

There's nothing to say that would stand alone as a reason. I loved it, that's all. Loved it, and hated it, because it didn't take long for me to see that something was wrong. Lethally wrong.

> "You're crazy, you know that, Gordon."
>
> "Just get me the jobs, Viv, that's all I ask."
>
> "It takes a special kind of training. I've told you it's not like learning lines from a holovid script!"
>
> "I'll learn."
>
> "But, Gordon, you'll have to improvise! That's all the whole thing is, except for the effects. You're given an outline and you bluff your way through it. It takes years to learn it right."
>
> "I've done it before, you know that. What's the big fuss? You'll get your percentage."
>
> "You don't get it, do you?"
>
> "I'll learn. That's all there is to it."
>
> "You don't get it at all."

There was a wave of nostalgia that had, for the briefest of lightning-lit moments, the old-style theaters rejuvenated, rejoicing, rehiring actors and producers and directors and such. Lord, how we tried. But the wave flattened, and by the time I was making those dream-tapes for children, nothing was left but the must, the dust, and the drifting in and out.

3

I went into my home: living room, bedroom, alcoves for lav and ovenwall. All in shades of black and white.

I ate, not tasting, and stared at the Keylofts across the street. I watched a news summary and discovered the playwrights I had attacked were recovering. Euphemisms abounded, but the message was the same: person or persons unknown.

God, I wished that hadn't been so bloody damned true.

And fifteen minutes later, Philip and Helena came for a visit and I fed them their eager rations of stories about my taping day. All the time watching Helena, as though Philip were only a ghost along for the ride.

"He sounds like an insect I worked for once," Philip said of the director. Philip was fifteen years older than my own thirty-seven (Helena was four years younger). He enjoyed reminiscing about the, as he called it, flesh-and-blood theater he had been in, but it was a dream that he lived—Helena told me he had been a minor bit player who seldom had lines and was lucky to find two weeks' work in fifty. I don't know why, perhaps because of Helena, but he liked me. "An insect, Gordon. Stamp him out. You won't miss him. I promise you."

"Oh, don't be a fool," Helena muttered. "He has to finish the contract." She was sitting cross-legged in the center of the floor, swirling a snifter half full of a brandy I had hoped to save for another, more special, occasion. Not that just being able to look at her wasn't special— and the moment I thought that was the first time I realized that I'd fallen in love. "Gordy, you can't pass up that money, you know. I mean, that's as far as it goes. No money, no food. How much simpler can it get?"

Philip, who was portly and conscientiously pompous, nodded and retrenched, scratching at his hairless scalp. "She's right, you know. There's no sense ranting about artistic integrity when you have to provide bread for the table."

"It isn't fair," I mumbled.

211

"Nobody said it was, man. But then, nothing ever is. There is no such creature as a Universal Fair, and I'm absolutely stunned that you haven't learned that by now. I mean, son, there you are, aren't you? Beating your head against the wall, trying to live on, of all things, the stage theater. You can scream all you want to about its lamented demise, but there's nothing you can do about it. Nothing at all."

I could only tug at my chin and gaze at the ceiling. It was true—God!—that the year of the Romantic had closed eons ago. No more traveling shows to the towns between the plexes, and only a single course in stage history at University, while the instructors told me sadly that the art was falling apart. But it wasn't. It was falling in, like a building whose inner supports had been dissolved in acid. A flurry of subsidies provided a revival or two, but essentially only prolonged the collapse, and when the charities took over most of the funding, there was a death knell unmistakable along the length of the aisles.

I closed my eyes and rubbed them, wishing Philip would banish himself so I could talk to Helena.

I smiled then when she crawled over to sit beside me, a gentle white hand resting on my calf, massaging absently.

"Gordy, if you drop out now—"

"Helena, I don't think Gordon wants to hear any more."

I sat up quickly. There was something in the big man's voice, a warning. I frowned and looked to Helena, who was brushing a finger idly through the carpet's low nap.

"Gordy, let's face it," she said without looking up, "if you cut from the contract. Vivian will let you go. And if she does, you'll end up like us. Like me. And like Philip."

"And what," he demanded loudly, "is wrong with the way we are managing? We hang in, don't we? We've been—"

"Starving, you idiot," she snapped. "And I won't have Gordy going the same way."

"Starving?" Philip's laugh was singularly mirthless. He punched lightly at his stomach and stretched out his hands to exhibit the fat that clung to them. "One doesn't starve, girl, and still look like that."

"You know what I mean. Starving for work."

"We manage, I told you."

"We manage, we manage," she mimicked in a high, child's voice. She looked back to me, and the gray in her eyes had slowly shifted to black. "One part between us, Gordy, since June. One stinking part, and the thing folded before the first week was over. He refuses to…what's the word? condescend?…refuses to condescend to do the work you do. He's a fine one to talk about artistic integrity. And he's fat because he takes most of the food dole in starches. He has a Falstaff complex, Vivian says."

"I refuse to listen to this—"

"Then don't," she yelled. "Go back to your loft and improvise something. Improvise thin. And don't call me, Philip. My vione is closed, for the duration."

"Helena, I will not be spoken to in—"

I'd had enough, more than enough, I unwound from the couch and moved to Philip's side. It helped that I was a full head taller and that my weight was distributed to give me at least the illusion of strength in my chest and arms. But the illusion was all I needed, and Philip fumbled into a meek silence.

"I can't help it," he finally said, almost whining. "Vivian fired us today."

I blinked dumbly, turned around to Helena, who was still on the floor. If I had been struck with a steel pipe I couldn't have been more stunned.

But: "True," she said. "She says she can't live on a percentage of nothing."

"But I am still man enough," Philip persisted as he looked for a way to regain the advantage, "I am still man enough not to have to condone the manner in which you two have—"

I shut him up by grabbing his arm and nearly dragging him to the door. He was too surprised to say anything. I slid the door back, eased him out, and stood there to be sure he entered the liftube.

"You'll pay for this, Gordon," he warned as he descended. "I am not without influence in some…"

I laughed and held on to the door frame. "That line is older than all of us put together, Philip. Why don't you just get yourself a job. In a restaurant." I had to shout the last, since he had already dropped from view, but the noise made me feel better. Somewhat, anyway. And I closed the door quietly, instead of slamming it.

Get a job.

Helena came up behind me then, reached to my shoulders and massaged them skillfully while she rested her cheek against my back. I closed my eyes for a moment, then took a calming deep breath and began talking. Explaining. Describing. Telling her everything and knowing that if she wanted to, she could run out to the Blues and probably collect a reward. The police were always giving out rewards. It was part of the system of mutual cooperation and protection. I stopped my confession only once, when her hands left my shoulder. But I finished. And when I was done, everything that had been keeping me upright deserted me. I sagged. She caught me and led me into the bedroom. And this time there was a catharsis of a sort. The weight of the attempted murders was, not lifted, but lessened. And I'm ashamed to admit that I was doubly relieved that she had not run to the Blues, for the reward.

And when we lay on the bed, each to a side, and did not touch or attempt to peel off our clothes, I knew she did not pity me, but loved me instead.

"I can't believe they're not really dead," I said into the darkness when the silence grew too long for me to accept. "But from the report I heard — and would you believe it was only just before you came here? — from what I heard, none of them will be the same when they recover. The worst part is: now that I've told you I don't feel guilty anymore. And that's got to be wrong! I wonder if I should stick around until I'm caught. I'm bound to be, you know. One of them must have seen something. And if my name and picture go out through the network, there's no place I can hide. Not for long, anyway."

"But Gordy, it's been nearly two weeks. If the police knew something, they'd be busting already."

I smiled. Grinned. Shook my head even though I knew she couldn't see it. "What's their hurry? I haven't tried to leave the country."

"Maybe…maybe you were lucky. Maybe they didn't know who it was, didn't recognize you, I mean."

I rolled over onto my side, one arm up against my cheek. I tried to see her, but couldn't. But I saw her anyway. "I keep telling myself that. It's a hope, I guess. I wish I knew."

―――――――――

"Gordy?"

"I'm awake."

"Are you wondering if I hate you for what you did? I mean, I did a show for one of them a year or so ago."

"A little, I think."

"Well, it's dumb, but I don't. I'm a bit frightened, though."

"I know that one well enough, don't I? Two weeks, and I still can't figure out why I did it."

"You were angry. Furious. That's obvious enough."

"Sure, but why? It wasn't the first time I was ever in a flop." I worked at a laugh, then, to take the sting out. "When you think about it, I guess, they're all flops, aren't they?"

"Of course they are. You just don't know why."

―――――――――

"Gordy, I want to help you."

"Escape?"

"No. I want to find out what's going wrong. I don't want it to happen. I...I have some scripts in my loft. I keep them under the bed, and when I get too depressed I read them."

"Scripts I don't need, believe me."

"No, not those kind. I mean real play scripts. Shakespeare, Williams, Miller, Chekhov...people like that. I'll bet I have more than two dozen of them. I got them...well, let's say they just gravitated into my gorgeous little fingers when I was visiting friends...places."

"God, Helena, you're a crook!"

"Look who's talking. It's funny, Gordy, but I'll bet I know almost every line of them by heart. It must have been nice, not to have to make up things as you went along. It's all down there, just like your cinema things. 'When beggars die there are no comets seen.' You sure can't improvise something like that, can you?"

"Who said that?"

"I don't know. Miller, maybe. I don't remember."

"You should."

"Why? Who cares besides you and me?"

"What about the guy who wrote it?"

I drifted back and forth from a sleep filled with candles and unicorns, and when I asked Helena about it, she told me the scene was from something about a hundred and seventy years old. She quoted me a long passage from the end of the play, about worlds lit by lightning and change and things like that. I'm no history buff, so I can't say how appropriate that might have been to the time it appeared, but I know about lightning now. And when I tried to explain it to her, all I could do was choke and tell her never mind.

Finally, just before dawn took the black from the ocean outside the plex, I cupped and pillowed my hands behind my head and whistled softly a song I once knew. It would have been nice if it had been a lullaby my father used to sing. Would have been. But it wasn't.

"Helena, there's one thing I know, now."

"What? And don't you ever get tired?"

"No, not often. And what I know is: we're dying. You and me and Philip and the rest of the whole stupid stable. Now that's a good word: stable. We're horses, Helena, in a motorcar world. One by one they're shooting us down. These tapes I'm making, they're supposed to be helping kids grow up. And what do I do? Me, the hero who survives floods and earthquakes and invasions of god-awful monsters? Just like a kid I lash out and hit someone just because I don't get it. I almost killed those guys, Helena. And they'll come for me. Someday."

A rustling. The bedclothes. Helena had finally given up and slipped in between the sheets. "Then we'll have to escape. It's as simple as that."

"We?"

"Oh, come on, Gordy! Do you think I'm going to let you have all the fun?"

This time the laughter was real, delightfully so, and I stretched out, gathered her to me, and we rocked, like children, until the spasms had passed and we were sober again.

"Look," I said, "there's no sense in my making some big dramatic escape until, and unless, the Blues come for me. It'll be easy to hide in a plex this big, right? And I want to finish the contract so I can get a job somewhere else if I have to. I don't need that blot on my work record, not now. And I have to find something else out. Like you said, sort of: I want to rate a comet. Even a small one. And to do it, I'll have to learn everything I can about why we're...dying."

"I know the answer already."

"Sure."

"The public doesn't like us anymore. It took a few thousand years, but they've finally decided they don't want us to live."

"No," I said, hovering close to an answer, yet not close enough to know what I was seeing. "No, there's something more. And before I start running, I want to know what."

"Then the first thing you're going to have to do is not to be so solemn. If we're going to hunt for this thing of yours, we'd better do it smiling."

"Why?"

"Oh, go to sleep, Gordon. You're no fun anymore."

Two days later a pamph came, announcing the limited engagement of a series of original material to be performed by players from one of the lunar domes. I had seen them before. I needed to see them again, knowing without knowing that they held the key. Vivian got me the tickets, and I repaid her by showing that simp of a director just how good an actor I could be. He loved me. I loved me. And, thankfully, I still wasn't picked up by a WatchDog patrol. I still jumped at shadows, still looked over my shoulder, but I was beginning to believe that I would always remain free. Or so I tried telling myself each night before sleeping.

The second day after the Lunar pamph came, I was stopped in the Keyloft lobby by my landlord, who told me there was a friend of mine waiting upstairs.

"He didn't have a latch, Mr. Anderson," he said, "but I seen him around here a lot of times so I figured you wouldn't mind that I tubed up and let him in."

I nodded thoughtfully, thanked him for his kindness, and spent most of the time in the liftube wondering if maybe it had been a Blue plant, and my dear old landlord would be collecting that reward.

But it wasn't.

It was Philip.

He was just signing off the vione when I came in, and as fast as I stepped around the couch to see who he was talking to, he shifted his bulk until the screen staticked into darkness.

"What?" I said, perching on the couch's arm.

Philip spread his arms in an attitude of peace-making. I didn't believe it for a minute. Without a single direct word, I had taken Helena from him, and had made him admit twice that he was living a deadly romantic lie. The friendship we had had was buried. Deep.

"Come on, Phil, I'm hungry, and then I have some studying to do for tomorrow." Half true. After eating, I was going to continue reading some of the scripts Helena had let me borrow.

"All right, then," he said, still standing by the vione. "I've come to inform you that I overheard something this morning that I believe you would be interested in. In return, I expect a favor."

"I don't get it," I said. "You want to make some kind of deal?"

He nodded.

"For what? A lousy favor? What do you need, money? A place to stay?"

"Just wait a moment, Gordon, and you'll find out everything. I am, as you well know, currently unemployed. According to procedure, just being part of Vivian's client menagerie marked me employed. When she unceremoniously, and without real cause, dumped me, I had to gain a measure of strength and make myself known to the nearest Blue Station Local to…to sign up for the complete dole." His hands fluttered, clasping at his stomach, grabbing at the baggy trousers he hadn't bothered to tuck into his boots. He was all in green today, his lucky color.

"I'm sorry, Phil."

His grin was short-lived and insincere. "I'm sure you are. But that's not the point, is it? While I was there I overheard a couple of the Locals—one was a 'Dog pilot, I think—talking about a series of criminal attacks down in the old district. Where you hang out, Gordon. I imagine you've heard about them."

I nodded, slowly, my face a masterpiece of serenity.

"Well, one of them was a regular patron of…" He rolled his eyes in an effort to display to me how distasteful his words were. To him. Not for me. "He enjoyed spending many off-duty hours in a joyhall." The words came in a rush, as if acidic on his tongue. "Arena stuff. You know what I mean. The sagas and things that you are always blathering about."

"Phil," I said, rising and heading for the ovenwall, "if you're going to be snide, just show yourself out, okay? I don't need that kind of aggravation today."

"I'm sorry," he said, standing behind me as I selected my lastmeal, and pointedly made the selection for one. When I turned around, he shrugged. "The Local was saying that he was sure that one of the actors fit the description of the man—they think those things were done by one man, you see—of the man who did them. Of course, I couldn't hear what the man looked like."

He stopped. I waited.

"I thought you might like to know."

"Oh? What for?"

"Well, really, Gordon, you holo folk stick together like I don't know what. I thought you might like to put out the word to your friends, have them watch their backs. So to speak."

I kept my hands in my pockets—clenched, to keep them from trembling. I nodded, hoping to appear contrite and grateful simultaneously, and led him toward the door.

"The favor?"

"What favor?" I said. "Oh. Well, sure. What is it?"

He took my arm at the elbow, his fat hand tight, the fingers pinching. "Please, talk to Vivian, won't you? I can't stand having to beg for a meal every day. I mean—really, Gordon, it's so demeaning, if you know what I mean."

"Philip, Vivian could get you a dozen parts tomorrow if you would only let her. But you won't. And until you do, there's nothing I can do, either."

He stepped back as if I had slapped him. Then, a scowl as dark as midnight crowding his face, he shouldered by me into the corridor outside the loft. He took a step toward the liftube, looked back over his shoulder, and smiled.

"You'd force me to do that, wouldn't you?"

"Phil, I'm not forcing you to do a thing. You want me to ask Vivian to let you back, you'll have to compromise. That, my friend, is all there is to it."

"I'm sorry for you then," he said, and left.

I waited for him to make a reappearance—waited, then hurried back into the loft and made a careful search to sec if he had taken anything, disturbed anything. The only evidence he'd been there, however, was the pamph. It had been picked up from my couch, obviously read, and tossed onto the floor. I retrieved it, folded it into quarters, and stuffed it into my pocket. It had on it the date Vivian had gotten me the tickets, and the man I was to see to pick them up.

I felt sorry for Philip and his nonsense ways, but had more important things to worry about at the time. I ate rapidly, watched the news for indications of impending arrests, then called Helena and we spent the rest of the night tying up the vione, reading random scenes from the scripts she had lent me. I would read a line and try to stump her for the next. I seldom won, but what was more important: I was learning them myself, and moving about the room grandly, until she snapped once that I kept disappearing from the vione's range.

It was, without a doubt or a worry, the single best way to pass the time—short of actually having her in my arms, of course.

That, I promised her a dozen times during the night, would come later. And often.

And all the time, that hovering I had felt drew more steady, closer, and the answering light more clear.

———————

At last, a week later, I stood in front of the theater in the park. It was a low dome, black and silver and sprouting several cowlike entrances through which people were already filing. A mosaic apron in blue, gold, and white led up to the dome, and from its center rose a tall post with four huge spotlights. Their soft glare was somewhat reassuring, but it turned the surrounding foliage into a dense black wall.

"Gordon!"

My name was like a slap across the back of my head. I stiffened, not knowing whether to run or surrender, then turned. It was Helena who stepped out of the shadows. Lithe, she looked uncommonly lovely in a plain gray tunic and trousers. Her auburn hair was almost like a veil. I held out my hands and she grasped them, pulled me close, and we kissed, once, lightly, forever.

Then I told her about Philip's visit, and she shattered her loveliness with a vicious scowl. "Relax," I said, rubbing at her arm. "The most he can do is swear a lot."

The floodlights dimmed twice.

"Time, great hunter," she said. "No more stalling."

———————

There were dozens of gold guidelights hovering at the head of each aisle. I held up my tickets and one of them brightened and led us to our seats, seats in an auditorium that radiated back from a traditional stage. I mentally blessed poor Vivian's efforts, crossed my legs, and held Helena's hand. Waiting. Staring at the proscenium, which was studded with holovid representations of the solar system, each planet revolving in truncated orbit, the moon in its center, dotted with blue specks that marked the colonist's domes. I was impressed, and depressed. I was cold, unusually so, and I could not figure out just why this was so.

I tried concentrating on the curtains, on the flecks of crimson that flashed whenever a guidelight flitted too close.

I tried listening to the audience around me, its muffled laughter, gossip, scoldings, coughing.

Something.

Something.

I knew it was there, but when I tried to drive it away so I could enjoy the show, it balked as if yanking on my arm to tell me something far more important.

Music, then, and I was distracted.

And three quarters of the way through the first act, it all fell into place, solidly, painfully, so that with some mumbled excuse to Helena, I crept up the aisle and hurried outside.

Walked. Paced, rather, in a large circle around the lightpost. There was no doubt that the performance was something I would never forget—if novelties are things from which memories are spun. The company was expert, the same I had seen those long months ago, and this particular parkdome had been reconstructed to approximate and give semblance to the absence of gravity the players were accustomed to on their own home satellite.

It was, in one dark sense, beautiful.

On the stage they were in all manner of costume. Free. Floating. Swimming. A freeform exercise complete with sets and speeches. The women were pale snowflakes drifting around men who were the same. I hadn't been able to follow the story very well—something about a starship lost around Andromeda—but many times there were long pauses in the action and in the flow of words, and the children in the audience grew restless and whispered. As did the adults by the time I had left. I could see, then, that before it was done, few would be listening to the dialogue magnified and booming. They would be watching only— and for that they all could have just as easily attended a joyhall show.

The play was a circus.

The Lunars were freaks.

That was why the people came. And that, I finally understood, was why they went to other plays, in theaters, on stages. I was a freak. A freak who happened to be around when volcanoes erupted or a ceilingstorm thundered or the sets changed so rapidly it gave one a headache. There was no longer any discipline, either in players or audience, no feel for words, because the words were instantaneous.

It was stupid. I should have seen it before. It was obvious, so obvious that I had overlooked it in search of something far more complicated, far less damning.

What did the man say? The man who broke the unicorn of my dreams and who tries now to blow out my candles? A world something by lightning. Well, I was struck.

And I was…I was mad.

———————

The nightwind chilled suddenly. An arthritic attendant with a small pouch at his side shambled around the area looking for debris to justify his pension. But the apron was clean and he vanished without once looking up at me, disappearing around the theater dome curve. A clock figure, I thought, with no hours to chime.

I scowled then, and shook myself like a drenched dog. I was falling too quickly into a self-pitying morbid mood that would do me no good if I wanted to devise some way to reverse the trend I had so belatedly discovered. I decided to get Helena and take us home, and had already started for the entrance when I stopped, a peculiar whining bothering my ears. I rubbed lightly at my temples, and the whining grew louder. Familiar. Another step, and I glanced up and saw the spiderleg spotlights walking a WatchDog toward the place where I was standing.

Frozen for a moment, I stood like an idiot until I realized they'd be landing not far from where I stood. I bolted into the theater and pressed myself against the door frame, watching as the sleek black-and-gold police machine settled onto the heart of the mosaic like a bloated dragonfly. A Blue leaped out, steadied himself, and reached up a hand to assist the others following. There were only eight that I could see, standing around in a curious display of alert watchfulness and indecisiveness. Then my nails dug unfelt into my legs. Philip lumbered from the exit, disdainfully brushing away an offer of assistance. I must have lost my temper, and a good part of my reason, because I found myself standing just outside then, and when a pinlight suddenly flared and caught me, Philip pointed.

A bell, small and unobtrusive, sounded behind me. Intermission had begun.

The Blues had already taken their stuntons from their waists, and I could see by the glowing tips that they were going to kill me if they had to.

Ah, you fat-bellied Judas, I thought, and spun back inside, fighting my way through the people seeking exit, grabbing at Helena's wrist when I saw her. I dragged her several meters before she tried to pull back, but all I had to do was yell "Blues" into her ear and she was with me, running down the aisle toward the curtains. Without bothering to stop and think, I vaulted onto the stage, hauled her after me, and raced into the wings and along the narrow corridor I knew would run the length of the theater's rear wall. There was a great deal of commotion back in the auditorium, and though I wanted just a moment to think things out, to ask Helena for advice, I slammed up against the fire exit and went through without stopping. A handful of Blues darted around the corner, yelling when they spotted us, but before they could set their stuntons for a firing charge, we were through the trees and into the underbrush so thoughtfully managed to make our flight easier.

Suddenly I stopped and Helena yelped. Except for the faint glow of the theater's lights, the darkness here was complete and, falsely or not, I felt a momentary safety.

"What?" she whispered as we heard the 'Dog's whining pitch as it lifted from the clearing.

The darkness was complete, I thought, and if we continued headlong as we were, we would be bound for injury that would make a mockery of our trying. I slapped impatiently at my thigh, then took her hand and made my way back, angling in a crouch toward the front of the dome.

The WatchDog whine screamed.

Handheld spotlights shattered through leaves and branches.

With only eight Blues immediately available, I knew my chances of at least getting to the park gates were fairly good. But it had to be done quickly, before reinforcements were summoned. I whispered all this to Helena as we moved, the words snapping singly, like those of a sprinter out of breath. Twice we had to duck out of the way of the thinly spread cordon, but soon enough we were at the clearing. The playgoers had already been herded back inside, and only Philip remained, talking quietly with an officer who was holding a comunit circuit in his hand. Instinctively, I took a step toward them, but Helena jerked me back.

"Later," she hissed in my ear. "And save a piece for me."

It was pleasantly obvious from the dour expression on the officer's face that we weren't going to be easily caught—if at all. Emboldened, then, I made my way through the trees to the pathway I had taken only a brief hour earlier. A minute's waiting that seemed twice a lifetime, and we broke from the cover and into a steady trot. We ran on our toes to keep the echoes from betraying us, and left the path only when we came to a bend too acute to enable us clear sight ahead, or to skirt the now unfortunately well-lighted gardens.

I thought of Philip, wondering how, until I remembered the mailer with dates and names scribbled on it.

I thought of him again, and wondered why, until I remembered his pride and the beating I had given it. Well, at least he would have the reward, I thought with a grin, though how much good it would do him was moot, since I had every intention of getting away.

I grinned even wider. Intentions. I had intended so many, perhaps too many things in these first thirty-seven years. And this was the first time I had actually been driven to action, to do something, to move. I almost felt good, I almost felt joyous.

And the feeling lasted until, only twenty or so meters from the gate, we had to veer sharply into the brush. A Blue had suddenly come from streetside and planted himself directly in front of the only way we had now of leaving the park. Dropping to the ground, I ground knuckles into my cheekbone, trying to force through the pain something I could use to eliminate that man before he was doubled, tripled, made unassailable.

We crept closer. The shouts behind us had separated, nearly vanished. Once, the WatchDog sailed above us, above us and beyond, back into the park. Then Helena jabbed me on the arm with a finger and pointed at the Blue. At herself. She made a steadying motion with her palm and rose to her feet before I could stop her. I tried a lunge, but it was too late. She was already in the middle of the path and walking toward the gates, her legs affecting a slightly drunken gait, one hand brushing through her hair, the other angled out from her side as if providing balance.

As she moved, then, so did I. Staying within the boundary of the hedging along the path, I made it to within five meters of the Blue before I had to stop—and watch—my hands pressed to the ground, ignoring the sharp digging of pebbles cutting into my skin.

Listening to the 'Dog still circling above.

Helena began an off-key whistling, and the Blue almost dropped into an offensive crouch, then saw her and straightened. She giggled, hiccupped—I thought she was overdoing it more than a little—and reached with one finger to unseam her tunic. The Blue raised a warning hand, cautioning her to remain where she was. She giggled again, lurched forward, and swayed. The Blue—a young man who should have known better, but didn't because he was young—took that first important step toward her. She swayed again, then allowed her knees to buckle. The Blue moved instinctively, catching her around the waist, allowing her weight to carry him around and down, his knees not quite touching the ground.

Immediately he moved, however, so did I again, this time racing from the brush to get behind him, and before he had completed his dipping motion, I had his stunton in hand. Fumbling with the studs on the handgrip of the cylinder, I tried to set the electric charge as low as I could. Then I lay the tip alongside the Blue's head. He jerked as Helena wriggled out of his grasp. He jerked, his arms snapping back, his hands almost touching at the base of his spine. Jerked, his tongue protruding and his breath inhaling in one explosive wheeze.

A silent dance while I was too dumbfounded to run.

Ending.

"Come on," I said more harshly than I had intended, and with Helena's assistance I dragged him into the bushes.

"Into the breach, isn't that what they say?" she asked me as we clasped hands once more and raced for the nearest Walkway.

"Who says?"

"Who cares?"

"You're not making sense."

It was apparent that neither of our lofts would be safe for us any longer. I had no doubt that Philip had also told the police about Helena's involvement with me. They'd be looking for her, too, once they'd discovered she wasn't coming home. But the Walkway had its terminus at the edge of the cityplex, and from there it was only normal highways for landcars and hovercats. They were only sparsely used, of course, for the villages and towns not linked into a plex, but walking them was unthinkable, especially at night.

So it was less a coincidence than has been reported that we ended up at Vivian's place less than an hour later.

"I'm leaving," I told her after we'd barged in and cornered her on a chair near her bedroom. "Sorry about the dream-tapes and all, but we're in rather a hurry."

She was too surprised to do more than blink, then quickly gathered her dignity about her like the gold-and-green robe she wore to cover her weight. "I heard on that"—she nodded toward the comunit—"that you were wanted. God, Gordy, what made you do a thing like that?"

"I don't know. I wanted to be a star."

"There aren't any anymore, but you're too thick to know it."

"I know one thing, Viv," I said, "and that's *why*."

"So? Tell me."

"Viv," I said when Helena coughed, "one last favor. The keys to your landcar."

"What will you do if I don't? Beat me to death?"

I shook my head, rose, and after a moment's long agony, she reached into a drawer in the table beside her and tossed me the keys as though they were hot. "I'll report the thing stolen, you know."

I laughed, moved as though to kiss her, then joined Helena, who was already in the hall.

"Listen," Viv shouted suddenly from the doorway, "if you get a job, remember you're still my client!"

The vehicle was an old one, but it got us through the plex tunnels to the outside, and once on the highway with no 'Dogs in our wake, I managed to slow down a bit. But we ran, through valleys of trees that had no hand to arrange them, past dimly lighted villages where we dared not stop. Twice in four hours we passed other vehicles, all going in the opposite direction, and each time I felt as if I would strangle until the headlights glared by and we were in darkness again.

Helena sat quietly in the passenger seat keeping watch on the starred sky. She was pale, far more pale than I had ever seen her now that the excitement had given way to realization. I kept telling myself that she had done nothing wrong, that she could easily go back to Philayork and claim I had taken her by force, or some such nonsense. I kept telling myself that as though it were a prayer.

And finally her weariness caught up with me and I had to find a small clearing at the side of the road. When I did, I pulled over and, without so much as a kiss or a wink, I fell asleep.

This time, there were no dreams.

4

We rode for two days more, swaying away from the main arteries, sticking to the tinier, less-traveled roads that webbed off the highway. It was difficult at first for several reasons. The hardest adjustment was to the continuing sky, the mountains, the sudden inducement of vertigo when the road would suddenly bend and drop and we were faced with a broad and green valley several kilometers wide. And now that we were running, we abruptly realized that we had no place to go. No friends. No contacts. Only the certain belief that should we attempt to enter a cityplex again, we would be trapped as fast as we walked into the first restaurant for something to eat.

Only Helena and I, then, and some half-formed hopes.

And finally, a small town called Eisentor, where we grabbed what courage we could and stopped. With what money we had we bought provisions, some clothes, and extra fuel for the car. No one asked us questions, no one paid us any more mind than they would a taxman drifting through his rounds. When it became obvious that we weren't suddenly going to be jumped and shackled, we relaxed, found a small eatshop, and had us a decent meal. We said little, however, because the

228

fear of the flight was still ghosting around our eyes. We ate, only, and drank what we could.

Then we walked awhile through narrow streets with wooden, brick, or clayboard houses. We sat on a bench and watched several children playing around a puddle left over from the previous night's rain.

Suddenly, without consulting Helena, I walked over to the children and asked them what their favorite shows on the comunit were. They didn't seem too eager to talk to a stranger, but they answered me anyway; and when I did a few lines from one of the plays Helena had given me, did a few lines and some comic strutting, they laughed. They were puzzled, to be sure, because they didn't really know why, but they laughed and asked for more.

I gave it to them, as much as I could, but when I saw their mother peering anxiously from behind a nearby house, I excused myself and hurried to get Helena.

"Did you see that?" I said excitedly as we made our way back to the car. "Did you see those kids?"

Helena kept nodding as I kept repeating the questions, and when she finally lay a hand across my chest to shut me up, I still couldn't stop grinning.

"Feels good, does it?" she asked smugly, as though she already knew the answer but was making me say it.

"Well, of course it does," I said. "But…"

"But what?"

"I don't know. It feels good, and it feels…funny." I scratched at my head, my throat, moved rapidly away from the edge of the sidewalk when a hovercat aired by, its skirts keeping down the blow of brown dust from its fans. "Things ought to be banned," I muttered as I brushed at my trousers.

"Progress," she said. "But what do you mean, 'funny'? You've acted before. What's…I don't know what's funny about it?"

When we reached the vehicle still parked in front of the eatshop, I hadn't yet found an answer. I thought about it, thought about what I had learned from the Lunar production, and from Philip and Vivian, trying right there in the middle of that town to squeeze in, in one way or another, the last piece.

To put together, as Helena said much later, years later, the last fragile piece of a broken unicorn.

And when I did I hustled her into her seat, slid quickly behind the wheel, and drove off much faster than I thought I was going. A few heads turned, a few faces frowned as we sped through Eisentor and back into the hills, and as soon as I realized it I eased the acceleration. The one thing I didn't need now was to have our faces remembered.

"All right," I said as I turned onto another side road, "I have to find a place where I can do some thinking."

"Isn't there anything else you do but think?"

Her bitterness amazed me, so much so that I almost stopped right there.

"I mean, Gordy, aren't you getting tired? Didn't those people...didn't they do anything for you?"

I made excuses for her. She was overtired—we'd hardly gotten the best of rest, sleeping in the car or on the ground beside it. She was still overwrought from our flight. She had not yet been able to accept the status she had willingly, knowingly, adopted when she came with me.

I made excuses, but for the next two hours or so we argued. About little things, dumb things, sniping and picking until it was apparent one of us was going to leap from the car if we didn't calm down.

By nightfall, I knew she was ready to give up. Maybe she had thought I had a meticulous plan already worked out; maybe she thought there was still some vestige of romance in weariness and hunger, dirt and thirst. Whatever it was, it angered me, and I was just about ready to turn around from wherever we were and take her back to Philayork when I realized that if I did, if I gave her up without some sort of trying, I would be no better than Philip and his incredible paunch.

I slowed and began to talk, ignoring her gibes as best I could, noticing after a while that they grew fewer and less acid. I talked, roughing out the idea I had had when prompted by the children. Her skepticism fed on it for nearly an hour, but I refused to give it up. And when I was done, with all her objections buried in the darkness around us, she was silent.

Shortly afterward, we came upon a solitary abandoned house, one of many that belonged to those who, having no direct contact with any of the smaller towns, decided that perhaps the plexes weren't so bad after all. Those we had come across before had been done in by the weather or vandals or a brutal combination of both, but this one had recently been vacated, and it didn't take me long to force my way in. There were scant provisions left in the ovenwall, but they were enough to fill us. The comunit still worked and, while I made some effort to hide the car, Helena watched the news for some sign of our escapade, and much later, years later, we both admitted that our egos were blunted sorely when nothing was broadcast. We were minor criminals then, it seemed, not worth the airtime.

We slept in the tiny bedroom. Apart. Alone.

I began to have doubts.

"We'll have to stay here for a few days," I said the next morning. "Just to be sure. I want to be completely sure before we go on."

"It happened too fast, Gordy," she said. We were sitting opposite each other in the living room. Her eyes were swollen and red, her hair in uncaring disarray. "Everything was moving just nicely, slowly. I guess that's what I mean. Then you showed up, and all of a sudden I couldn't blink without something happening. You know, we didn't even have time to say—"

"We had no one to say it to, really, you know."

"There was Vivian, I suppose. I guess we said good-bye to her. In a way."

"But she fired you!"

"She was still someone I knew."

"Well, for all that, so am I."

"Yes, but you're here."

––––––––––––––

"You really think we can get away with it, don't you?"

"Why not? We won't have some thirty-room loft overlooking the ocean, but we'll manage. It all depends on your priorities."

"We'll have to change, then, won't we?"

"I'm afraid so. Not radically, mind you, but enough to confuse anyone we might happen to meet that knew us."

"Now what are the odds of that, Mr. Anderson?"

"Fantastically small."

"Do you have any idea how many years it took for this hair to get this long? You're asking an awful lot of me."

"That, too, depends on your priorities."

"If you're not careful, Gordon Anderson, you're going to get as pompous as Philip. Hand me that knife."

"The food's running out. They must have disconnected the supply when they moved. Must have? Of course they did. I must be getting stir crazy or something. It's all that practicing you're making me do."

"Well, if the food's running out, then we might as well start planning to make our first move. You know, Philip said he was starving. I wish he'd walk through that door right now. I'd tie him permanently to a chair and face him to the ovenwall. Then I'd smash the thing and let him watch the food rot while he shriveled."

"You're vicious."

"I have a sense of the dramatic."

"Do you like the color of my hair? Black sets off my skin rather nicely, don't you think?"

"Do you like my beard? Vivian kept telling me I had an agreeably weak chin."

"Helena!"

"What's the matter, don't you like it?"

"Where…where did you get it?"

"There's a storage room upstairs. I was looking for some clothes, those over there, and I found this little chest. I think there must have been children here sometime. A long time ago. Anyway, I opened it, and there were all these baubles and things. This one was at the bottom."

"I can't…it would look better on you."

"No. It's yours. See? It has a chain around its neck, just like a halter. You can wear it around yours. For luck."

"It's too small, Helena. I'll break it."

"I'm not going to argue with you. You'll wear it and like it. If someone asks you, you can tell them you have a fetish for horses."

"They'll know it's not a horse."

"I wouldn't bet on it. Besides, you and I are the only ones it'll matter to, anyway."

"It matters to you?"

"If it doesn't, I've learned all those parts for nothing, haven't I? You know something, Gordy, you really can be dense sometimes. You really can. Now put it on."

"I feel funny."

"Don't. Just wear it."

"It's so small, it's buried in my palm."

"Wear it! It'll keep the beasts away."

It did.

5

I stood at the rear wall of the meetinghouse. I think, that year, it was somewhere in Michigan. In front of me were several rows of static chairs dragged in by volunteers from the attics and storerooms that had been opened to us when we arrived. Already there was a fair crowd waiting. Talking. Nudging with elbows. Pointing with only half-hearted disdain at the crudely painted backdrop on the far wall. It depicted, rather impressionistically, a forest none of them believed existed, but a forest nevertheless. They drifted in and smiled when handing me their admission, but promptly forgot I was there once the money had changed hands. Which was perfectly all right with me. I had worked toward that end. Now I could watch them without fear of being rude—gauging, searching their faces, estimating their average age and income, style, and education.

Most of the time my conclusions were correct, and the material that would be presented to the audience, numbering just under fifty, would be geared to whatever imagination I thought they possessed. It was a skill, and a necessary one, that I had developed over the years after we nearly landed in the clutches of the local Blues the first time we tried our little show. We had hoped that anything in those scripts Helena had stolen would be sufficient to enthrall. Sadly, and realistically, it didn't work out that way. Luckily, however, we'd been given a second chance, and after I had had an opportunity to talk with those who had come to see us that night, I knew which of our plays they would enjoy the most.

We did it.

And they did.

It was simple, actually, once I understood that even in the towns the audiences had been…not spoiled, but despoiled.

We worked out a routine then, which grew into a science. A week or so in each community. The first night an informal education. The second a performance with intermittent explanation. The third through the fifth or sixth something done in earnest.

No gimmicks.

Just words.

And that crudely painted backdrop became a forest indeed.

We grew. A boy here, a young woman there, an elderly couple with young stars in their eyes. But it was, as always at the last, Helena and I—and our children when they grew.

Philip came to see us one evening, trailing behind a representative of some official or other who, having heard of our little troupe, had come to see. I had been nervous throughout the entire performance, thinking that fat and now enfeebled old man had pursued his idiot revenge to the extreme. But when we were done, Helena and I were given some papers in which, with much legal phrasing and hyperbole almost sickening, we were granted our pardons. Artistic merit had rehabilitated us, I gathered. The only catch: we were not allowed back in a cityplex, for any reason, at any time. And I think Philip was truly enraged when both Helena and I accepted the terms. Laughing.

I sighed silently. I waited until I was sure there would be no late-comers, then lifted a finger, which dimmed the lights. Working swiftly and carefully then, I adjusted the makeshift spots that had been bolted for us over the lintel of the meeting-room door. And once lighted, the forest became natural, and once populated, it lost what was artificial in the words of the players.

There were no curtains, so we walked our exits.

There were no musicians, so we improvised our songs.

And the costumes we used were bits of rags, shards of cloaks, and sometimes only the clothes on our backs.

I watched from the back, waiting for my cue, and as I did, I took from beneath my shirt the gift Helena had given me when we had given birth to our dream. It sat in my palm, glowing, its eyes catching the light like two miniature candles.

And when my cue came from Helena, the laughter was real.

"When beggars die, there are no comets seen," Helena has said. It was her favorite line.

Helena.

Is dead.

Last year.

She was eighty.

But my favorite line…"I didn't go to the moon—I went much further—for time is the longest distance between two points."

She was eighty.

Prologues and epilogues.

I give them alone.

But no matter how often my world is lit by that lightning—I'll not now, nor will I ever, blow out my candles. When all is done, and done…and done, a tiny glass unicorn still sits on my palm.

About the Author

Photo by Jeff Schalles

Charles L. Grant taught English and history at the high school level before becoming a full-time writer in the '70s. He served for many years as an officer in the Horror Writers Association and in Science Fiction Writers of America.

He was known for his "quiet horror" and for editing the award-winning Shadows anthologies. He received the British Fantasy Society's Special Award in 1987 for life achievement; in 2000, he was the recipient of the Lifetime Achievement Award from HWA. Other awards include two Nebula Awards and three World Fantasy Awards for writing and editing.

Charlie died from a lengthy illness on September 15, 2006, just three days after his birthday. He lived in Newton, NJ, and was married to writer/editor Kathryn Ptacek for nearly twenty-five years.

Book List

Horror
Novels
Black Oak: Genesis
Black Oak: The Hush of Dark Wings
Black Oak: Winter Knight
Black Oak: Hunting Ground
Black Oak: When the Cold Wind Blows
Fire Mask
For Fear of the Night
In A Dark Dream
Jackals
Millennium Quartet #1: Symphony
Millennium Quartet #2: In the Mood
Millennium Quartet #3: Chariot
Millennium Quartet #4: Riders in the Sky
Night Songs
Raven
Something Stirs
Stunts
The Bloodwind
The Curse
The Grave
The Hour of the Oxrun Dead
The Last Call of Mourning
The Nestling
The Pet
The Sound Of Midnight
The Tea Party

The Universe of Horror Trilogy
The Soft Whisper of the Dead
The Dark Cry of the Moon
The Long Night of the Grave

Collections
Dialing the Wind
Nightmare Seasons

The Black Carousel
The Orchard

Science Fiction
A Quiet Night of Fear
Ascension
Legion
Ravens of the Moon
The Shadow of Alpha

As "Geoffrey Marsh"
The Fangs of the Hooded Demon
The King of Satan's Eyes
The Patch of the Odin Soldier
The Tail of the Arabian, Knight

As "Lionel Fenn"
The Quest for the White Duck Trilogy
Blood River Down
Web of Defeat
Agnes Day

The Kent Montana Series
The Really Ugly Thing From Mars
The Reasonably Invisible Man
The Once and Future Thing
The Mark of the Moderately Vicious Vampire
668, the Neighbor of the Beast

The Diego Series
Once Upon a Time in the East
By The Time I Get To Nashville
Time, the Semi-Final Frontier

The Seven Spears of the W'dch'ck

As "Simon Lake"
The Midnight Place Series

Daughter of Darkness
Death Cycle
He Told Me To
Something's Watching

As "Felicia Andrews"
Moonwitch
Mountainwitch
Riverrun
Riverwitch
Seacliffe
Silver Huntress
The Velvet Hart

As "Deborah Lewis"
Eve of the Hound
Kirkwood Fires
The Wind at Winter's End
Voices Out of Time

Curious about other Crossroad Press books? Stop by our website:
http://crossroadpress.com
We offer quality writing
in digital, audio, and print formats.

Subscribe to our newsletter on the website homepage and receive a free
eBook.